LOU ABERCROMBIE

Coming Up For Air

Part 1

APNOEA

APNOEA *[AP-nee-uh]*

Noun
The scientific term for holding your breath.
Literally meaning 'without air'.

Pathology
The suspension of breathing as occurs in diving
mammals.

One Full Breath

Picture this: a girl lying under the water, body relaxed, her fair hair floating serenely while her last full breath pulsates in her veins. Calmly, she contemplates her life, enjoying the stillness and sense of peace that washes over her. The seconds pass by into minutes and still she doesn't come up for air. Is she a fish or perhaps a mermaid? Whatever she is, she seems to belong under the water.

Cut to a shot of me trying awkwardly to stay beneath the five centimetres of water that I'd managed to run before it got cold. Most definitely not the glamorous image that I'd imagined. Wearing nothing but goggles in the bath isn't exactly a strong look.

Holding my breath underwater while going over the events of my day, the way a director might run through the dailies of a film shoot, is my absolute favourite thing to do. With my view limited to what's right in front of me, and only an inner monologue to narrate the story, it's like viewing my life through the lens. It gives me a new perspective and enables me to focus on what's really important. It's funny how much I can relax like this.

I'm forever imagining myself in a movie. A montage of best mates giggling over a burger; the lone main character, i.e. me, running in a city park; the main character, me again, staring out of the window pensively, with some sort of emotive music to accompany the shot. Wouldn't it be great if we actually did have soundtracks to our lives? You'd certainly know what was coming next if you heard the ominous sound of violins striking up...

Mississippi eighty-two, Mississippi eighty-three.

So goes the count in my head while I focus on what the sequel to my London life is going to look like.

Min, my insanely creative, chaos-inducing, fun-loving, stuck-in-adolescence mother, has lost her job – she was a producer for a large Soho post house – and is relocating us to her hometown, some 300 miles away from everything I love and cherish. It's somewhere I've never been and – cue the violins – the place where my dad died before I was born. Min calls it a hellhole on the edge of the world and had vowed never to go there again, but she's rather prone to dramatic outbursts, so you can't take her word for anything. That reminds me: I should look the town up. As an aspiring documentary maker, it's important to have more than one point of view.

The thing is, I love where we live. It might only be a tiny one-bed apartment, but it's on Wardour Street, slap bang in the middle of everything. It's Min's favourite story actually, how it was purely down to her having the gift of the gab that we got to live here. How, when starting out as a runner, she made friends with Bob, an up-and-coming director, who also dabbled in property development. Quite how she talked him into letting her rent our one I don't know, but they've been friends ever since and here we are fifteen years later…

Mississippi one-thirty-one, Mississippi one-thirty-two.

When she first told me that her boss had sacked her, my immediate thought was that it was my fault. Robin's never really liked me hanging round the edit suites and as of last month, when I asked a visiting celeb for an autograph, I've been banned. Not surprising I suppose, given it's a sackable offence and I'm just an annoying fifteen-year-old hanger-on. But it was the presenter from a TV show I'm obsessed with: *Big Mother,* a reality show where children who think their mums are the best get them to go on telly and compete, doing things like baking, running and the odd outdoor extreme sport thrown in for good measure.

Mississippi one-fifty-two, Mississippi one-fifty-three.

This change has been coming for some time. Min's been burning the candle at both ends and has said for ages that post-production is a young person's game. I just wasn't prepared for her to make such a big alteration to our lives.

I've got friends here, a Saturday job, school even. But, with Bob selling our flat to release equity for a film he's planning, and Min without a penny of savings, we've got no choice.

Mississippi one-seventy-five…

I've been under for nearly three minutes now and my insides are spasming, telling me to come up for air. But I hold on, and just about make it to three and a half minutes before I burst to the surface, gasping for breath.

"Yes!" I yell with a triumphant punch, ignoring the slosh of water over the side of the bath.

"You still in there?" asks Min, picking her way over to the loo where she perches, knickers round her ankles – she'll take any audience she can get – the hem of her vintage dress soaking up the spilled bathwater like a sponge.

"Personal best," I pant, still recovering my breath.

She frowns. "I hope you didn't use up all the hot water."

She tiptoes over to the sink where she begins the long and laborious process of getting ready for a night out. I used to love watching her do it while lying in the bath. An immaculate beehive hairdo, thick black eyeliner that wings out almost as far as her perfectly shaped eyebrows, pale foundation, dark eyes and barely there lips. It's a look all right. And she doesn't have any kind of skincare routine – except soap and water – at the end of a night. How she never breaks out in spots is beyond me.

"Come on," she says, chivvying me out of the bath. "Last night on the town. Let's make it one to remember…"

Piscary Bay

Town in England

Description

Piscary Bay is a small bustling fishing harbour in south-west England. Known for its picturesque-postcard appearance, with candy-coloured houses nestling into the hillside surrounding an aquamarine bay that has been known to light up with bioluminescence under the right conditions. It has become an increasingly popular destination for tourists and city types looking to relocate for a quieter life. And who could blame them? Cheap housing, excellent waves for surfing and day trips along the coast to see the copious amounts of wildlife, including seals, dolphins and puffins. Just watch out for the rips *and* the locals…

<u>Weather</u>: 22 °C, Wind NE at 9 mph (14 km/h), 61% Humidity
<u>Population</u>: 20,342 (<u>2011 census</u>)
<u>Local time</u>: Sunday 23rd June 18:04

A Night to Remember

That evening we do a walking tour of our favourite spots. This involves Min standing by patiently while I record little pieces to camera so that I never forget them. I think it's her way of saying thanks-for-not-going-teenage-ballistic on her. Not that I ever really do. That's more her area of expertise.

There are so many hidden places in London that tourists don't know about. Gothic churchyards where you can sit beneath the gaze of eerie gargoyles. Side streets leading to gardens bursting with flowers and wildlife. Min and I have a whole lifetime of memories in these spaces.

"D'you remember when we schlepped all the way to the Regent's Park playground and I immediately fell out of a tree you'd told me not to climb? And then you had to rush all the way back home, with me screaming in your arms and blood gushing over your shoulder."

"Never did get that out of my coat," laughs Min. "It was my favourite as well."

I squeeze her hand. "Sorry."

She shakes her head. "Don't be silly. You were only four, darling." She says this with an accentuation on the 'ah' in the transatlantic-movie-star-from-the-golden-age-of-Hollywood sort of way. We have a shared passion for films, and we've been watching black-and-white movies every Sunday afternoon together since I can remember.

"D'you remember when I ran away and hid here?" I ask, as we arrive at our favourite bench in Phoenix Garden.

"Is that where you went?" gasps Min in mock horror, humouring me because we've replayed this scene many a time. "I was going spare by the time you got home. It was dark and I—"

"Had a client dinner you needed to get to," I finish. "Yes, I remember."

Min grabs my hand, her eyes urgently searching my face. Did I mention that she's a bit dramatic? "No, it wasn't like that," she gasps. "I was worried about you."

And so continues our reminiscing. Both of us trying not to discuss what comes next, though questions keep floating unbidden into my head. Like what am I going to do in a small fishing village where I know no one, losing all the friends I've worked so hard to make? But I push the worries away – I need to find a silver lining.

"If we're going to live by the sea, we could get a dog," I suggest tentatively, because Min's always been against the idea. She doesn't like the idea of more responsibility...

"Darling!" she shrieks, doubling over with laughter. "You crack me up!"

"I wasn't joking."

"Neither was I," she retorts. "Now are you gonna put that phone down? Can't eat and film, you know."

Looks to camera – speak for yourself...

~~~

After dinner from our favourite Taiwanese street stall and then dipping into the Nellie Dean for Min to say goodbye to the landlord, we head home to face the daunting task of finishing packing up the flat. We find Bob waiting in the street, leaning against the door, dressed like half the TV industry in jeans, suit jacket, shirt and trainers.

"You've got a nerve," Min spits venomously.

"I've come to say goodbye. Sunshine..." he coos, his gravelly voice catching on his nickname for me. "I'm gonna miss you."

Min flounces past him, angrily shoving the key in the door. "Make it about *her*, why don't you? You're making *both* of us homeless if you hadn't noticed."

Bob sighs. "I'm sorry. You know how hard it is getting a foot in the door of the film industry. I don't want to be making entertainment shows for the rest of my life."

He turns to me, producing a milkshake from behind his back. "You gonna invite me in or what? I brought your favourite…"

My eyes pop like saucers. "Peanut butter with extra whipped cream? Oh my God, Bob – I love you!" I shriek, pulling him into a hug.

"He's not coming in," mutters Min sulkily.

"Yes, he is," I laugh. "Ignore her. Wouldn't be our last night without you."

"'S'all right," he says cheerily. "I brought something for her too." And in the other hand he produces a bottle of wine.

Change of Scene

I don't know what time Bob leaves, or when Min makes it to bed, but what I do know is that it's an effort to get her up in time for the 11 a.m. coach from Victoria Station. We have a mad dash to the Tube at Oxford Circus, made more nightmarish by the record player that Min insists on us bringing and the four suitcases rammed full of our belongings. We own a lot of clothes.

"Come on," I moan. "We can't miss the coach."

Min rolls her eyes, tutting like a stroppy teenager. "I'm doing my best, all right?"

"I know you are," I hiss.

Cut to the Tube journey. Min and I are bickering while I try my level best to stay calm by holding my breath. But, by the time we get to the coach station, I'm ready to let rip with a whole gamut of emotion ranging from yelling

16

my head off to bawling my eyes out. The latter winning through when the coach pulls out of the station and the London life that I adore becomes all but a blur...

~~~

"How long till we get there?" mutters Min, rooting around in her vintage leather handbag for her sunnies, both epic charity-shop finds at which she is an expert.

"Ten hours," I reply, gloomily looking out of the window as my beloved London whips past. "Did you remember the sandwiches I made?"

She shakes her head. "Sorry, forgot."

"But I made those specially," I groan. "It isn't payday yet."

"Yes, I'm well aware, thanks. No use to me anyway. I'm not eating wheat or dairy at the moment."

Looks to camera – this is gonna be a long journey.

If my life were a movie, the next scene would be a jumpcut to us arriving fresh-faced in the station, being met by an overjoyed Uncle Henry – Min's brother – or a montage of shots of us chatting and laughing, the countryside whizzing past, accompanied by a twangy guitar soundtrack. The reality is so much more boring and, after an hour of us both staring out of the window, I can't bear the moody silence any longer and suggest a game of I Spy.

"What are you, eight?" sneers Min.

"It's only a suggestion," I reply testily. "Favourite thing then. What was—?"

"I have the mother of all hangovers. How about some quiet time so that I can get some shut-eye?"

I silently zip my lips and go back to staring out of the window, shoving my headphones on so that I can at least have a soundtrack to accompany my boredom.

It's late by the time we arrive, my stomach rumbling like mad and my patience with Min wearing thin. God only knows how she's feeling, since she turned down my offer of sharing my lunch and spent the last of our money on chewing gum.

Piscary Bay is tiny. High street on one side, beach and sea on the other and I can literally see from one end of the bay to the other without moving my head. OK, so that's a bit of an exaggeration, but it's a big change of scene from London.

"There's the sea," I gasp, catching sight of it just as the sun breaks through the clouds, sending shafts of golden light over the water as if they're heaven-sent. "It's beautiful," I murmur.

Min, still in her sunnies, shrugs. "It's just the sea. Help me with the bags, will you?"

"Where's Uncle Henry?" I ask, looking about us at the empty bus stop on the seafront – equally as abandoned save for the odd dog walker and surfer.

She shrugs listlessly. "Dunno."

"How far is it?"

She points to the left of the bay, where the sun is setting behind row upon row of brightly coloured houses nestled into the hillside. Above them sits the silhouette of a large house in prime position on the cliff overhanging the sea.

"That's it?" I gasp. "Wow! You never said you grew up in a mansion."

Min snorts. "Wait and see."

"I guess we'd better start walking then," I say brightly. "Let's hope Uncle Henry's got a nice dinner waiting for us." And I set off at a pace, dragging the two large suitcases behind me, record player shoved painfully under my arm.

"Come on, Min," I call sometime later. She's walking at a snail's pace, thanks to her four-inch heels.

"I'm doing the best I can," she mutters. "These bloody suitcases."

Looks to camera – yeah, that's the problem.

"Should've left the whole lot behind." Even though she's got the lighter load by far, she seems to be weighed down.

"Here, let me," I say, lifting the smallest suitcase out of her hand.

"Thanks, darling," she murmurs and trots off ahead, seemingly oblivious to the load I'm now carrying uphill. A metaphor for my life if ever there was one!

But it's as if the scenery won't let my mood slip as the

19

sunset continues to deliver. Tones of pink, orange and yellow mingle like watercolours, turning the sky into a sheen of rose-gold delight.

And I can't take my eyes off the sea. The way it looks like a piece of silver-blue crumpled satin rippling in the breeze. It's so inviting. Especially after a ten-hour coach journey. I could just dive in and let the cool water envelop me. But that's tomorrow's promise and I can almost sense the tension in my shoulders slip away at the thought. For the first time since Min told me we were coming here, I actually feel excited about what the summer might hold.

Out of the Blue

The stark white clapboard house is much gloomier close up. It's surrounded by a thin stone wall bordering the cliff path and fronted by an overgrown garden, knee-high with nettles and grasses through which I can just about make out a stone path leading to a sad-looking wrap-around porch and an enormous front door with a sign saying *The Cliff House*. It looks like it's been suffering from years of neglect.

"Is anyone in?" I ask doubtfully, peering through a cracked window into darkness.

"Bloody hope so," mutters Min, ringing the doorbell impatiently.

Nothing. "Bell must be out of order," I say, checking my phone. I've got just enough charge left to film my first-ever sighting of Uncle Henry.

Min bangs loudly with her fist and, when still no one

comes to answer, she stands on her tiptoes and yells through the letter box, "Henry! Stop talking to your bloody fish!" Then finally, after another succession of impatient bangs and more expletives, a light flickers on somewhere within and we hear slow footsteps shuffle towards the door.

"Who is it?" comes a gruff voice. "Minnie, what the devil are you doing here?" And suddenly, with a jump, I notice a pair of hooded eyes blinking at us through the letter box.

"Don't call me that," whines Min, sounding like a petulant child. "Come on, open up."

After another lengthy delay, the door slowly creaks open to reveal a slight, gaunt man who looks far more like Min than I do, with dark brown hair and pale skin, who'd be quite tall if it weren't for his withered stoop. A distinct lack of fashion sense marks him out as the antithesis of his sister.

Looks to camera – my uncle, everyone!

"This is Coco," says Min, pushing me forward. "Your niece."

"Ah yes," he says, cocking an eyebrow. "Named after your favourite designer."

"No, she wasn't!" she shrieks, overreacting a little if you ask me. I mean, it is true…

Uncle Henry snorts, seeming to enjoy her reaction.

"Hi, Uncle Henry," I say.

"Get that phone out of my face," he mutters.

"Sorry. I just wanted to record the moment."

He stares at me. "Why?"

"Because it's the first time I've met you.'

"No, it isn't," he scoffs. "I came to the hospital when you were born." He pauses. "Did you know that shark pups can be born in three different ways? And, in some species, they have to survive gestation without being eaten by their siblings."

Looks to camera – er…

"Yeah, all right, Dr Fish," sniggers Min.

"D'you think we can come in?" I ask. "It's been a really long journey and we're famished."

Uncle Henry shrugs indifferently and turns on his heel, shuffling back down the darkened corridor to a lamplit room, where he sinks wearily into a well-worn armchair. I know this because I follow him. Min, on the other hand, stays stubbornly on the threshold, looking like she doesn't want to enter.

Funny – in my head, I'd imagined my uncle answering the door to us, me shouting, "Uncle Henry!" and him welcoming us with open arms. But, as I stand there awkwardly, wondering when he's going to show us around or serve dinner, I suddenly realize: Min hadn't told him we were coming.

Uncle Henry

"You can't just turn up out of the blue after fifteen years without so much as a phone call or a letter or even an email!"

And freeze-frame!

That's Uncle Henry's shocked face. A furious brow making a craggy line delve deep between his wide I-can't-believe-you're-here eyes and snarling lips, half hidden by a remarkably untidy brown beard flecked with white. From what I can tell in the hour we've been here, he's been living a hermit-like existence in this large, draughty house. And, now that we're here, things have gone from bad to worse.

"Well?" he demands angrily. "Haven't you got anything to say for yourself?"

"Min's hungry, Uncle Henry," I explain, glancing nervously between them. "Hasn't had anything to eat all

24

day. Not even a bit of my six-inch from the Subway at the services. She doesn't eat wheat."

Uncle Henry scrunches up his face. "Doesn't eat wheat? Six-inch? What?"

I laugh, hoping to lighten the atmosphere. Fat chance. "Oh, it's a sandwich. My favourite's a tuna melt with gherkins and honey mu—"

His glare forces me into silence.

"Minnie, what are you doing here? You could've warned me."

"So that you could avoid answering the door?" she sneers. "No thanks." She falls back into silently glaring at him and no amount of wide-eyed glances from me produces any further explanation. Quite frankly, it's not helping.

"Minnie," barks Uncle Henry.

"It's Min," she growls through gritted teeth.

Guess it falls on me to explain everything then. He takes it remarkably calmly, as if he's always been expecting it, until I say – cautiously I'll admit – "So, we're coming to live with you."

"You've got to be joking," he mutters angrily.

I'm stunned. I mean, I know our arrival has come out of the blue, but we're family. His only one as far as I know. Surely he should be happier to see us.

"This is my house too. What's left of it," mutters Min, looking round at the dilapidated kitchen, where bowls and mugs and plates are scattered across every surface.

"Coco, find us something to eat, would you? I think I might faint if I don't eat soon."

"Get back," hisses Uncle Henry as I make a move towards the ancient-looking fridge-freezer. "I've got bloodworms in there and the last thing I need is you spoiling them. There's nothing to eat anyway."

"Is there anywhere we could go?" I ask hopefully.

"Not at this time of night, no," he says. "It's late. I was on my way to bed." Then, sighing heavily, he says, "Follow me," and shuffles out of the door. "Mind that step," he mutters. "Tread's loose. And that one... That one... That one..." He continues on like this until I'm virtually hopping up the two flights of stairs. No mean feat when you're dragging *two* suitcases with no offer of help. Not that Uncle Henry looks all that strong. More of an old man shuffling in his slippers and threadbare dressing gown. I wonder how old he is. Funny, Min's always talked about him as if they were close in age and she's only early thirties...

"In there," says Uncle Henry, giving a cursory nod to a battered door. "Bathroom's down there. Goodnight."

"Uncle Henry," I call. "What's the Wi-Fi code?"

He snorts. "Never you mind." And off he shuffles to the room at the end of the corridor, leaving me to make myself at home, such as it is. The guest room is just an unmade double bed, with frayed curtains and wooden floorboards through which seems to creep a horrendously cold draught considering that it's summer.

I set my suitcases down, feeling as if a tornado has swept through my life, leaving nothing recognizable. Too weary to think about what lies ahead, I curl up on the bed, pulling the musty-smelling duvet over me, and slip into an exhausted sleep.

Fade to black…

Finding Nemo

Last night I imagined that I was a character in Narnia – Lucy, obviously. My uncle was the professor, which I guess makes Min the White Witch. Anyway, it made me wonder whether there might be some wonderful rooms to explore. A wardrobe even. Preferably with a magic portal to take me to a far-off land or, even better, back to London. But flinging back the curtains reveals not the winter wonderland of Narnia, but a summer scene that makes me gasp in delight.

From my clifftop viewpoint, the town beach can barely be seen in the dawn light, save for the reflective pools of water defining its edge as it stretches upwards along the coastline. Boats bob in the harbour beyond, where I can just about make out the early risers beginning their day. And on the horizon an intense strip of orange collides with the rippling satin-silver sea dotted with white horses, as the early-morning sunlight hits the incoming tide. Wow. That is a view and a half!

I'm half tempted to go for a swim, but the gust of cool, salty air that attacks my senses when I open the window suggests I should wait for the day to warm up. So instead I turn my attention, and my phone, to the house…

Camera rolling. And action!

Fade up on an external shot, the house sitting pretty in pink as it glows under the spotlight of the rising sun.

I survey the scene, the wind whipping at my face, enjoying the peace and quiet bar the roaring of the waves crashing at the foot of the cliff. But, as the spotlight broadens, the grim reality of the house comes into focus. Its dreariness. Its bedraggled state – full of cracks and holes that shouldn't be there. Pieces of clapboard half hanging off the walls, broken windows and rotting wood. It feels like a place without a soul.

Cut to the interior.

Endless corridors of cold and decaying rooms full of dated, dusty furniture, windows smeared with dirt, peeling wallpaper and cracked paintwork.

On the first floor, I pass a peeling white door with giant red letters spelling *KEEP OUT, MIN'S ABOUT*, coupled with a half-ripped poster of Amy Winehouse and a Surf's Up vinyl sticker. I tiptoe in, my curiosity getting the better of me, and find Min fast asleep in the corner, curled up in a foetal ball, surrounded by her teenage life. Walls decked out with posters of pop stars I barely recognize and fairy lights whose bulbs have long gone. It's like seeing a snapshot of her life from before I was born.

Further along the corridor, I find more bedrooms piled high with bin bags and cardboard boxes, and a mouldy bathroom where the shower curtain hangs limply from its rail, while a dripping tap has turned the white ceramic sink green. I open the door to my uncle's room, just a fraction, because I'm curious. But I can't see much. The blackout curtains cut out most of the light, though I can just about make out the mess. Clothes scattered over the floor, books and papers piled teeteringly high against the walls. Another teenage bedroom if ever there was!

At the top of the creaky staircase winding its way up the middle of the house, I push open a heavy door and gasp with delight as a sudden influx of daylight hits me from huge windows on three sides, giving me a glorious panoramic view of the sea.

The large, open-plan attic is laid out like a science lab and, judging by the amount of dust and cobwebs, one that time forgot. Bare light bulbs hang from the wooden rafters, swaying in the breeze. Shelves wedged in this way and that are packed with brown bottles and glass containers of differing shapes and sizes, filled with all manner of brightly coloured powders, liquids and what look like fish spines.

In the middle is a giant workbench on which sits a large metal frame housing test tubes galore, as if a very important experiment has been abandoned. Bunsen burners, goggles, tongs and glass beakers are scattered everywhere.

To the left, under a window looking directly out to sea, is an ornate wooden desk piled high with yet more books and paperwork, and a large, ancient-looking computer plonked like a cherry on top. On the wall behind, scrawled across it in black ink, are formula after formula. Some scrubbed out carelessly, with expletives beneath them. I can almost feel Uncle Henry's frustration at being unable to find the right answer.

My attention is drawn to the far end of the room where a light gently flickers on, and an underwater scene suddenly comes to life. The fish tank is enormous. Full of brightly coloured rocks and seaweed slowly swaying in the water. And the fish! Yellow and black, purple and blue. There are even a couple of orange-and-white stripy ones like Nemo. But it's the pufferfish that comes to stare at me. Blowing his cheeks out – I can tell it's a he – big googly eyes staring sadly at me as if to say, *I don't belong here!*

Looks to camera – I know the feeling...

"What d'you think you're doing?"

I whip round to see Uncle Henry glaring blearily at me. In the sunlight, he looks younger. Dark brown beard, with only a smattering of white, and a full head of wild brown curly hair and very few wrinkles.

"Morning, Uncle Henry," I say brightly, allowing his moodiness to float over my head. Good job I've had a lot of practice at this. "Didn't hear you come up... I love your fish tank. It's beautiful."

"You didn't touch it, did you?" he gasps, his eyes bulging like the pufferfish. "The fish can feel the vibrations... What on earth's that noise?"

"I haven't eaten since yesterday lunch." I wince as my stomach continues to grumble loudly.

Uncle Henry recoils. "Fish only need to eat once a day."

"Well ... I'm ... not a fish," I murmur. "And I'm really rather hungry."

"Go and get something to eat then," he says, rolling his eyes. "The supermarket will be open by now."

I grin nervously. "I, er ... I ... don't have any money."

"Ask Min then."

"Neither does she," I reply.

"What, and you think I'm made of money?" he retorts, exhaling heavily. "Fine. But I'm giving you a list. I couldn't get an online slot until next week so you may as well do the weekly shop while you're at it."

Zombies

Stepping out of the front gate on to the cliff path, I am once again hit by the glory of the sea, now glowing a turquoise blue in the full light of day. It's so gorgeous and appealing that, if it weren't for my growling stomach, I'd be heading straight in. I sprint downhill to the shop we passed last night, enjoying the feeling of the sea breeze in my hair and the sun on my face. Maybe being here isn't so bad after all.

"Morning," I say brightly to the first person I meet, a teenager stacking shelves, who doesn't reply. Maybe they didn't hear me. "Smells divine," I add, inhaling sharply. "Is there an in-house bakery?"

The teenager nods mutely towards the back of the shop, where I spy a rack of fresh bread and pastries that makes my stomach gurgle with anticipation. I love fresh bread – it's that home-baked aroma. At least I imagine it is.

Min hasn't cooked for me since I was little and even then it was limited to omelettes and baked beans on toast with shop-bought sliced white.

I buy a croissant and wolf it down with a pint of chocolate milk, sitting on the wall outside, watching the tide roll in and revelling in the sounds of the sea. Can't do this in London, can I?

The town is finally waking up and with it the odd dog walker and early-morning surfers. I see a curious-looking cyclist draw up in front of the supermarket on a bright red BMX. With a matching bright red helmet, white shirt and black tie, and giant black trainers, he seems to be yelling, "Look at me, look at me!"

"Hey," I say, with a friendly wave.

He glances at me, pulling off his helmet to reveal a mass of golden-brown hair that flops over his eyes, which he immediately brushes back, raising his face to the sun while he does it. The kind of thing you'd see in a Coke advert.

"I like your bike helmet," I say. "Never seen one like that before. Most of the cyclists dash round Soho – that's where I'm from – in full black leather gear, like they're extras in a superhero movie."

The cyclist responds to my giggles with a grunt as he continues into the shop. I'm a bit tempted to call him out on his rudeness but, since I'm trying to make friends not enemies, I keep my comments to myself. I follow him inside to finish Uncle Henry's shopping – a list the length of my arm – hoping to strike up a conversation with someone. But the bored girl stacking the shelves now has headphones on, and the lad on the till is more bothered about talking sea temperatures with the rude cyclist than taking my money. After several minutes' standing there, my throat-clearing is getting a bit obvious, but they still haven't stopped gassing.

"So sorry to interrupt," I say with my twinkliest smile, "but d'you think I could pay?"

"Flippin' Zombies," mutters the cyclist, standing aside.

I giggle. "Oh, has the apocalypse started without me?"

He rolls his eyes. "It's the summer, isn't it? Happens every year. Place gets overrun, rubbish and plastic tat left on the beaches and then you lot sod off back home."

Looks to camera – I think he means tourists.

"I'm staying up at Cliff House," I tell him.

"Big house that," he scoffs, with narrowed eyes. "This place has changed since the Cuckoos moved in and turned everything into an Airbnb."

"Cuckoos," I murmur, feeling confused. I decide to try a different tack and paste on an even bigger smile to see if it will soften him. "So, what's there to do around here?"

He returns my grin with a death stare, then gestures to the beach. "Would've thought that was obvious. Just make sure you stick to the lifeguarded areas, yeah? And stay away from the rocks. People like you come out here thinking you're invincible in the sea. The rips don't care who you are… And don't leave your litter on the beach either."

I exhale slowly. He's making an awful lot of assumptions considering he doesn't even know me. Funny, after a bit of a conversation, I can usually win people round.

"Not invincible," I say with a cursory nod. "Got it. Can I have a bag, please?" I ask the shop assistant, realizing that I can't carry everything.

"That'll be five pee extra," he sneers.

I stare at the coppers in my palm. "Will four do?" I ask. "I can come back with the extra penny in a bit."

"Sorry, shop policy."

I'm left with no alternative but to gather everything in my arms and leave the shop, hearing them mutter, "Flippin' Zombies…" in a not-so-subtle way.

Siblings

Eventually, I stumble into the kitchen with the shopping. Min is slumped over her coffee at the table, swamped by a navy-blue fisherman's jumper pulled over her drawn-up knees, her hair messily scraped back and yesterday's make-up smeared across her cheeks. A look she somehow manages to pull off.

Eye-roll to camera.

"You forgot the milk," she grumbles.

"Sorry, but they didn't sell oat milk and they were all out of soya. She's lactose intolerant," I explain, pouring myself a cup of coffee as Uncle Henry unceremoniously dumps a bottle of milk on the table in front of her.

He frowns. "You always were a fussy eater."

"It's not fussy if you're allergic," she retorts. "Fine, I'll drink it black. What did you buy me that I can eat, darling?

37

I'm famished."

"Oats," I say, triumphantly plonking the box in front of her.

"And what am I supposed to eat them with?" she moans. "Water? You know I hate that."

"Oh yeah," I say, feeling like an idiot. "Sorry. I didn't think."

Min tuts loudly. "You never do."

"She's just got a week's worth of shopping in." Uncle Henry frowns. "I'd say the problem's with you, *Minnie*."

"It's Min," she retorts, her eyes flashing. And, when Uncle Henry smirks at her, she picks up a handful of oats and flings them in his face, hitting him squarely in the eyes. I try to muffle my giggles, but the coffee spurting out of my nose is a dead giveaway.

Uncle Henry scowls at us, wiping away the beige flecks stuck in his eyebrows. "What are you?" he sneers. "Twelve? You're pathetic ... *Minnie Mouse*."

Min's face darkens, as if he's called her the worst thing possible. Probably has. I feel like I've stepped back in time and I'm watching a scene from twenty years ago. I half expect my grandmother to walk in, slap them both round the head and tell them to stop fighting. Or so I imagine – I've never met her.

"No more pathetic than you," retorts Min. "And I told you – don't call me that. Not ever. D'you hear?"

"Mi, mi, mi-mi, mi," says Uncle Henry, resorting to an

irritating, high-pitched whine.

"Shut up," snarls Min.

Uncle Henry smirks. "Mi?"

"I mean it," she says and launches a croissant this time. But he's ready for it and ducks out of the way, the pastry landing on the floor behind him.

"You're tragic, you know that?" he snorts.

"No, you are," says Min. "Idiot."

"Takes one to know one."

Bewildered look to camera…

I grab the croissant from the floor – five-second (ish) rule – and slip out of the room unnoticed. If I had a sibling, or any kind of family, I'm pretty sure I'd never behave that way towards them. If you ask me, they're both a bit tragic.

Mesmerized

Outside Cliff House there's a little white gate half hanging off its hinges, with a sign saying *PRIVATE PROPERTY: KEEP OUT*. The pathway down is pretty steep and a bit nail-biting in places, but it leads to a small, deserted, sandy cove, separated from the main stretch by an enormous pile of jagged rocks gradually diminishing in size as they disappear into the sea. It looks like a dinosaur has stuck its head in the cliff face with its tail in the water.

Watching the sea hurl itself against the rocks, and with the rude cyclist's angry words still ringing in my ears, my resolve to swim suddenly loses momentum. And it's not helped either by the breeze whipping the hair from my face, treating me to a blast of salt and ice-cold spray, as the freezing waves crash round my ankles. I'm not sure I *can* get in.

I sprint up and down the beach, running barefoot so that

the sand squidges between my toes. Running is what I did in London when I had a problem. I'd weigh up the pros and cons until my head felt clearer. But it doesn't help today, and I collapse on the sand, drenched in sweat, the worries piling up in my mind. So many unanswered questions, like are we just here for the summer? When are we going back to London? Why is Uncle Henry a Cuckoo? And why was that cyclist so rude?

My eyes are drawn back to the sea and I find myself mesmerized by the blue, blurry line across the empty horizon, the waves lapping gently against the shore, the seagulls gliding effortlessly on the breeze. And, before I know it, I strip down to my bikini and confidently wade in.

Cut to a shot of my eyes widening with shock as my feet and ankles grow numb.

I press on, determined to get through it, gritting my teeth as the freezing water laps at my thighs and grimacing as it hits my stomach. I pause, teetering on the brink of going back to the beach. It's way too cold to swim, surely. No, I can't let a bit of icy water defeat me!

I dive under – it's the only way to get my shoulders in – and resurface with a howl as the cold shoots down my spine, feeling like I'm being stabbed all over.

I swim to and fro, throwing my arms into a fast and punchy front crawl, kicking my legs madly. It's certainly not pretty but slowly and surely my body gets used to it. Begins to feel warm even. Then something catches my eye on the bottom of the seabed. A shell or a pebble twinkling in the sunlight. I take a deep breath and plunge under into a handstand, the rocking of the waves making it hard to stay submerged. Without goggles on, the saltwater burns my eyes and it's harder to see so I just grab at the first shell I find. I come back up for air, the sparkling curiosity no longer looking quite as pretty now that it's removed from its watery bed.

I dive down again. I can't resist. It's even better than being in the bath. So peaceful and so much to explore. Ignoring the sting in my eyes, I pull myself along under the water, eventually resurfacing to swim the length of the cove shoreline, taking in every little detail that I can. Like the fact that Cliff House, now gleaming white in the sunlight and with distance hiding its flaws, looks like a doll's house from down here. Above it, the pale blue sky is dotted with hazy white clouds while seagulls swoop and dive in the wind. One dive-bombs suddenly into the sea at the foot of the cliff, which is dotted with rock pools, growing smaller as they peter out into the sea. There I spot a series of official-looking signs. Guess my uncle is serious about keeping trespassers out.

I roll on to my back and cloud-watch, the sun making the exposed parts of me prickle with its heat. As I relax, so too does my mind. This is amazing. I feel so alive! Because for all the things I love about Soho – my mates and social life, the hustle and bustle of a happening city – the suffocating traffic, the crowded streets of aimless tourists, the thick, cloying summer air where you can see the haze rising from the pavements are claustrophobic.

I can't do this in London. So, just like that, I know what I need to do. With two months of summer stretching ahead of me, a huge house with my own bedroom and a private beach to explore, plus unlimited free access to the sea, there's only one thing for it. I'm going to make the most of this unexpected holiday.

Screams

It's as if I'd pressed pause on the scene of Min and Uncle Henry when I get back. They're still fighting, and I get the feeling they've picked up where they left off some fifteen years ago.

"It's my house!" shouts Uncle Henry.

"It's *ours!*" Min screams back.

"Ma didn't want you living here. Not after all the trouble you caused."

"Well, she should've changed her will then," Min counters. "You've let this place go, Henry."

He snorts, casting an eye about him at the pots and pans shoved in the sink, plates and bowls piled high.

Someone really should clean up.

"You're too busy talking with your bloody fish," says Min. "Not that they can answer you."

"As a matter of fact," he shouts back, "they can communicate with each other by vibrating their swim bladder!"

Looks to camera – ew.

Min bursts out laughing. "I'd forgotten how lame you are. That fancy office of yours is not exactly paying for itself, is it? If Ma knew how much it's going to waste, she'd be turning in her grave."

"Yeah, well, at least there's something to show for the money," he retorts. "Yours got wasted on childcare. Anyway, I'm ill," he mutters, scratching the back of his head.

"I'm ill," repeats Min in a grating voice.

"Stop it, Min," warns Uncle Henry.

"Stop it, Min," she smirks. Well, if being annoying is her aim, she's on to a winner.

"And cut!" I want to yell, but I don't think it would go down very well. So I head straight back out, armed with a tenner I found shoved in my jeans pocket. After all, there's a whole new town to explore, people to meet, films to create!

Fade up on a long panoramic shot of the bay.

To my left, there's the sea and a steep path down to the high street. Across the road from the beach, on a raised pavement bordered by black railings, there's not exactly much to it. The harbour and a pub, the Flying Fish, are at one end and Devi's Deli, the supermarket I was in earlier at the other. A smart-looking pink hotel called Burbank

House marks the centre point with the in-between filled by a surf shop, gift shop, wine bar, newsagent, Plaice 2 Be chippie and an ice-cream parlour called Screams.

This last discovery fills me with joy because I love ice cream. I'd eat it for every meal if I could, not that there's anyone stopping me. I used to have a Saturday job in Soho at Rai's Parlour. He was an easy-going kind of guy and let me have whatever I wanted after my shift. My favourite was a mouth-watering combination of salted caramel and pistachio in a wafer cone. Best. Job. Ever.

"Hi," I say brightly to the woman behind the counter, pressing myself against the glass to look at the ice-cream flavours, not that there are half as many as in Rai's. Oh well.

"What can I get you?" she asks. She's middle-aged with grey-streaked hair swept back in a bun and wearing a Screams apron, and she's staring grumpily at my phone.

"I'm filming my arrival here," I explain. "Wanted to remember it, you know? I was just admiring the ice-cream flavours."

The woman's face scrunches up in confusion. "They're just the usual ones. Bennie Khatri, where d'you think you're going?" she throws at a tall dark-haired boy with light brown skin.

"Off for a dive," he says.

"No, you're not. Delivery's arriving in a minute and I need you here."

"But, Mum," he moans, gesturing frantically out of the door.

"There'll be plenty of time for all that later. The sea's not going anywhere. Now can you please serve this customer?" And, with that, she hangs up her apron and disappears into the back of the parlour.

"Sorry," I say, with an apologetic grin that he doesn't return.

"What can I get you?" he sighs.

"Got any pistachio?" I ask.

He wrinkles his nose. "Just the flavours you can see, I'm afraid."

"How about salted caramel then?"

"We're all out," he says and, with a weary shake of his head, leans against the counter. "Look, just choose from what's here, all right? Queue's out the door."

"Um," I say, feeling surprisingly indecisive. "Vanilla. No, chocolate. No, fudge. No, wait!"

"Seriously?" he groans.

I laugh. "Sorry, just not used to being under such pressure. I'll stick with fudge, thanks."

I hesitate, ice cream in hand, wondering whether it's too soon to ask him if he fancies hanging out, but he's already moved on to the next customer.

Wariness

My next stop on the high street is Hej! – a small, dark Aladdin's cave of a space, crammed artfully with anything that you might need for the kind of house you see in magazines. Zinc buckets and old wooden fish boxes arranged as flowerpots, sheepskin rugs displayed on rickety oak ladders, brightly coloured cushions scattered on chairs and, in the middle of the room, a giant wooden table, painted distressed grey, covered with lamps and glassware, books and candles. I instantly want to buy everything.

At the end is an old-fashioned glass cabinet displaying chunky necklaces, dangly gold earrings, socks, scarves, you name it. And sitting next to it in a high-backed armchair, reading, with a dog curled at her feet, is the fiercest-looking old woman I've ever seen.

She's dressed in a black military-style jacket casually

done up over the top of a delicate gold dress, with a pair of gold flip-flops on her feet. To top it all off, she's wearing a beanie and thick turquoise-green glasses through which, I suddenly realize, she's watching me closely...

"*Hej*," she says in a sing-song accent. She sounds sort of Swedish or Danish. I'm not sure which.

"Hi," I say brightly. "Oh, what a gorgeous dog! What's she called?"

"*He* is called Ned," she replies. "What are you filming in here for?"

"Oh, just recording my day. D'you mind?"

"Yes, I do."

I lower my phone quickly. "You've got lovely things in here," I say.

"*Tak*. Looking for something particular?"

I wish! "Just window-shopping," I say, taking a swift lick of melting ice cream as it tries to make its escape.

"*Fint!*" she sighs. "Just what I need. Can't you read?" she asks, nodding at a sign on the shop door saying *STICKY HANDS STAY OUTSIDE* that I hadn't noticed.

"Sorry," I grimace. "I didn't see it."

"No, this appears to be a common problem around here. Well?" she asks, holding up the book that she seems desperate to get back to.

I smile. "I'm sorry to have bothered you. I just got here and wanted to explore, that's all." At the door, I turn to wave, but she's already lost in her book again.

A stone's throw away, I reach the harbour, a bustling area fenced in by a low stone wall. There's a large concrete ramp leading into the water from which stems a labyrinth of wooden jetties, where wader-clad fishermen rub shoulders with designer-dressed boat owners, while suncream-smeared tourists clamour for a piece of the action. I count four signs advertising different boat tours, all claiming to be the best with promises of dolphin-spotting and seal sightings.

I walk the length of the jetty, enjoying the cool breeze, until I reach a small wooden kiosk marked *Piscary Bay Sea Safari* where a spotty lad, clad in a checked shirt and a bucket hat squishing his fringe in his eyes, looks like he'd rather be in the water.

Looks to camera – I know the feeling!

"Hi," I say brightly.

He frowns at me. "Are you filming me?"

I nod. "Is that OK? I'm just recording my arrival here in Piscary Bay. I want to be a film director one day. I'm going to start out in documentaries first, then maybe end up shooting features like Bob. He's my … sort-of dad. He says it's tough, that everyone in media wants to be in film, but what he's forgetting is that I'm determined."

Looks to camera – TMI?

The kiosk boy stares at me incredulously. I'm being too much, as usual.

"So whatcha doing?" I ask, changing the subject quickly.

But his grimace deepens. "Working. I sell tickets for the boat trip."

"Nice," I say, fiddling with the leaflets on display. "Can I take one of these?"

He shrugs. "You're a Zombie, aren't you? We're sold out for today though. You'll have to come back another time..."

There's that term again. I hate it!

I smile anyway, determined not to let my irritation show. "Can't believe how busy it is," I say. "Beats being in school though."

He doesn't return my smile.

Labels

By lunchtime, I have filmed the entire town and bought a cheap snorkel mask from Alf who runs the *Surf Shack*, wolfed down a portion of chips from the Plaice 2 Be and hovered outside Screams, contemplating another ice cream. The story's been the same wherever I've gone. Wariness. Of my questions, my openness, my smile even. I'm just trying to be friendly! But, as the high street swarms with yet more tourists, the locals' unfriendliness starts to make sense.

I wander on to the beach. It's so packed with people marking out their territory now that you can hardly see the sand beneath the brightly coloured picnic blankets, windbreakers and tents. I feel shocked – and this coming from someone who's used to the crowds in London! Who knew you needed so much stuff? Little kids scatter their plastic buckets and spades, inflatables and shoes far and wide, and I can see what the rude cyclist meant about his home being overrun. When, for the millionth time, someone mindlessly kicks sand over me and doesn't apologize, I'm beginning to feel pretty grumpy myself.

"Hello!" cries the doorman as I trudge miserably past the Burbank Hotel. Dressed in a well-cut silver suit with a grey shirt and dark grey tie, he's very striking-looking, out of place somehow on this high street. Kind of how I feel at the moment.

"Why the long face?" he asks, his light grey moustache waxed into curling tips that make him look like he's permanently smiling.

I peer past him into the dark depths of the reception area. Kind of reminds me of London hotels and I'm suddenly filled with homesickness.

"Let me guess," he laughs. "You're a ... how they call? Zombie?"

My shoulders slump. It feels like I'm playing a not-so-happy interactive game of Happy Families, a game I adored as a kid when I used to dream of having a stay-at-home mum who'd bake me cupcakes. I'd imagine Min and Bob married with a newborn brother for me. Although, given Bob's gay, it was never going to happen.

"I'm just a person." I sigh and walk away, feeling even more miserable. Something that doesn't improve when the camera on my phone suddenly switches off with an incoming call from school.

"Hello?" I answer briskly.

"Coco James? It's Miss Garvey from the school office."

"Oh, hi, Miss Garvey," I say. "How are you?"

"I'm very well, thank you for asking. Where are you?"

"In Piscary Bay."

"So not London then." She sighs. "It's not holiday time yet, Coco. Your mother should have filled out the appropriate authorization form. I've called her numerous times now and left messages to no avail."

"Yeah, she's not the best at answering her phone," I admit. "But we're not on holiday. We've been kicked out of our home. Min was supposed to tell you."

"Yes, well, she didn't," says Miss Garvey a little more sympathetically. This isn't the first time we've talked because of something Min has or hasn't done. "I'm sorry to hear about your troubles, Coco. Are you OK? Do you have a place to stay? Is there another adult you can speak to?"

"Yes, thanks." Does Uncle Henry count as someone I can talk to? "I'm fine," I say. "You don't need to worry about me."

"Well, that's reassuring to hear. Now, can you please tell your mother to confirm this is in writing? An email will do. And she'll have to transfer you to the new school authority. You're fifteen. You should be in school regardless of how few weeks there are left of term…"

A History Lesson

The house is dead quiet when I get back and Min's door is firmly closed. I suppose their row didn't end well. Guess I'll tell her about school tomorrow.

I creep up to the attic. I like it there – it feels homely and lived in, while everywhere else seems neglected. Sitting high above everything, so that all you can see is the sea, it's as if I'm in a ship. Oh, and I like fish and I'm dying to get a proper look at the aquarium. Min had one at work – a giant one between two edit suites. It was gorgeous. I used to spend hours chatting to them – much to Robin's disapproval.

I stop short when I see Uncle Henry sitting in an armchair facing the fish tank, talking. "It made sense. How could I have been convinced so easily without backing up my arguments?"

He glances up, pausing as if the fish are going to answer, and in my imagination the pufferfish does, making me splutter with laughter and causing Uncle Henry to whip round.

"What are you smirking at?" he demands.

"Oh, er…" I mutter, trying desperately to remove my grin. "It's just… Were you talking to the pufferfish?"

"I was dictating a voice memo," he says, holding up his phone. "Working."

"Oh." I take a tentative step forward and nod at the pufferfish. "What's his name?"

Uncle Henry's brow wrinkles. "Name? Er … the scientific name for pufferfish is Tetraodontidae."

"That's not much of a name," I laugh. "Too much of a mouthful for a start. How about … Brian? Brian the pufferfish. Yeah, that'll do. You've got a couple of Nemos too. The orange-and-white ones," I explain.

"Amphiprioninae," says Uncle Henry.

Looks to camera – wow, he really knows how to suck the fun out of things…

"Pretty sure they were called clownfish in the film," I say. "D'you mind if I sit here? I'll be as quiet as a … fish."

"Actually, fish are capable of making a whole variety of sounds," he says. "Keep quiet then. I'm working…"

I walk over to the tank, being careful not to touch it, and peer in. "Hello, Brian," I whisper. "Why d'you look so sad? It's not all that great out here, you know."

Uncle Henry tuts loudly, rustling his papers pointedly at me.

"Sorry," I mouth, and tiptoe back to the armchair where I pick up the binoculars lying on the table between us, letting out an involuntary gasp when I think I see a dolphin. But it's just a piece of driftwood and a glance at Uncle Henry makes me put them down quickly with another mouthed apology.

"Uncle Henry?" I ask a few minutes later because I'm dying to have a proper conversation.

"I'm working."

"I was just wondering…"

"I'm working."

"It's just that…"

Uncle Henry flings down the paper that he's reading. "What?"

"Um… Well, I met someone earlier. A few people actually. They called me a Zombie and you a Cuckoo. Didn't make any sense."

He frowns out at the sea, the sunlight making his watery green eyes sparkle like emeralds. "None of it does," he snorts. "Min and I are Cuckoos because we weren't born here. We relocated from the States when I was fourteen and Min was eleven. The name's derived from the summer visiting bird that steals other bird's nests, i.e. anyone who's come to live here from anywhere else."

I frown. "So, the rest of the community are…?"

"The Fish," he sighs. "Or, as they see it, the true locals of Piscary Bay, but only if you've got three generations in the grave." He frowns. "Zombies is a new one on me though. Probably something to do with the way the tourists wander around, leaving a trail of destruction behind them."

Having seen it for myself, I can't argue with that last point, but…

"It's a hateful term!" I gasp. "We all live and breathe the same air, don't we? In London, we celebrated our differences. I had loads of friends from all over."

I hesitate, wondering suddenly about my family ties on my dad's side. "What was my dad then?" I ask. "Min's only ever talked about him as if they were the real-life Romeo and Juliet by the sea."

"I'll bet she has," he snorts. "A Fish, a Cuckoo and a forbidden love." He sighs. "Billy coined the terms as a joke just to wind Min up – and it worked too – but he certainly never meant for them to stick like this."

"So, what does that make me when we're only here for the summer?"

Uncle Henry thinks for a moment. "Have you ever heard of the remora fish? Eight species of fish from the Echeneidae family who attach themselves to sharks and other large marine life including ships."

"No," I murmur, wondering where this might be going. But the punchline never comes and he remains silent.

"Erm…" I say. "What's that got to do with me? I'm not a fish."

"No, you're a mammal. You'd be eaten by the shark. The remora attach themselves for protection. Sharks don't eat them."

My frown deepens in confusion. "Are you saying I should just suck up to them then?"

But Uncle Henry shrugs as if the idea hadn't occurred to him. Quite what he's suggesting, I have no idea!

"Billy was a fun-loving guy," he says suddenly. "A social butterfly who just wanted to be in the water. You're just like him actually. The looks, his temperament – God help us. You'll find a way to make friends, I'm sure."

"D'you miss him?" I ask hesitantly, fearing that he might respond in the way Min usually does when I try to delve deeper beyond the love-at-first-sight bit. It's like she's edited her life and slapped a caption on saying, *Fifteen years later…*

As a result, I don't know as much about my dad as I'd like to, other than the aforementioned romance, that I look like him and that he died in a freak sea accident before I was born.

"Every day," answers Uncle Henry, patting my hand absently. "Now, d'you think you can bugger off? I'm trying to get some work done."

PISCARY BAY TIDE TIMES

Wednesday 26th June

LOW TIDE:	06:34	HEIGHT:	2.30 m
HIGH TIDE:	12:29	HEIGHT:	4.90 m
LOW TIDE:	19:02	HEIGHT:	2.50 m

Waning Quarter Moon

SUNRISE:	05:13	SUNSET:	21:36
MOONRISE:	01:59	MOONSET:	14:26

Panic

I'm up super early the following morning. Kind of hard to stay awake with the sunlight pouring into my bedroom, the curtain rail having fallen off in my hands last night. Min and Uncle Henry don't appear to have the same problem as their bedrooms remain dark and silent, making the house feel like a morgue.

I pick my way carefully down the steep pathway, taking care on the narrow spots and watching for stray rocks. My new snorkelling mask dangles in my hand along with an old towelling robe that I found in the utility room, hidden among a load of mouldy old wetsuits that must've been Min and Uncle Henry's back in the day.

It's quite a nerve-wracking drop down to the cove beach and, since no one knows I'm here, I'm being extra-cautious and trying to ignore the fact that I'm desperate to get in the sea, the lure of which is really quite magically compelling. It was the last thing I looked at before I went to sleep last night, staring out at the incoming tide, and it was the first thing I jumped up to look at this morning.

I'm hooked. So much so that last night I found a website for Piscary Bay tide times. I don't know what's come over me. I used to swim occasionally at the Oasis back home, but the chlorine always hurt my eyes. And I've only been to the beach at Brighton a handful of times. Maybe it's all that time I spent relaxing underwater in the bath. It must have seeped under my skin…

I fling my towel over a large, smooth rock, strip down to my bikini and get ready to sprint along the beach to get warm. Then I notice the pile of someone else's belongings folded neatly on the sand. My eyes search the water, suddenly *very* alert to the fact that no one knows I'm here.

The tide is going out and it takes me a while to spot them. Two heads bobbing about in the sea. All of a sudden, they disappear underwater and I automatically hold my breath as if I'm there too, counting the Mississippis in my head. By three minutes, I'm desperate to breathe. They haven't resurfaced and I'm suddenly full of panic. Have I just witnessed two people drown?

I impulsively dash into the sea, my feet slapping noisily against the wet sand, my eyes firmly trained on the spot I'd last seen them. And, as the water gets deeper, my strides get larger until I'm bounding over the waves and

I dive straight under, hardly noticing the freezing waves I'm so focused on finding the missing people.

I'm swimming now with a choppy front crawl, the outgoing tide making me feel like I'm an Olympic swimmer, and I reach the place where they went under in no time. Taking a deep breath, I dive down, but the snorkel mask floods with seawater and I have to resurface, my eyes burning from the salt.

Treading water, I glance around me helplessly. Where are they? I turn this way and that, trying hard not to cry, but the fact that this is how my dad died flashes in front of my eyes.

"You all right?"

The voice comes from behind me and I turn quickly to see none other than the rude cyclist swimming towards me, accompanied by Bennie from Screams.

"Oh thank God," I gasp, gulping down my tears.

"What are you doing swimming out here on your own?" asks the rude cyclist. "There are dangerous rips along this shoreline, you know. Typical flippin' Zombie. Never listen."

"Yes, I do," I mutter, my hackles rising. "You were under for over four minutes. I was worried."

"We're fishing," he says scornfully, holding up his spear. "Why don't you toddle off back to your mansion? Leave us alone."

Bennie frowns. "That's a bit harsh, Leo. She was only trying to help."

Leo starts laughing and jeers at me. "Her, save us?

Yeah, good one."

"Oh, whatever," I retort. "Should've left you to drown."

I start to move away from them, but the outgoing tide is strong. It's like swimming upstream and they're still only a few metres away. At this rate, they're going to have to *save me*.

"Need some help?" asks Leo smugly.

"Not from you, no," I snap.

"Well, if you're not careful, you're going to find yourself caught in a rip that you can't get out of. You shouldn't be swimming alone."

"You're here, aren't you?" I say.

"You're swimming in circles," says Bennie.

"Because she's wearing that piece of crap," snorts Leo, gesturing dismissively at my mask.

"I bought it from the Surf Shack," I protest.

He laughs. "That Zombie trap. You should really be wearing a proper mask if you're going to swim out this far."

"You're also rotating when you breathe. Try this," says Bennie and he demonstrates his arm position in the water. "Yeah, that's better. Don't kick so hard either. You'll burn out at that pace if you're not used to it."

"Should be wearing fins too, if you ask me," mutters Leo.

"I didn't," I reply, pointedly fixing my twinkliest smile on Bennie. "Thanks for your help, Bennie."

Back on dry land, I collapse on the sand, my legs feeling wobbly at the effort it's taken to swim back to shore. But I feel exhilarated too, in a way that running has never quite done for me.

"So, d'you guys freedive too?" I ask as the boys stride out of the water. "I've only ever seen that in the movies. I'll bet there are some interesting places to explore around here, aren't there?"

"What's with the twenty questions?" snarls Leo.

"I'm just being friendly," I say, my hackles rising again. I've never struggled to make friends like this before. I turn my charm offensive on Bennie. It feels like I've got more chance getting through to him. "I used to work in an ice-cream parlour. Rai's in Soho?"

He shrugs. "Never heard of it."

"It's award-winning," I say. "He makes his own gelato."

"Good for him," Leo says.

"It was actually. Anyway, if your mum ever needs a spare pair of hands, I could always help out. Got nothing else to do and I could use the cash."

Bennie grimaces. "Thanks, but you're a Zombie. You'll be gone in a few weeks. It's not worth the bother."

"Oh, I'm here all summer," I say

"Still," he says, unconvinced. "Well, see you then."

I watch them pick their way up the path, feeling intensely irritated by how they're judging me when they don't even know my name.

Bloodworms

Min's in a foul mood to match mine when I get back, crashing about in the kitchen. Half of me hopes she might be attempting to make some pancakes. The other half knows fat chance. A domestic goddess Min is not. If I want something, I have to do it myself.

"D'you have to make all that racket?" demands Uncle Henry, appearing at the bottom of the stairs.

I hold my hands up. "Not me, Uncle Henry. It's Min."

"Hmm," he grunts and disappears into the kitchen. "What's wrong with *you*?" I hear him ask. Then, "My bloodworms! You can't take those out of the freezer!"

"You care more about those bloody fish than you do about us!" yells Min, hurling something at him.

Looks to camera – I hope it's not defrosted bloodworms.

Taking a deep breath, I peer cautiously round the

kitchen door and come face to face with the situation. Standing in the corner, hair half tied up with a bright red bandana, Min appears to be trapped by a sea of pots and pans full of lumps of ice, thawing bags of peas and plastic pots of... Oh yuck, bloodworms. She's been defrosting the freezer and, by the looks of the water everywhere, it's something that hasn't been done in years.

"Where've you been?" mutters Uncle Henry, taking in my bedraggled state with a frown.

"Swimming," I say, holding up the snorkel mask.

"On your own?" he gasps. "There are rips around here. You shouldn't—"

"It's OK," I interrupt. "I normally stick close to the shoreline. But there were a couple of local lads fishing down there anyway."

"That's a private beach," he splutters. "They're trespassing." He shakes his head angrily. "They'd better not be trying to get at that…" He stops abruptly.

"Get at what, Uncle Henry?" I say, my curiosity spiking. I do have a nose for a good story after all. But, much to my disappointment, he won't be drawn on it.

"Never you mind," he mutters. "I'm going back to bed."

"What happened, Min?" I ask, watching him leave with a bowl of sugary cereal.

"Don't you start," she snaps before bursting into tears.

"I wasn't going to," I say quietly, recognizing signs of the end-of-her-temper tantrum, which always involves lots of crying. It usually doesn't last, as long as I keep it together and don't make it worse. "Why don't we leave this for a minute," I say, leading her into the front room and settling her into the armchair by the window.

I disappear into the kitchen to clear up the mess. Mainly shoving everything back in the freezer and shutting the door on it so that I don't have to stare at the box of frozen bloodworms.

"Thanks," she sighs when I return with a mug of fresh filter coffee. She looks a lot more at peace sitting there in the morning light, as if the sea and the sunlight have a calming influence. "You been swimming?" she asks.

I nod.

"I used to do that too," she replies with a sad smile. "Used to meet Billy down there, just as the sun was rising. We'd swim together, then lie in each other's arms until we were warm again. Sometimes he'd bring me coffee in a flask, or he'd cook us breakfast on an open fire. He was amazing at doing that sort of thing. So thoughtful…"

Looks to camera – see what I mean about the epic romance?

Don't get me wrong, I love hearing her stories, but part of me does wonder whether they're all completely true. I mean, no one's that perfect, are they?

"Did I ever tell you the story of how he and Uncle Henry got into trouble with the police?" says Min suddenly. Now this is a new one. "There's this small beach further down the coast. It's great for surfing. Anyway, we'd been going there for years and all of a sudden the tourists got wind of it. Billy and Henry were so furious when they found out, they covered a tourist's car windscreen with board wax."

"No," I gasp. "But Uncle Henry's so serious."

Min chuckles. "Yeah, time's changed us both. Don't think he's ever got over his failed scientific career."

"Which was?"

"Oh, he threw himself behind some idea about apes and water," she explains. "It's a popular theory among the Fish. They're freedivers. Been doing it around these parts for centuries. Anyway, it got disproved or something. I dunno – school was never my strong point."

"Speaking of which," I say, "my school rang yesterday. You didn't tell them that I'd left." I try to keep my voice neutral. "And you're supposed to get in touch with the local authority here."

Min, as ever, overreacts. "And you're only telling me this now?"

"I'm sorry, I forgot," I reply, bristling. "You're the mother here!" But I don't say that last bit because I'm keeping the peace and I don't need her to start crying again.

"You've had a lot on," I say quickly. "Miss Garvey wants you to email her." But Min looks exhausted, as if the idea of doing anything other than sitting there is beyond her, so I pat her hand. "It's all right," I say. "I can log into your email. Leave it with me. And I'll look up the number of the local authority for you." I hesitate. "That is if we need it?"

Min frowns. "How d'you mean?"

"Well, I won't bother if we're going back to London…
Are we?"

She shrugs. "Don't ask me."

Looks to camera – who should I ask then?

My Name is Coco

Put off by the idea of swimming alone, I've taken to spending my time on the town beach. As early as possible so as to avoid the inevitable summer crowds. Which means it's just me, the dog walkers and the surfers, and the odd yawning parents, who sit staring blearily out to sea with their takeaway coffee cups while their young children dig hopefully in the sand.

I used to love people-watching back home. Soho's full of them coming and going, and I liked to imagine what inner monologues were going on in *their* heads. Bob said that's why I'd make a good documentary maker: I'm very observant. I miss him. He was always the person I could talk to when Min was in one of her moods.

Swimming has become my new ritual, along with people-watching and the quiet contemplation of the sea, trying to assess the currents before stripping down to my bikini. Then leaving my clothes and phone in a neat pile under a rock, jogging across the sand before I wade into the sea, the waves lapping against my thighs, sending shivers down my spine. I feel better there. More so than in the bath. As if all my focus is on getting in and under the cold water, temporarily suspending any other thoughts.

Doesn't feel like that today though. More like wading through mud. The outgoing tide is too choppy and I can't seem to get my stroke right, the way Bennie showed me, resulting in a lungful of water. So I give up and look out at the waves, the wind lashing against my wet skin, forcing the hairs to stand on end. No amount of swimming can shift the anxiety looming over me. The question of whether or not we're returning to London preys on my mind, mixed with intense loneliness and homesickness. It feels like, no matter how hard I try, I just can't fit in here.

"Penny for them," says an old woman, striding past me with a surfboard tucked comfortably under her arm, a gleeful smile of anticipation on her face. She looks kind of like Maggie Smith, if I scrunch up my eyes and imagine her wetsuit as a witch's cloak.

"Just enjoying the view," I sigh.

"It's a good one," she agrees. "Waves are tremendous today."

"Yeah, too big to swim in though."

She nods. "You were hoping to get some thinking done?"

I glance at her. "Yeah, how did you know?"

"The long face," she replies. "And the far-off look."

"Not much *to* smile about."

"You know," says the old woman, inhaling deeply, closing her eyes to the sun and beaming as if it's the best thing ever, "I think that sometimes bad things are sent to test us … our sense of character and who we are." She sighs. "Being in the sea is the one place where I feel I can come up for air and just breathe again." She pauses to look at me. "The sea will be different tomorrow, and so will you."

We contemplate the water together in silence, as if we're both saying a prayer for something we've lost. And then the moment is gone and she's grinning wildly again. "I don't mean to rub it in," she laughs, "but the sea is absolutely spot on for surfing today. If you'll excuse me, I'm off to catch me some of those right-handers. See you."

I watch as she strides into the sea, her long grey hair tumbling down her back.

Cut to a shot of her pulling herself on to her tummy on the surfboard.

She begins to paddle towards the white water, expertly manoeuvring herself just as the waves crash. She's quickly out to sea, scouring the waves for the right break. Then, all of a sudden, she's up on her board, riding one in with a huge ecstatic grin plastered on her face. I think she might be the coolest old lady I've ever seen. Well, the second one.

Looks to camera – how many can one small town have?

When I get back to my clothes, I find that Bob has sent me a message – a lengthy essay in that way adults seem to text.

29 June

Bob 10:34

Sunshine! How's my favourite gal doing? Has the whirlwind settled? You got that dog you always wanted yet? What's the house like? And Uncle Henry – is he like Min? *Christ, I hope not* I know you'll have a ton of friends eating up your time, but don't forget your old pal Bob! Send me an email … or a text … or an emoji 😬 and don't spare any of the details… I miss you so much. Listen, can you get Min to call me? I've tried a few times but either her phone's off or she's ignoring me on purpose. *We both know it's that* She's being a drama queen and we need to talk! XOX

Things suddenly don't feel so hopeless any more – funny how a few kind words can do that. It's exactly the cue that I needed. I plaster a smile on my face, feeling determined to make people see past those silly labels. I'm not a Cuckoo or a Zombie or a Fish! I'm Coco James, the girl who doesn't give up…

"Morning," I call out to the owner of Hej! "Nice outfit."

The fierce woman smiles. "*Tak*."

"I'm Coco, by the way," I say. "I'll be in later, minus the ice cream."

She nods. "Ingrid. See that you do, Coco."

"Hi, Bennie," I yell across the street. "I'll be in later for some salted caramel! Oh, and I never told you my name. It's Coco!"

He half raises his hand in reply, a smile automatically flashing across his face before he can get himself in check. I continue on like this, waving at everyone I meet and introducing myself properly. My theory being that if I act as if I've got lots of friends then eventually I will have. One thing's for sure: they'll all know my name!

"Let me help you with that!" I cry, jumping to open the door where the Burbank doorman is struggling with two armfuls of cases, the owners of which stand to the side, staring obliviously at their phones.

"Thanks!" He beams, reaching into his pocket. "Here." And he hands me a slip of paper. "For your troubles. Client gave it to me, but I don't really like sea. Not out on it anyway." He stares at me, half dressed in a falling-apart towelling robe and sand-covered legs. "Something tells me you do."

I laugh. "Yes, very much. And thanks. I'm Coco."

"Jan," he replies. "I'm from Poland. Where you from?"

"Soho," I reply. "But living here currently."

"Ah, the land of jazz," he gasps. Then he sings, "*Booby-doo bop-bop,*" in a deep, raspy voice, which makes me laugh and him smile even more.

"See you around. And thanks!" I call, waving the voucher in the air. Suddenly everything feels like it's going to be OK. Because yesterday was my final payday from the ice-cream parlour and I know exactly how I'm going to spend the money...

PISCARY BAY SEA SAFARI

The ultimate way to experience the beauty of Piscary Bay!

Join us on one of our catamarans as we explore our stunning coastline in search of wildlife. Seals, dolphins, porpoises, puffins and maybe even the odd mermaid!

THIS VOUCHER ENTITLES THE BEARER TO A 50% DISCOUNT ON ANY OF OUR TRIPS.

BOOKING ESSENTIAL DURING THE SUMMER MONTHS

In association with **Part of our World.**

Children are deemed to be 12 years and younger.
Any person with a child ticket must be accompanied by a responsible adult at all times.

PISCARY BAY TIDE TIMES

Sunday 30th June

HIGH TIDE:	03:51	HEIGHT:	5.80 m
LOW TIDE:	10:22	HEIGHT:	1.70 m
HIGH TIDE:	16:15	HEIGHT:	5.90 m
LOW TIDE:	22:46	HEIGHT:	1.60 m

Waxing Crescent Moon

SUNRISE:	05:15	SUNSET:	21:35
MOONRISE:	03:31	MOONSET:	19:08

The Big Blue

I'm at the harbour bright and early the next day. The old woman was right – the sea is calmer and everything seems different. Well, kind of. The spotty boy with the plaid shirt and bucket hat is still looking bored in his little wooden kiosk and the harbour is still buzzing with people, though perhaps a little quieter on a Sunday morning. The main thing is that *I* feel different. Like I could conquer the world.

"Morning," I say, glancing at the inviting cool sea shimmering calmly in the sunlight. "Perfect day for it, don't you think? Is there space available on your boat this morning? Only I've got this voucher."

"Who d'you know to get that deal?" frowns the spotty boy. "The Burbank normally only gives that to VIPs."

I smile. "What, don't I look like a VIP?"

He stares incredulously at my carefully selected outfit

of bright pink culottes and an off-the-shoulder crop top. "No."

I laugh nervously. "Wasn't sure what to wear, to be honest. Never been on a sea safari before. I'm Coco, by the way. We didn't formally meet the other day."

"The other day?"

"Yeah. I came and got a leaflet off you. Anyway, you are?"

The boy blushes. "Seth. Why d'you want to know?"

"Just being friendly. Which way's the boat?"

The sea-safari boat, a white catamaran named *Seals the Deal*, is docked at the front of the harbour down some small, steep steps leading off the giant concrete ramp. It's packed full of tourists, including a group of lads laughing and jostling each other as they sort through their diving equipment, and a group of giggling women, one of whom is wearing a bridal veil. It looks like I got the last ticket!

"Hi, I'm Coco," I say, taking a seat next to a family smartly dressed in fleece-lined hooded coats, so cosy they look like duvets. The mother, a Black lady with braids, smiles a vague greeting, then returns to looking out to sea so I turn my focus instead on the skipper of the boat. A thickset red-faced man with grey hair and white stubble who doesn't appear to like the presence of my phone camera.

"What are you doing?" he asks gruffly.

I smile sweetly. "I'm making a wildlife documentary. This one's called *The Big Blue*."

"Think you're the next David Attenborough, do you?" he snorts.

"Something like that," I laugh. "It's busy today. Did I get the last spot?"

"'S'always busy this time of year. Just waiting on two more and then we'll get going. Ah, here we are."

I follow his gaze in time to see Leo dumping his bike on the jetty and taking off his helmet to reveal perfectly messed-up blond hair. He certainly knows how to make an entrance. Dressed in cut-off jeans and a hoodie, he looks about as fashion-conscious as a … fish! Next to him, on an old-fashioned bike with a basket full of wetsuits and flippers, is a tall, lanky girl with long blond hair, dressed in a similar outfit. She climbs onboard, brushing past me as if I'm invisible, despite murmuring hello. Then Leo sees me and his face falls into a scowl.

"Hi, Leo," I say, deciding to ignore it and adding with a giggle, "we must stop meeting like this." But my joke doesn't go down well and he stomps over to his friend who clearly wants to know who I am, which I suddenly realize he doesn't know either.

"I'm Coco," I say, walking over to him on wobbly feet like a toddler taking their first steps. "Whoa," I laugh, clutching wildly at the handrail and missing so that Leo has to put an arm out to stop me from going head first into the sea.

"Careful," he mutters.

"Ladies and gentlemen – please take your seats and no standing while the boat is moving," calls the skipper, staring directly at me. "There are plenty of seals out today, so I've no doubt that you'll be swimming with them within the hour."

"Seals?" I gasp excitedly.

"Yeah. What of it?" sniggers Leo.

"Oh, I just didn't know we could *swim* with them. What are they like?" I ask, my eyes sparkling with excitement. "I'll bet they're like big cuddly dogs, aren't they? Oh, I can't—"

I'm stopped in my tracks by Leo's look of disgust. "They're not pets, you know," he says sharply. "The male ones can get quite aggressive, especially if they think they're under attack. Don't put your hand out to stroke them, whatever you do. And don't corner them either."

He turns his back on me to talk to his friend who gives me such a dirty look that I hold back my impulse to ask her name. Something tells me she wouldn't tell me anyway. So I go back to making my film. With the sun on my face, the sound of seagulls serenading me and the gentle rocking of the boat as we head out into the big blue, this feels just like my kind of scene…

Siren Call

Fade up on a long panning shot of the boat anchored in a bay, a short distance from shore, surrounded by the sparkling turquoise sea and a ragged coastline where giant grey rocks stick out like claws and thin stretches of yellow sandy beach lie scattered with seaweed and pebbles.

It feels like I'm in paradise.

"Wetsuits on," calls the skipper. "Seals are out in force today. You're in for a proper treat."

I watch as everyone springs into action, except me. I don't want to wear a wetsuit. They're clingy and unflattering, and besides, I've been swimming fine without one.

"Do I have to wear one?" I ask.

The skipper stares at me and chuckles. "Rather you than me. It's still cold at this time of year, you know."

"Yeah," I say, "but the sun'll soon warm me up."

"Well, OK. But go careful, eh? Twenty minutes max. Don't want you getting hypothermia. You do want the snorkelling gear though, right?" he adds, pointing to a bench in the middle of the boat, where there's a large plastic box full of enormous flippers, masks and snorkels.

Attempting to move in the giant flippers has me hooting with laughter as I stumble round the rocking boat, continuing to look like I've only just learned to walk.

"How do you manage in these things?" I ask the duvet-clad woman from earlier as I collapse on to the bench beside her. "I look like a clown. Oh my God, there's one!" I squeal as I spot a seal popping its head up in the water. "And another!"

My enthusiasm is infectious and soon we're crying out with every new sighting as if we're playing whack-a-mole at speed.

"I take it this is your first time swimming with seals," laughs the woman. "You're going to love it. We come every year to see them. You sure about not wearing a wetsuit though?"

I laugh. "I'll be all right. I'm baking."

"You won't be in there," she says. "Here. At least have my gloves and boots. I never stay in for long anyway."

"Oh, thanks" I say, grinning happily.

We chat lots after that, me and Tania. About how nice

and peaceful it is to be out on the water. It turns out she knows Min. Guess that's a small town for you. They went to school together apparently and she had a massive crush on Henry for years too.

Leo and his friend, both now wearing hooded wetsuits, gloves and flippers, snorkels and masks, brush past me and jump in.

"He can hold his breath for more than four minutes, you know," I tell Tania.

She nods. "It's all the freediving they do. The Fish have been doing it for centuries in these parts. Enjoy the seals, Coco, and remember: don't stay in for too long." Then, with a wave, she jumps in too.

I'm the last one left onboard, save for the skipper and his mate. Having heard the shrieks from everyone else, all of whom are wearing wetsuits, I'm suddenly feeling a bit reticent. Wading into the cold sea and taking my time over it is one thing but jumping in knowing full well that it's going to be an icy blast is quite another.

I point my phone at the water instead, trying to focus in on the seals, but the reality is that they're too far away and just look like blurry dots, so I have to give up.

Then, poised with my toes curled over the edge of the boat, I survey the idyllic scene, my senses coming alive. The calm green-blue sea where the sun makes it sparkle like a carpet of stars. The squeals of wonder and delight from the snorkellers seeing their first seal up close.

The sharp, fishy tanginess of the sea air. The tingling of my skin as the midday sun begins to burn it, mingling with the coolness of the sea breeze. It's as if the sea is luring me in. A siren call to swim and be at one with the sea life. All of a sudden, it's the only thing that I know is right and I can't wait to get in.

And ... action!

Damsel in Distress

Flipping hell, it's freezing!

I burst to the surface, seawater erupting from my mouth as the salt burns the back of my throat, and swim wildly in an attempt to warm up, throwing my arms into an aggressive, punchy front crawl, while trying to put into practice what Bennie told me the other day. My feet and hands are OK thanks to Tania. The rest of me, however, feels like there are knives digging into every part of my body.

"You all right?" calls the skipper anxiously from the boat.

I raise a hand, nodding that I'm OK. If I just keep moving, I'll be fine. I swim towards the group of snorkellers, all face down in the water, watching the seals. Then one pops up suddenly just a few metres in front of me, looking startled, and dives back under, darting right beneath me. Or so I imagine. I miss it because of fiddling with the mask that sits uncomfortably on my face, steaming up with my breath, while the snorkel keeps flooding with water. I'd be better off holding my breath. So I swim back towards the boat.

"Coming out already?" chuckles the skipper. "Knew you would."

"Can't see with this thing," I say, grabbing hold of the steps. "Got any normal goggles?"

"Sure. Want a wetsuit too?"

"No thanks," I say because I'm getting used to the cold now and it's not so bad. Besides, I don't want to miss out on the seals.

The next seal I spot, I don't even realize is one. It's so far below the surface, it looks more like a giant stingray. But then I see its little pointed head, black nose set into a white snout of whiskers, and beady eyes staring up at me, and I realize the water is teeming with them. I could stay here for hours, just watching. And they are like dogs, whatever Leo says.

It's fascinating watching them play. I can almost hear a David-Attenborough-like commentary describing their every move: "See how the young, playful seal pup dives beneath its captivated human audience..."

I swim towards where the divers have gone and, holding my breath, plunge under to explore the hidden rocks. It's so beautiful. With the sunlight streaming in, the water is a clear, tropical aquamarine today. The bright green seaweed sways as if in a breeze and shoals of silver fish dart round me, while seals occasionally dash past.

I kick around for ages, floating on my back, feeling the most relaxed I've felt in a long time. It's like I've escaped from all the worry and angst of the last few weeks and I can be myself again. The cold sets in suddenly, emanating outwards as if my core is made of ice. But, unwilling to leave this paradise quite yet, I kick my way to shore, where countless more seals lie in rows like sunbathers.

I choose a smooth, flat rock some distance away, so as not to disturb them, pulling myself on to it for a breather. The stone is hot – almost too hot – but as I'm so cold it's welcome, and I take a seat, gingerly pressing my skin against the burning rock until I'm used to it. Then I sit, looking out to sea, watching with delight as the seals continue popping up like meerkats. I blink my eyelids slowly like a camera shutter, taking a deep breath, inhaling the moment so that I can remember it forever. God, I wish I had a waterproof camera. This would make excellent footage.

Getting back in the sea after baking in the hot sunshine is refreshing for all of five seconds and then I'm shivering down to my bones. I should've worn a wetsuit. Trying to ignore the cold, I take a deep breath and dive down under for one last look at the rocks to see if there are any more seals down there. I pull myself along, my fins propelling me forward as I rifle through the brightly coloured seaweed and sand for shells. I could stay down here forever if it weren't for the cold.

Just as I think I'd better resurface and get out of the water, I see Leo swimming quickly towards me. He makes some kind of hand gesture that I don't understand and, all of a sudden, his arms are round me and he's pulling me to the surface and trying to flip me on to my back.

I impulsively push him away. "What are you doing?"

"We need to get you out of the water and fast," he says. "You've got hypothermia."

"No, I haven't."

He looks confused. "But you were underwater for ages."

I smirk at him. "I was freediving. Why don't you toddle off back to the boat and leave me alone?"

"Because you shouldn't ever freedive alone," he retorts.

"How come you are then?"

"I'm not," he growls. "Amy's gone back with the other divers. I was coming to look for you. Wish I hadn't bothered now. Well," he says, gesturing towards the boat, "after you."

I'm actually feeling very cold now. My front-crawl technique is embarrassing, my arms don't move in quite the co-ordinated way they should and it's only thanks to the enormous fins that I manage to move at all. As much as I hate to admit it, I'm kind of grateful that he's here.

The panic fully hits my chest the moment I climb out of

the boat and collapse thankfully on to the floor out of the wind. As my body catches up and I breathe in, it's a weird gasp.

"You all right, Coco?" asks Tania, concerned.

"I will be," I say, my teeth chattering.

She quickly pulls off her coat and flings it over me, the warm fleece snuggling against my clammy skin. "You need it more than I do." Then together we sit on the boat floor, Tania chatting quietly, her arms wrapped round me for extra warmth, the gentle rocking motion making me feel like I'm a child.

"I warned you about staying in too long," says the skipper gruffly. "You OK?"

I nod gratefully as he passes me a steaming mug of coffee.

"Zombies don't listen, Dave," pipes up Leo, smirking cockily at me. "No fashion statement to be made in the sea, you know."

I grimace in reply.

"Ignore that Leo Tremain," whispers Tania. "Just another Fish puffed up with his own importance."

Her comment jars with me though. I'm allowing myself to fall into the very label trap I'm trying to avoid. If I don't want to be thought of as a Zombie – shudder – then surely I can't go around judging others for being Fish. I can see that I'm going to have to stand strong in the face of their indifference and convince them they're wrong about me.

Charm Offensive

Back on dry land, Tania insists on my keeping her coat even though I've fully warmed up, and with promises to see me around town she walks away with her family, leaving me to ponder how to continue with my charm offensive. As I spy the queue of families with whinging children winding out of the door at Screams, I realize if ever there was a moment to prove myself – this is it.

"Hi, Bennie," I call. "Need some help?" And, before he can argue, I jump behind the counter and grab an apron and gloves. "What can I get you?" I ask the next customer with a sparkling smile so infectious that they can't help but smile back.

"Hey, you're good at this," cries Bennie as I expertly craft an ice-cream flower to an accompaniment of impressed cooing noises.

"Thanks," I reply. "Happy to be of service."

I-told-you-so look to camera...

"Nice dryrobe," he says, nodding at my coat.

"It's Tania's. D'you know her?"

Bennie laughs. "I know everyone. That's the problem with living in such a small town."

"Being anonymous isn't all it's cracked up to be," I say. "You can go days in London without seeing anyone you know. Anyway, I went on the seal cruise," I explain. "Got a bit too cold. My own stupid fault for swimming without a wetsuit."

"You went swimming without a wetsuit!"

"Don't you start," I laugh. "Your mate Leo tried saving me. Thought I was a damsel in distress."

Bennie chuckles. "You don't strike me as the sort."

"No. That's what I said. He doesn't like me, does he?"

He shrugs. "I wouldn't take it personally. He's like that towards all the Zombies."

The irritation rises up in me all over again, but I don't want to spoil the moment so I let it go.

We get through the queue in no time and, after a couple of hours, it's finally reduced to one. My charm offensive is working like a dream and Bennie and I are chatting as if we've known each other forever. Along with the freediving, he's a keen surfer and swimmer, and, being in the year above me, he's just done his GCSEs.

"I'm doing science and maths A levels next year," he

tells me. "I want to study marine biology eventually."

"Whoa," I say. "You'd get on with my uncle. He likes fish too."

Bennie snorts. "It's a bit more than liking fish. Their behaviour and interaction with the environment can teach us a lot. For example, did you know that life can be hard for a fish, which is why they don't go it alone? Their tendency to group together results in shared patterns behaviour in the face of external threats that can benefit marine conversation and even help us understand human behaviour."

I giggle. "Yeah, you'd definitely get on with him."

"Listen, thanks for helping out."

"No problem," I say. "Like I said, I've got nothing better to do until I go back to London. And who knows how long that will take!"

He frowns. "Why don't you know?"

"My mum got the sack," I say. "Then we got evicted by Bob. He's a TV director who's a sort-of dad to me. Anyway, he wanted to sell our flat to make some money for a short he wants to make. Half the people in the industry aspire to work in films. I want to be a director some day," I explain. "That's why I've got this," I say, pointing at my phone. "Got to start somewhere. So anyway we're stuck here until then, living with Henry."

Bennie frowns. "Henry? What did you say your surname was?"

"James," I say. "Min never married so I got her surname."

Bennie's face suddenly falls. "You're Henry James's niece."

I nod.

"As in *the* Henry James?"

Looks to camera – is there more than one?

"Haven't seen him in years," he mutters, looking quite disturbed. "Didn't know he had a niece. Well, you'd better leave before Mum sees you then."

"What? Why?"

"Because you're a James," he sighs. "Look, I'm sorry," he adds, smiling sympathetically and shoving a tenner in my hand. "There's a lot of history between the James family and my mum. The whole community actually. I don't want to get involved. Sorry."

∼∼∼

The comedown hits me hard as I traipse along the seafront. Even the spectacular sunset, shooting crepuscular rays through the clouds into the incoming waves, can't stop it.

Down on the beach, there's a group of kids setting up a fire. Kids in hoodies laughing and chatting, while others fool around in front of them, vying for attention. It's exactly my kind of scene. The sort of thing me and my mates might do, though in a park and without the fire. Any other day, I'd jump at the chance to go and say hello, try to integrate myself, make some new friends. But today I can't face being shunned by anyone else.

Not being given the chance for them to get to know me.

So I trudge on past, shoulders hunched, hands shoved in my pockets, feeling a lonely despair, which for once I can't reason myself out of.

London Calling

The first sound I hear when I get back to Cliff House is Min sobbing. Along with my usual what-is-it-now? feeling, the panic immediately wells up inside me, the hairs standing up on the back of my neck, and I hold my breath. It's my only way of coping with the helplessness and guilt.

"Oh, Coco," she gasps. "He didn't pay me what I was owed. The conniving sod." She sinks back into the armchair, looking deflated, like all the fight's gone out of her. Eyes streaming, black eyeliner running down her pale, gaunt cheeks. Her usually immaculate beehive hairdo is skew-whiff and half tumbling down.

"What am I going to do?" she wails. "I don't know what to do. Tell me what to do."

"You're the mother, not me," I want to say after the day

I've had. Instead, I continue holding my breath, trying to think what *the right thing* is to say. "You could … call Bob?" I suggest cautiously. "He texted earlier. Said you hadn't been answering his calls." I try, and fail, to keep the testiness out of my voice.

"Yeah, all right," snaps Min, rising to it as always. "He probably just wants to shout at me like you're doing."

"I'm not shouting," I retort, my voice automatically rising. I take another breath. I'm not helping myself here. "Look," I say, softer this time, "you two are like siblings. You're always fighting, but you make up in the end. Why don't you go to London? You could speak to Robin in person. Convince him he made a mistake and that you're the best post producer he's ever had. You could meet up with Bob while you're there too."

Min stares thoughtfully out of the window and I actually think I might have hit on something.

"This isn't forever, is it?" I say, motioning about us. "This place is falling apart and Uncle Henry doesn't want us living here."

"What he wants and what he gets are two different things."

"Yeah, I know," I reply, "but we're not staying here…"

"You're not making any sense," sighs Min. "Where else would we go?"

"Back to London," I say, my frustration bubbling to the surface again. Why doesn't she get it? "It's where we belong, Min."

"I don't know," she murmurs.

Yes, but I do.

"You've worked for Robin for years," I tell her. "That's got to count for something. We're city girls, Min – that's what we've always said. Being down here is a nice change, but all the sea views and sunsets can't compete with being able to see our mates whenever we like. Don't you miss the hustle and bustle of home?"

Looks to camera – now I'm feeling really homesick.

"So, will you go?" I press on. "Bob sounded like he wanted to talk to—"

"Coco, can you shut up for two seconds?" snaps Min. "I can hardly hear myself think!"

I flinch, feeling like I've been slapped. I've pushed it too far. As always. "I'm sorry," I mumble. "I'm just trying to help."

Her face softens. "I know… Did Bob really say he wanted to talk to me?"

I nod. "Maybe he's changed his mind about the flat. Wouldn't be the first time, would it?"

"It's worth finding out, I suppose."

"Does that mean you'll go?" I ask.

Min smiles. "Yes, I'll go to London. Sort this out once and for all. I'm not letting Robin walk all over me. We James girls are made of sterner stuff."

"Oh, Min!" I squeal. "That's great news. The best I've

heard all day."

She frowns. "Where's that coat from?"

"Tania lent it to me," I explain, leaving out the bit about nearly catching hypothermia. Don't think Min could handle it, though *I* could really use a cuddle. "She lives in the close below. In the pink house between the blue and the yellow ones."

"Yeah, I know where she lives. Why'd she do that?"

"I was too cold," I reply. "And we got chatting. She seemed quite surprised about me being your daughter actually."

Min shrugs. "I skipped town before anyone knew I was pregnant… Why were you cold?"

"I went swimming with the seals. Oh, Min, it was magical!"

She laughs. "Yeah, Billy and I used to go out round that coastline all the time."

"Really?" I say, my eyes lighting up at the idea that I've done something my dad used to do. My head is suddenly full of questions about him. Things I've never even considered asking. "What else did he like doing? Did he live nearby? Did he—?"

Min exhales heavily. "Now's not the time, Coco. It's too painful a subject. I just … can't."

But it's like a door to the past has been opened and, quite honestly, I don't want to shut it.

PISCARY BAY TIDE TIMES

Thursday 4th July

HIGH TIDE:	06:51	HEIGHT:	6.60 m
LOW TIDE:	13:18	HEIGHT:	0.90 m
HIGH TIDE:	19:12	HEIGHT:	6.80 m

Waxing New Moon

SUNRISE:	05:18	SUNSET:	21:34
MOONRISE:	07:02	MOONSET:	23:09

Holding my Breath

It's with trepidation that I walk with Min to the bus stop. As much as I can't wait for her to go back to London and resolve this mess, I'm feeling nervous about being left here on my own. Leaving aside the fact that we've never been apart for more than a couple of days, I've made no further progress with the locals, and Uncle Henry is ... eccentric and closed off, to say the least.

"Why are you holding your breath?" asks Min.

Looks to camera – funny, she's never noticed me doing that before.

I puff out the air. "Feeling anxious."

"Why?"

"Because nobody likes me," I say. I gasp out my exasperation at Bennie dropping me like a hot potato when he found out who I was, and how, when I took the coat back to Tania, her son Abe had merely shrugged when I'd suggested he might like to go for a swim sometime. "I'm struggling to fit in."

Min snorts. "You? Yeah, right."

"It's true," I say, then whisper, "I'm not a Fish or a Cuckoo, am I?"

Min rolls her eyes. "That old nonsense. Look, maybe dial it down a bit," she suggests, nodding at my outfit, a sparkly black playsuit I bought in Camden Market. "You can be a bit … much, darling. Rather like that outfit."

Looks to camera – says the woman who wore a floor-length kaftan to breakfast yesterday!

"Turn the camera off and talk to them," she suggests. "This community's stuck in the past. They don't like change. Give them time."

"Well, with any luck, we won't need that," I sigh. "Say hello to Bob for me. Tell him I miss him."

"Tell him yourself," she laughs. "That's what phones are for."

I'd look to camera again if I had the energy…

"Are you sure I can't come with you?" It's a question I've asked a thousand times since she made her decision. And, once again, she shakes her head firmly. She can be just as determined as me unfortunately.

"It's best if you to stay here," she says. "I'm sleeping on a mate's sofa. Cheaper that way. Besides, Henry needs you."

"Does he?" I reply. "I haven't seen him all week.

He's always in bed or working at weird times. He was up at three this morning, shuffling round the attic. What's he even doing up there?"

"Walking apparently. He's got ME. Told me he's barely been out of the house in ten years."

She turns to me, taking hold of my face and planting a kiss on it. "Look after him for me, will you? Someone needs to. Talk to him about fish – he likes that."

I laugh. "Yeah, I noticed… Did he used to be someone?" I ask. "Only I've heard a couple of people talking about him in a legendary kind of way."

Min splutters with laughter. "Legendary? Lame, more like. Look him up on Wiziwisdom. That'll give you something to laugh at." She stops by the coach. "Now, give me a hug and wish me luck."

I laugh. "OK, bye then. And good luck. Come back with great news!"

I wave until the bus has disappeared over the hill, imagining twangy guitar music providing the background to her journey.

~~~

The spell of hot weather breaks the following morning, just as I'm on my way down to the shop for more cereal. Uncle Henry eats a lot...

Cue plonky piano music to accompany shots of me happily skipping down the hill, pausing to look up at the sky. A look of

*elation as the raindrops pitter-patter on my face, then jumping
in the fast-forming puddles, high-pitched giggles at the splashes
I produce. Jumpcut to a long pan of people huddled under the
shop awning, waiting for the downpour to stop, staring at me
as if I'm mad.*

I'm suddenly joined by a little girl with curly brown
hair who comes rushing over, landing with both feet in a
particularly large puddle that makes an impressive splash
and completely soaks us both, making her squeal with
delight.

"Hazel Quartermain!" yells a woman in a matching
bright yellow anorak, her perfectly coiffed short brown hair
beginning to flatten in the rain. "Get out of that puddle this
second. You're ruining your school uniform."

"Don't want to," mutters the little girl, pointing at me.
"She's doing it. Why can't I?"

The mother sets down her shopping basket and peers at
me with frosty green eyes, momentarily lost for words as
she takes me in. I suppose I do look a little odd wearing
a fake fur coat over the top of my shorts, but it was the
warmest thing I could find. I'm sure Min won't mind.

"That fur will be ruined in this weather," says the woman.

"It's only rainwater," I laugh. "It'll dry." I smile down at
the little girl. "I think you may have created the biggest
splash I've ever seen with that jump."

She laughs. "Really?"

"Yes, really. In fact, if there was an Olympic medal for

puddle-splashing, you'd definitely get gold. I'm Coco," I say, extending my hand to the mother. "I'm staying at Cliff House."

The mother's face softens. "Cliff House, you say? Prime estate that. Rather wanted to look round it but got told in no uncertain terms that it wasn't for sale. It used to belong to some famous, lauded professor, though that's before my time. Who lives there now?"

"The same one, I believe," I laugh. "Uncle Henry's my mum's brother. We're staying there for … well, a few weeks at least."

"Adele Quartermain," says the woman suddenly, thrusting her hand decisively into mine. Then, prompting her daughter with a nudge, she murmurs, "Say hello, Sprout."

Sprout doesn't seem to take kindly to being told what to do.

"That's an interesting name," I say, dropping to her level. "Is it cos you're a fan of Brussels?" She wrinkles her nose and I laugh. "Good, cos they really make you fart and that would mean you're more of a herring," I add, thinking of a fact Uncle Henry told me the other day. "That's how they communicate apparently. Bit smelly, if you ask me."

Sprout giggles and grabs hold of my hand. "D'you want to play with me?"

"Well, er," I say, glancing nervously at her mum. "Sure. I mean, I've got nothing better to do."

Adele tilts her head. "How d'you fancy doing a spot of babysitting?"

"I'm not a baby!" shrieks Sprout.

"It's just a term," snorts her mum. "We've recently moved back into the Old Barn," she tells me. "Renovation job. Took an age to get done thanks to the so-called builders and their surfing habits. Anyway, we're in now and I've got my first Airbnb guests arriving this afternoon. I've got to get the rooms ready. I don't suppose you're free now…?"

Grand Designs

The Old Barn sits in prime position in the middle of town, set back into the hillside with views to rival Cliff House and a whole separate wing, known as the annexe, for Airbnb guests – every inch of it renovated to the highest standard. It's the most beautiful home I've ever seen.

"Did you design all this yourself?" I ask, indicating the enormous stainless-steel kitchen, immaculately kept and gleaming in the sunlight. Everything's been meticulously thought through and I feel like I'm sitting in a magazine spread. Where's all the mess? "It's just gorgeous. I love it."

Adele blushes. "Thank you. And yes, I'm trying to set myself up as an interior designer. The Airbnb is supposed to fund it. I'm on the lookout for my next project actually. Don't suppose that uncle of yours would consider selling, do you?"

"No idea," I laugh. "He's not the most approachable of people."

"Don't I know it," she says ruefully. "That house is wasted on him. Those views, those features."

"Yes, it could certainly do with some attention," I agree. "It's positively falling apart at the seams. Rather like my uncle."

"How so?" asks Adele.

"He's got ME," I say. "Though I don't know what that is."

"It's a long-term illness," she replies. "Extreme tiredness among other things. Has he tried changing his diet? There's lots of information online. He should look it up."

She sets a glass of juice and a plate of home-made biscuits on the kitchen table – a vast slab of oak decorated with a collection of wildflowers poking out of vintage milk bottles.

"How old are you, Coco?" she asks.

"Fifteen," I say. "Doing my GCSEs next year."

"Shouldn't you be in school now then?"

"We needed to leave London," I explain. "Temporarily. Min's back there now, sorting it all out. I'll probably only miss a few weeks at the most. Doesn't matter."

"Course it matters." Adele frowns. "Siobhan is your age. She's not home from school just yet. She's a boarder." She leans in and whispers, "I can't wait to see her, but honestly … I'm dreading the rows between her and her sister. They're like chalk and cheese unfortunately. I'm sure I didn't use to argue that much with my sisters.

Do you have a big family?"

"Just Min and my uncle," I say with a shake of my head. Though, come to think of it, maybe I do have other family here…

Adele checks her wristwatch and stands suddenly. "Why don't you go up to Sprout's room? Top of the stairs, then take a left. I must get those guest rooms ready."

A flight of wrought-iron stairs lead up to a glass-lined walkway high above the kitchen, off which is an internal hallway – immaculately decorated in midnight-blue wallpaper – lit only by a set of windows high up in the roof. There are six doors to choose from and behind each I find yet another stunning, magazine-spread room with its own balcony looking out over the sea.

"Sprout!" I cry, finding her at the end of the corridor and discovering at last where all the mess is kept.

Sitting on the floor in front of a giant doll's house, Sprout's reaction to seeing me is one of pure delight. This must be what it's like having a sister.

"That's the prettiest doll's house I think I've ever seen," I gasp. Not that I've come across many.

"Flynn Rider is about to marry Rapunzel," explains Sprout.

"Ooh, my favourite of all the Disney movies!" I gasp. "And I'm an expert at setting scenes. Shove over."

I go on to tell her all about my plans to become a film director, regaling her with stories of my time spent hanging out in the edit rooms of Soho. She sits, rapt with attention, and I have the most fun I've had in ages. Finally, someone to talk to! Even if she is six years younger than me.

Looks to camera – well, it's a start, isn't it?

~~~

"You will come back, won't you?" asks Sprout, looping her arms round my waist as I try to leave.

I laugh. "Yes, I promise. But it's your dinnertime and I've got to get back to cook for my uncle. He'll be getting hungry."

Sprout furrows her brow, unconvinced.

"Let her go now, Sprout," says Adele firmly. "She's never been this enthusiastic with Siobhan."

"That's cos Shiv hates me," mutters Sprout. "She's always yelling at me. Calling me names."

"Oh, I'm sure she's not that bad," I say.

"Yes, she is."

Adele laughs nervously. "Um, Sprout, can you run and get the box on the kitchen table for me? I made some courgette cupcakes for Coco and her uncle."

As Sprout runs off, Adele hands me a twenty-pound note and a couple of printouts of a Wiziwisdom information page and a blog about ME.

"There are loads of links on there," she says. "I'm sure something will be useful. I always find a well-balanced diet is the best place to start. I hope it helps."

WIZIWISDOM

CHRONIC FATIGUE SYNDROME (CFS / ME)

Chronic Fatigue syndrome (CFS), often referred to as ME (myalgic encephalomyselitis) is a long-term illness with its most common symptom being extreme tiredness. It can affect anyone, including children, though it is most commonly found in women.

Contents
1. Symptoms
2. Diagnosis
3. Treatment
4. Living with ME

Symptoms (edit)

1. Sleep problems

2. Joint and muscle pain

3. Low immune system – headaches, sore throats, flu-like symptoms

READ MORE V

Diagnosis (edit)

There isn't a specific test and CFS / ME can look like many common illnesses. Speak to your GP…

READ MORE V

Treatment (edit)

There are a whole host of treatments available though none so far have a proven 100% track record:

* **Cognitive Behaviour Therapy**
* **Graded Exercise Therapy**
* **Nutrition-based suggestions**

READ MORE V

5th July 16:04
This page was last edited two days ago

Excerpt from Cottonwoolhead *blog:*

You are what you eat!

A balanced diet is crucial for everybody, but for someone struggling with CFS/ME it's crucial. And, when you've got the kind of foggy brain that I have, it's hard to focus on what the best thing to do is. That's why I got in touch with a local nutritionist who was able to tailor-make an eating plan to ease my symptoms and boost my well-being.

DO!
- Eat little and often.
- Include at least five portions of fruit and veg.
- Choose anti-inflammatory foods such as salmon, strawberries, olive oil and nuts.
- Choose foods with a low GI (glycaemic index) for a slow burn – that means more porridge, sweet potato and wholegrain pasta.

DON'T!
- Eat inflammatory foods such as sugar, fried foods and processed meats.

For details about creating a personalized diet plan, click <u>here</u>.

ME

"What d'you want for dinner, Uncle Henry?" I peer round his bedroom door. Staring listlessly into the dark, he lies spread-eagled on a pile of pillows as if he hasn't even got the energy to move his limbs together.

"You look exhausted," I say. "Bad night?"

He scowls at me. "You have no idea."

"Why don't I bring dinner to you then?" I suggest. "That way you can lie like a starfish *and* eat."

"Starfish extend their stomachs out of their mouths to eat," he snorts. "Are you suggesting that's what I do?"

I frown. "Er … no. How about a walk on the beach? Might do you some good to get out of the house. Certainly seems to be the only thing keeping me sane at the moment. I'll bet Cove Beach has some interesting…"

My voice trails away as Uncle Henry stares as me as if

114

I've suggested we fly to the moon and, yet again, I have a sudden longing for a jumpcut to my life. One that would have me at the station, meeting Min off the bus, her throwing her arms round me, me laughing as she tells me we're moving back to London…

"We could watch the sunset together," I say as a pathetic last resort. "There's something rather magical about seeing a day end over the sea, don't you think?"

For once, it's the right thing to say and Uncle Henry wearily climbs out of bed.

With the rain now all but forgotten, the bright blue skies sit above a fluffy white nest of clouds sprawled across the horizon, the sun peeking through, casting a deep orange hue across the silky-smooth sea. As it sinks lower, a pink warmth emanates from the sky, turning the clouds indigo and leaving only a yellow spot of sun reflected across the water, accentuating the ripples of the incoming tide. I sigh happily, letting the magical light wash over me, making it feel as if everything is possible.

"Ooh, it's a good one," I say, snuggling into what's fast becoming *my* armchair.

Uncle Henry remains silent, staring at the view, his expression unmoved as he tucks into another bowl of cereal, having turned down my offer of baked beans. Has he lived as a hermit for so long that he's forgotten how to speak and react to people?

"What's your favourite thing?" I ask him, resorting to a game I often play with Min when she's in a mood.

"Excuse me?"

"Your favourite thing?" I say. "About the day, I mean. I came up with it as a way of seeing silver linings when things are tough."

"Let me see," he says sourly. "I went to bed early last night because I was exhausted, but couldn't sleep for love nor money, so I got up and did some work in the middle of the night. Saw the sunrise as usual, then went back to bed. Got woken up too early by you clomping around. Came back upstairs to find one of the Amphiprioninae had died…"

I gasp. "Oh, which one? I hope it wasn't Laurel."

He stares at me as if I'm mad. "Laurel?"

"Yes, the other's one called Hardy," I say. "Thought it suited them. You know, being clownfish."

"Anyway," sighs Uncle Henry, "after I threw it down the loo—"

"You didn't give it a funeral?"

He fixes me with his steely eyes, the crease between them deepening. "As I was saying, after I disposed of the body, I went back to bed. Been there all day and I feel horrendous for it."

He turns his stare back on the sea, leaving me wondering whether I should tell him my favourite thing.

It is fish-based after all.

"So, my favourite thing was spotting a dolphin this morning," I say eventually. "I've never seen one in the wild before. Or it could have been a seal, I suppose. Either way, it was still special. And it was a really nice sunrise. I kept the window open last night. It seems to help me sleep—"

"D'you think you could stop?" asks Uncle Henry, rubbing at his temples. "This incessant chatter. Take a breath, would you?"

"I'm sorry," he mutters after an extended silence. "I've just grown used to my own company." He smiles at me, a gappy grin – the same as Min's only it looks out of place on his face, as if he hasn't used it enough.

"Wouldn't it be wonderful if we saw a mermaid right now?" I muse.

"No such thing," he scoffs.

I frown. "Yes, I know that, but imagine there was…"

"Humans can't breathe underwater."

"But they can hold their breath," I counter.

"There are no buts," snaps Uncle Henry. "Humans would freeze to death if they lived underwater. And you can't be both a fish and a mammal. Evolution wouldn't have it. Mermaids could *never* exist. They're just a romantic notion of what a child thinks lives under the sea."

He sighs. "I'm sorry. Again. It's been a bad week. This damn illness keeps me tired all day and awake all night."

My heart leaps. Because, spurred on by my conversation

with Adele, I think there are some changes he could make. "I was talking to someone about your, er … condition," I begin nervously. "She gave me some information and said you should look at your diet. Anti-in-something-or-other. Apparently, you ought to eat things like porridge and not so much sugary cereal. You can even get a personalized—"

Uncle Henry's slams his bowl on to the coffee table between us, splattering milk everywhere, making me jump out of my monologue.

"D'you think I haven't tried?" he hisses. "That I've just been lying in bed for the last ten years? I've seen you look at me," he continues. "Thinking that nobody needs *that* much sleep – even teenagers. Assuming I'm lazy and can't be bothered to get myself out of it. Mind over matter! If I could just think more positively, I'd get better soon enough. You're just like everyone else…" And he shuffles from the room, leaving me to stare guiltily after him.

Note to self: talk to Henry about fish, not medical conditions…

HENRY JAMES

WIZIWISDOM

Henry **JAMES** is a marine biologist most noted for his papers: *Fish Who Climb* and *Fish Who Cling*. He is also the two-time winner of the Neptunian Award, considered by many as the only award worth having.

He hasn't been seen on the science circuit in over a decade. Could it have something to do with being born with scales…?

READ MORE V

Contents
1. Early life
2. Career
3. Bibliography
   3.1 Fish Who Climb
   3.2 Fish Who Cling
   3.3 The Woeful Tale of the Fiffer Faffer Fish

Bibliography (edit)

Fish Who Climb (2002)
Fish Who Cling (2003)
The Woeful Tale of the Fiffer Faffer Fish (2004)
Life and Times of the Aquatic Ape (never published)

7th July 01:49
This page was last edited 5 days ago

Scientist or fish enthusiast?

Once upon a time, Henry James – no, not the ground-breaking American-British author, though this guy's also transatlantic – was an upcoming marine biologist set on a stratospheric course towards the Scientists' Hall of Fame alongside such greats as Curie, Einstein and Darwin. He was widely expected to bring the exciting world of fish to the masses and he almost did…

Born in Boston, Massachusetts, USA, where he went to the prestigious New England School for Boys until his parents relocated to Piscary Bay, England. Living by the sea, it was perhaps only natural that he become fascinated by fish and thus his desire to become the country's, nay the world's, number-one marine biologist was born.

After graduating with a first from Exeter University, James's career certainly looked promising. He burst on to the scene with an explosive paper revealing the unlikely phenomenon of fish that scale waterfalls, for which he won the much-coveted Neptunian Award. He then went on to win it for an unprecedented second year with his follow-up paper, Fish Who Cling, following the remarkable tale of the remora fish. A bright future looked doubly certain.

His third paper, somewhat fantastically titled The Woeful Tale of the Fiffer Faffer Fish, however, was not as well received and, when James let his love of the sea cloud his judgement, he declared his belief in the Aquatic Ape Theory (AAT). I hear a collective gasp! And you would be right. For what person in their right mind would fall for such pseudo-scientific nonsense? Well, to his discredit, James did. Oops…

Excerpt from The Woeful Tale of the Fiffer Faffer Fish *by Henry James:*

With only five per cent of the world's oceans explored, many scientists believe there are literally millions of animals and fish still waiting to be discovered. One such creature is the Fiffer Faffer fish. With its spotted skin, teeth the size of a human's rendering it incapable of closing its mouth, and an obsession with its reflection, it could be argued that the Fiffer Faffer fish is, in fact, a gormless teenager…

Iron Man

I sneak up to the attic the next morning. With the sea pounding turbulently against the coastline, the stormy skies are back: dramatic black clouds looming outside the windows making it feel strangely cosy to be inside. I guess the next best thing to being in the sea is staring wistfully at it.

"Morning, Brian," I whisper as the aquarium flickers to life. "How are you today?"

"He can't answer you, you know," says Uncle Henry, making me jump because I hadn't seen him in the shadows.

"Oh, morning," I reply with a nervous laugh. We didn't exactly leave things on the best terms last night. "You're up early."

He shrugs. "Couldn't sleep."

"Me neither," I sigh, pulling a blanket round my shoulders.

I wave at Brian who stays in the same spot, transfixed, as if he's watching TV through the aquarium window. The idea makes me giggle. What if our world is like a soap opera to the fish? Is Brian miserable because all he gets to see is Uncle Henry's sad face?

"Can fish be depressed, Uncle Henry?"

He frowns. "Yes. There's a whole study about developing antidepressants for them actually. Though I missed out on that one thanks to my head being full of cotton wool. Why?"

"It's just that Brian looks so sad all the time."

"You're anthropomorphizing him," he sniffs.

Sidelong glance to camera...

"You're assigning a human emotion to an animal," he explains.

"Oh," I gasp, realizing I might be able to score a few brownie points with my newfound knowledge. Turns out Uncle Henry *is* someone. Well, if science is your thing anyway. "But isn't that what you did with the Fiffer Faffer fish?" I say, feeling rather clever. "By calling them gormless teenagers, I mean?"

The silence that follows is immense, punctuated only by the urgent calls of the seagull family who have taken up residence on the roof. Uncle Henry's brow furrows deeply, his expression matching the dark clouds outside, making me wish the floor would swallow me up whole. Perhaps I should have read the whole article before commenting...

"Sorry," I whisper. I don't like people being angry with me.

Uncle Henry nods curtly and returns to reading. A short moment later though, he looks up sheepishly as if he feels bad. "So, er … what's your favourite … fish?" he asks.

"Er," I mutter.

"Oh, come now," he says, warming to his topic. "We've all got one."

Looks to camera – have we?

"Mine's a seahorse," he says excitedly. "What about the pointed sawfish with its pair upon pair of lateral teeth you might ask? Nope. Or perhaps the world's most beautiful yet poisonous mandarinfish? No again! Because the seahorse is an evolutionary wonder," he explains passionately, eyes wide with awe.

"Hippocampus is the scientific term. They've got eyes that move independently. The males have a ventral pouch that allows them to give birth and –" he pauses for dramatic effect, throwing his hands around to demonstrate his point – "with thirty-six bony sections in their tails, each of which have four corner plates connected by small joints, they are super strong. Kind of like a suit of armour, if you will."

"Oh, like Iron Man, you mean?" Uncle Henry's face goes blank. "He's a billionaire industrialist and one of the Avengers," I explain. Nope, still nothing.

"Actually, I quite like starfish," I say, steering the conversation back to safer ground.

"Not a fish actually."

"Oh. Jellyfish? The ones in the London Aquarium are stunning."

Uncle Henry shakes his head. I begin to wish I'd searched fish rather than him.

"Dolphin then."

"Technically, they're mammals," he grimaces. "They're warm-blooded, you see. They breathe air, using their lungs not their gills."

I nod. "Kind of like mermaids," I giggle. "Sorry, couldn't help myself."

He doesn't smile. Doesn't even flicker with the hint of one.

Note to self: never joke about fish with Uncle Henry…

PISCARY BAY TIDE TIMES

Tuesday 9th July

LOW TIDE:	06:29	HEIGHT:	1.90 m
HIGH TIDE:	12:26	HEIGHT:	5.50 m
LOW TIDE:	18:56	HEIGHT:	2.00 m

Waxing Quarter Moon

SUNRISE:	05:23	SUNSET:	21:31
MOONRISE:	14:55	MOONSET:	01:27

External Threat

The rain keeps me indoors for the next few days and I'm relieved when I finally get out, what with the tense atmosphere around Uncle Henry. He's definitely forgotten how to behave in the company of other human beings. And there's been no word from Min about how her mission is going. I head straight for the town beach.

At four p.m. every day, like clockwork, the local kids arrive, throwing their school uniforms in a pile on the sand, and wade into the water as if they've been thinking about it all day. Which they probably have. They throng round each other, splashing and laughing and watching closely while several of them take it in turns with the snorkel masks to float face down in the water.

After several days of watching this ritual, my temptation to mingle finally outstrips the fear of being rejected.

"Hi, Amy," I call, spotting Leo's friend. "I'm C—"

"Yeah, I know who you are," she replies dryly. "The one who films everything and has no idea."

I laugh. "Yeah, not wearing a wetsuit was a bit stupid."

She stares at me. "I'll say."

"What are they doing?" I ask, nodding at two boys floating next to each other, their hands outstretched as if they're in a Mission: Impossible film.

"Last Fish Floating," she replies. "The last person to come up for air wins."

"Can I try?"

She laughs. "You? You're not a Fish."

"Well, no," I laugh. "I'm a mammal. We all are…" I falter into silence when her face doesn't even crack a smile.

"Most people can't hold their breath for longer than thirty seconds," she says. "Two minutes max."

One of the boys bursts to the surface and splashes his fist furiously into the water as the other boy, Bennie, slowly and triumphantly pulls himself to standing and accepts pats on the back as the winner.

"Well done, Bennie," I coo. "How long did you hold your breath for?"

"It's called static apnoea actually," sneers Amy.

Bennie pants for breath as he wipes his face with his hand. "Dunno. Four minutes, maybe more."

"Wow," I gasp.

"Oi, Cassie," calls Amy as a slip of a thing paddles over.

"She wants to play Last Fish Floating. You game?"

"Really?" gasps the little girl as if she can't believe her luck.

Cut to a shot of me lying face down in the sea next to her, the sea gently rocking us to and fro. Long pan of the seabed as I search it for shells to distract me. Jumpcut as I slowly come up for air the moment I see her burst to the surface, thinking that I'm finally in with a chance of being accepted.

"What did you do that for?" snarls Amy, her arms wrapped round a now snivelling Cassie. "She's only nine. You were supposed to let her win."

"But you said it was a game," I say.

"It is," she hisses.

"You looked pretty comfortable out there," says Bennie.

"I've been practising," I reply. "So, what's the record for this?"

He shrugs. "About five minutes? Leo holds it. Still can't beat Billy though. No one can."

"Billy?" I ask, my heart beginning to beat a little faster.

"None of your business," snaps Amy.

"He was one of us," says Bennie. "Died years ago."

"D'you mean Billy Pengelly?" Surely there can't be more than one who died. "Did you know him? What was he like?"

"What's it to you?" replies Amy. "Who are you anyway?"

"She's a James," says Bennie before I can answer. "Staying up at Cliff House with her uncle."

Amy frowns. "Henry James has a niece? I thought that was just gossip?"

"No, I'm real," I laugh, feeling as if I could maybe sweet-talk them now that I know more about Henry. "Though definitely not as obsessed about fish as my uncle is." I giggle. "He started to tell me how the male oyster toadfish calls for females to come and spawn."

Their faces are a picture of horror. Presumably what I must look like when Uncle Henry tells me these things. "Apparently, they moan and—"

"Min's back," interrupts Bennie and it's like there's an echo as the words ripple through the group.

Amy's face drops. "Does Leo know? His mum won't be happy. Neither will mine."

"Not yet," he replies. "But in this town it won't be long."

I frown. "Look, I don't know what it is that you think I've done, but I'm not Min. I'm just trying to be friendly. Why don't we go for an ice cream?" I add, thinking maybe that will crack their unfriendly veneer. It would me.

Amy turns on me. "I wouldn't hang around with a James if you were the last person on earth. Come on, guys," she calls. "Let's go to Screams. Bennie says he's paying."

"In your dreams!" he shrieks, and I watch as they quickly move away en masse, leaving me all alone.

Taking a Breath

I hold my breath the whole way home, using the feeling of the remaining oxygen pumping in my veins, pounding in my ears and throbbing at my diaphragm, to stop myself from crying. Then I fling myself on to my bed and all bets are off as I bury my face into my pillow, finally allowing the sobs out. How could they be so mean? They don't even know me. I'm not Min! I know she's not everyone's cup of tea but what on earth did she do to make half the town hate her?

I replay the footage in my head over and over again, hoping I might find answers to the questions queuing in my mind. Fat chance. I end up wailing at the top of my lungs, sounding exactly like an oyster toadfish, for want of a better comparison.

The knock is so quiet I almost don't hear it, then Uncle

Henry's face appears in the doorway. "Coco?" he says quietly. "Are you OK?"

I try doing what I'd normally do with Min. Grin and bear it and pretend that everything's fine. He doesn't need to hear my troubles; he's got enough of his own. But with his continued silent presence and intense look, as if he's reading me like a book, I find myself doing the opposite and blurting out what happened on the beach.

"I'm only trying to be friendly," I cry. "Why can't they see that? I haven't heard from Min either. I think she's abandoned me… And you!" I gasp. "You hate me."

Uncle Henry frowns. "No, I don't."

"Yes, you do," I sob. "I've been trying my hardest to figure out how to get through to you. How to help with your ME. I've even been reading your science papers about fish and I *hate* science. What did I ever do to you? It's not my fault Min lost her job and that we needed to move here…"

Uncle Henry holds up his hand. "Do you ever take a breath?" he asks.

I giggle. "Sometimes."

"How about you take one now then?" He smiles. "Shove over, would you?" And he climbs on to my bed and puts an arm round me. "I'm sorry if I've given you that impression," he says. "I'm just not used to having people around… I don't hate you. How could I? Look, Min's a complicated character. Of course she hasn't abandoned you. You mean the world to her. You and I both know she never answers her phone. Why d'you think we lost touch? It wasn't for want of trying, then this damn illness took hold."

His voice changes as if he's telling me a bedtime story. "It was like a lightning bolt from the blue," he says. "Ma had just died and I was burned out from all my research. It felt like an uphill battle to get anything done. Then I woke up one day and everything hurt. The tiredness that engulfed me – it was like a power cut. I had no energy. Brain turned to mush too. I went from being able to write a whole paper of research to sitting in bed in a foggy haze."

"Why didn't you ask Min for help?" I ask. "Oh." Then we both laugh at the ridiculousness of what I'd just said.

"She'd long since cut all ties with this place," explains Uncle Henry. "Ma's housekeeper stood by me for a while, unlike any of my friends. As soon as they realized I wasn't getting better any time soon, they got bored." He snorts. "Or maybe it was me who got fed up with them and their suggestions. Eat this – do that. If I could just put my mind to it, surely I'd get better."

I cringe. "So me coming up with ways to fix it was…"

"Nothing I haven't tried," he sighs. "I researched them all. Believe me."

"What changed?"

He laughs. "My fish. I hadn't seen them in over two years. I set myself a tiny challenge, to take one step at a time. Took me months to make it up those ten stairs to the attic. Each day I told myself I couldn't do it, but somehow I convinced myself to give it one more day. That turned into weeks, then months and, for the first time in ages, I felt like I was doing something to help." He pauses. "It was your grandma's idea actually."

Looks to camera – wait, what?

"I have a grandma?" I say incredulously.

Uncle Henry nods. "Yes. Wanda Pengelly. She lives above the harbour. She doesn't know about you, mind."

"I can't believe Min hasn't told *me*," I say. "She's always been pretty tight-lipped about the specifics. Apart from the—"

"Epic romance." He rolls his eyes. "What d'you want to know? Ask me anything."

I sit up, feeling excited. "Can you tell me about my dad? What was he like?" I pause. "What really happened to him?"

Cut to a sequence of scratched sepia images of yesteryear. A young Min and Henry James meeting Billy Pengelly on the beach for the first time. Their instant connection. Their adventures swimming, diving and surfing together. How Billy planned to go to art college in London. Then it turned into a horror movie, and a freak accident took his young life too soon.

"He died in a rip tide," says Uncle Henry. "Down on Cove Beach. It's why I don't want you swimming there alone."

The very place where I have been swimming, unaware

of its importance. I frown, feeling confused. "How can that be Min's fault?"

"Who's to say?" he replies. "I was away when it happened and, by the time I got back, the rumour mill had started. How someone had heard them arguing. Another person even claimed to have seen Min storm into the…" He stops short.

"Into the what?" I ask. But he shakes his head, refusing to say more.

"You know, when I want to know about something," he says suddenly, "I do some research."

"Research," I say with a decisive nod. "Got it."

Uncle Henry smiles, then, taking a deep breath, creaks to standing and gestures for me to follow him next door to a bedroom rammed so full of dustbin bags and boxes, you can hardly see the floor.

"What is all this?" I ask.

"Ma's things," he replies, scouring the boxes. "Ah, here they are." He opens the top box and pulls out a set of dusty-looking photo albums. "My advice is to start your research here…"

Memories

Looks to camera. "OK, this is the first day of finding out who I am."

"Really?" interrupts Uncle Henry with a snort.

It's tipping down so we've decamped to the attic, he to continue his research and me to start mine, though I can't help but stare longingly at the sea, wishing I could be in it.

"I'm making a documentary," I say. "It's what I want to do when I'm older. Like Bob."

Uncle Henry laughs. "Explains why you've always got that blasted camera phone aimed at something. Just don't film me."

"Wouldn't dream of it."

Cut to a close-up of the box I've lugged upstairs.

The photo albums are ordered by year and labelled in meticulously neat handwriting. I vaguely remember Min moaning about her mum being a super-organized person. Guess the tidy gene skipped a generation then.

Each photo has a title, like *Min – first steps, aged 13 months*, and *Henry – new bike, aged 3*. It's so well documented that it gives me a real glimpse into what their childhood was like. Min and Henry playing together on the beach, building giant sandcastles with their pa. Henry, with floppy hair, teaching a fresh-faced and spotty Min to surf.

Looks to camera – so she did *get spots!*

I come to a photo of Uncle Henry grinning at the camera, a bubble-shaped object held proudly aloft. His eyes are sparkling and he looks like a young Leonardo DiCaprio, only with darker hair and much paler.

"What *are* you holding?" I laugh, but he's fallen asleep, snoring lightly, his own research lying dormant on his lap. I glance between him and the photo. He looked so young and carefree then.

I come to a particularly bad year for fashion and text it to Min, hoping it might jolt a response out of her. Surprisingly it does.

12 July

ME 10:34
What are you wearing?? LOL

MIN 10:35
OMG where did you get that picture from?

ME 10:35

Uh, found your mum's photo albums... BTW, when were u going to tell me about my other grandma?!?

MIN 10:40

Coming home on late bus tomorrow

ME 10:40

OMG that's great! Good news I hope!

MIN 10:50

. . .

The three torturous dots sit there, tormenting me with what she might be replying. Then all of a sudden they're gone, leaving me wondering what it was she was going to say, and playing out the different scenarios in my head. All of them good. I figure that it's such exciting news she'd rather tell me in person. To see my reaction, that sort of thing. I know I would.

I absent-mindedly flick through the photo album, giggling to myself. Guess Min's fashion sense came later and Uncle Henry's, well... The less said about that the better. Then I come to a series of photos of them with their mates. Min looking insanely young, though still with her trademark eyeliner and beehive, sitting round a beach campfire next to my dad, cracking up at some long-forgotten joke off-camera. Friends who look vaguely familiar with faces I've seen in the town. Laughing and fooling around for the camera.

There's even a shot of them all in the water, gathered round a couple floating on their fronts, perhaps playing Last Fish Floating. As much as I can't wait to get back to London to see my mates again, there's a whole side of life in Piscary Bay that I haven't explored yet, including finding my grandma.

Lost for Words

Town is swarming. The harbour and streets throng with holidaymakers arriving in their too-wide-for-the-lanes SUVs, while families wander obliviously in front of me, dragging their bodyboards behind them. I'd quite like to get back in the sea but I'm on a mission and I don't even stop for a chat with Jan, other than to ask if he knows Wanda.

"Of course, *kochanie*," he laughs. "Everybody knows her."

I spot Bennie on my way past Screams. "Hi, Bennie!" I call. "Looks like the surf's good today."

"What would you know about it?" he laughs.

"Nothing. Haven't been in actually. It's too rough to swim today… D'you know Wanda Pengelly?"

He snorts. "Course. Everyone knows everyone here. She's in there," he says, nodding behind him.

The bell announces my entrance into the ice-cream

parlour, not that anyone notices, and all of a sudden I feel ridiculously nervous. Maybe I shouldn't film this.

"Back again," says Bennie's mum.

"Oh, hi, Mrs Khatri," I trill. "I'm not after ice cream actually. I was looking for Wanda Pengelly."

"Over there," she replies briskly, throwing a glance at the corner where a woman is sitting by the window, staring out pensively from behind her black-rimmed glasses, fussing nervously with her plait.

"Oh," I frown. "Is there more than one? She looks too young."

But Bennie's mum is too busy serving customers, so I go up to the woman anyway. Can't hurt given that everybody knows Wanda Pengelly…

She looks up. "Hello. Are you here to find out more about our mermaid course?"

I shake my head, too scared to let go of my breath. But it results in a bit of face-off between the two of us.

"What did you want then?" she asks, looking puzzled.

I exhale slowly and take another breath for courage. "I'm trying to find Wanda Pengelly," I say. "Mrs Khatri said that's you, but you're not old enough."

She splutters. "That's because I'm not. She is." And I spin round to come face to face with the old woman I met surfing the other day. That's my grandma. I have a grandma. Oh my God.

I stare, transfixed, the scenarios running through my

141

head of what might happen next. I'm terrified. Because, although I've always dreamed of having a family, a dad, a sibling, a gran even, it's not going that well so far, is it? It's taken over two weeks for me to get to know Uncle Henry and that's been a route fraught with bumps and I'm still very much working on it. What if my grandma's the same? What if she doesn't want to know me? It's not like I'm a cute newborn bundle of a grandchild.

"You all right, lovey?" she says, giving me the kind of twinkly smile that I have.

That's my grandma…

"Do you mind?' says the woman with the plait. "We're having a business meeting here."

I nod politely as Wanda steps round me and takes a seat by the window, while the younger woman speaks about numbers, and all I can do is stare at my grandma, hardly able to believe my eyes.

"Look, what d'you want?" asks the younger woman, shooting an irritable glance at me.

"Sarah," scolds Wanda.

"She's been standing there for five minutes, Mum," she replies testily.

Looks to camera – Mum? Does that make her my aunt?

I take a deep breath, then swallow the inordinate amount of saliva that's built up in my throat. "Well, it's just… I wanted to meet Wanda because … well, she's…"

"Spit it out, would you?" snaps Sarah.

142

"Sarah!" Wanda turns to me and fixes her icy blue eyes on me. The same colour and shape as mine. "What is it, lovey?"

"Look, who are you?" demands Sarah.

OK, I'm just going to have to say it.

I blink. "I'm—"

"Coco! Where've you been?"

I spin round for a plot twist I hadn't anticipated. The spotlight shifts on to Min, looking stunning in a brand-new pair of ruby-red four-inch heels peeping out from the wide leg of a white silk trouser suit that I haven't seen before. "I've been waiting ten minutes at the bus stop," she moans. "You were supposed to be there."

I frown. "But you said the late bus."

"I caught the earlier one. What are you doing?" Her gaze moves past me to Sarah who looks equally shocked.

"Well, would you look at what the cat dragged in?' she spits at Min. "Didn't think you were ever going to 'set foot in this hellhole again'. I believe they were your exact words."

Min shrugs. "Yeah, well, times change."

"For you maybe," says Sarah, bristling. "Some of us don't get to move on." She throws a pointed look at Min. "And certainly not as quickly as you apparently did. You're not welcome here, Min. You should leave."

"Sarah," mutters Wanda. "Too much."

"Since when did you change your tune?" she snorts. "After what she did? I'm sorry, but I want nothing to do with the James family."

"Feeling's mutual," throws back Min. "Come on, Coco. We're leaving."

"But…" I say.

"Now," she hisses and stalks out of the door, me scurrying after her.

Well, one thing's for certain: if my life really were a film, that scene would end up on the cutting-room floor with an urgent call for a reshoot.

Taking Sides

Min's shoulders are bunched up round her ears as she clomps up the high street, dragging her suitcase noisily behind her. I don't know why she's so angry with me.

"Min, stop!" I cry. I've never seen her walk so fast in my life.

"How could you?" she demands.

"Me!" I protest. "You're the one who interrupted. I was about to let Wanda know that she's my grandma – thanks for telling me by the way… That was supposed to be my moment and you spoiled it."

"Your moment!" she shouts. "After what she said to me? How she's treated me?"

I shake my head. "Why don't you just explain what happened? It's not your fault he tried to fight the rip."

Min grunts. "Oh, I see my brother's been giving you

a history lesson, has he? Obviously, I've tried explaining. I'm not that stupid. It's a painful subject," she mutters. "You're to have nothing to do with them, you hear?"

"But why? They're my family."

"Family!" she shrieks, causing numerous tourists to stop and stare.

She motions angrily for me to follow her – with her suitcase and shopping, I might add – as she continues her frogmarch up the hill, stopping briefly to fumble in her handbag for her sunglasses.

"*I'm* your family," she snaps. "The one who's raised you, clothed you, fed you. It wasn't my fault what happened to Billy, but they've never been willing to hear my side of the story."

"Have you listened to theirs?" I ask.

By now, we've reached the supermarket, where Min stops to catch her breath on the bench. Her face is full of such fury. I don't think I've seen her this angry in a long time, not even when Robin sacked her.

"Are you saying you don't believe me?" she says. "You are, aren't you? You're taking their side already. I knew this would happen. I knew there was a reason why I should never come back here."

She starts off up the hill again and it's all I can do to keep up, especially carrying her suitcase and four shopping bags. Under normal circumstances, I'd be excited to find out what she's bought, since it usually means something for me too.

"Min," I call. "Min! Wait!" But I don't catch up with her until we're outside Cliff House. "I don't understand!" I cry. "Of course I'm not taking sides, but any decent documentary maker knows that you should fully research a story."

"Is that all this is to you?" she snorts. "You're to have nothing to do with them. D'you hear? I forbid it."

Looks to camera – this coming from the woman who's barely ever told me no.

"You've got be kidding!" I shriek in disbelief. "Min, that woman's my gran—"

"Lower your voice," she hisses, glancing anxiously around us at the now curious tourists wandering past on the coastal path.

"She's my gran," I whisper. "Which presumably means Sarah's my aunt."

"She's nothing but a stranger to you," growls Min, passionately grabbing hold of my hand. "You saw the way she talked to me. How much she hates me. Coco, please? You can't do this."

"But they're my family," I say helplessly.

"Me and Uncle Henry aren't enough for you?" she says. "It's been the two of us your whole life. And I intend to keep it that way."

"So what are you saying? You can't expect me to keep it a secret."

Min nods. "It's too painful for me, Coco. Please. You can't…"

I've never seen her like this. And, being the people-pleaser that I am, I keep my mouth shut and nod mutely. Because, apart from anything, I don't want to spoil the moment she tells me we're going back to London. Besides, it's been fifteen years of Wanda *not* knowing me as her granddaughter. A few more days can't hurt, can it?

Min's face softens. "Let's go in. It's about to rain, and I don't want to ruin this new fake fur."

"Oh, I noticed that," I gush.

Looks to camera – good job because the rain really did ruin her other one…

"It's gorgeous," I murmur. "Where'd you get it? Did you get me anything?"

Min smiles, making me feel relieved that we're back on safer ground. "Yes, love. Wait and see, eh? Did you get on all right with my brother?"

I wrinkle my nose. "Yeah. And I learned a lot about fish."

Min pauses in the doorway, as if she's still not sure whether she wants to be here. Runs her hands distastefully along the walls like she's seeing the house in it's true light for the first time. "This place is filthy," she mutters.

"So, did you see Bob?" I ask, dumping her shopping bags on the kitchen table. "How did it go? Did Robin accept your apology?"

"What's with the twenty questions, Coco?" snaps Min.

148

"I'm tired. It's been a long journey."

"Sorry," I say, trying not to bristle. "I'm just interested. It's my future too." But whether Min hears me, or just chooses to ignore me, I don't know. She clomps upstairs, yelling out a greeting to her brother, and then I hear her bedroom door firmly shut and I'm still none the wiser as to what's going on.

The Wrong Scene

With no sign of Min coming back down, I decide to go for an early-evening swim to clear my head because boy do I have a lot to think about! Going back to London, knowing I've got a whole family here, keeping my existence a secret from a gran who looks really quite nice. Where do I begin?

These questions float to the back of my mind as I concentrate on the job of getting in the water, though I'm much more confident these days. No longer do I tiptoe in for fear of catching my toes on a shell or rock. Nor do I wince at the first touch of cold water as the waves rush round my ankles. No more squealing when the waves splash against my bare midriff either. With a deep breath, I dive straight in, enjoying the feeling of power as the force of my strokes pulls me down, down, down.

It's so peaceful exploring the seabed. Brightly coloured

seaweed swaying slowly to and fro, each individual frond dancing to its own tune. Tiny silver fish darting in and out beneath the rough grey rocks covered in barnacles and mussels. Crabs creeping among the sparkling shells that peek out of the gravelly sand. It's like being part of another world.

Holding my breath, I'm super aware of my other senses. Can feel my heart banging against my chest. The tension in my shoulders. The grittiness in my lungs. I've been doing this for as long as I can remember; it's like a coping mechanism, making me feel in control. Pulling myself down under the water, leaving the chaos of the world above me, seems to accentuates that feeling even more. As if I should have been a mermaid in another life – regardless of what Uncle Henry thinks!

I swim around underwater, briefly coming up for air, then eagerly diving back down to explore this alternative world. And, when I'm ready to come out, I resurface to the gentle pitter-patter of raindrops and the dark sky.

The scene is set. The one I've been waiting for. The kitchen is dimmed with low lighting from candles I found in the utility room. The table is laid immaculately with a white cloth, a jug of water and a bunch of wildflowers in an old milk bottle. Music is coming from Min's record player next door, giving it a kind of French film atmosphere.

It's perfect!

The first thing Uncle Henry does is flick on the kitchen lights.

"Don't," I grumble.

"Can't see a damn thing," he mutters.

"I'm setting the scene and you're spoiling it."

He laughs. "And what scene would that be?"

"Our last supper," I say. "I'm hoping this is the moment that Min tells me we're going back to London."

"One can but hope," he retorts. "What are we eating?"

I wrinkle my nose. "Beans on toast? It's about all I can do. Oh, hi, Min," I say. "Come and sit down. I made tea for us. Sorry it's a bit late. I went for a swim."

She eyes me wearily. "You know I don't eat wheat."

"'S'all right," I say, refusing to rise to the bait. "I got you some gluten-free bread from the shop."

"Well, I'm not eating that," she says, pushing her plate away untouched. "Tastes like cardboard."

I give her my twinkliest grin, barely able to contain the excitement. "I suppose we could have celebratory fish and chips," I say. "You know, as if we're really on holiday… When does Robin want you to start by the way? I thought we could maybe spend another week down here, two weeks tops. Perhaps we could go on that seal trip together? You could show me the places that were special to you and Billy." I gasp as another great idea hits me. "We could even go for afternoon tea at the Bur—"

"Coco, would you shut up!" yells Min.

Uncle Henry winces while I'm stunned into silence. This isn't the reaction I'd imagined earlier when I was swimming at the bottom of the sea.

I thought that if I kept my end of the bargain, remained quiet about the existence of my grandma, then Min would jump at the chance of telling me that we're going back to London. But her face doesn't look as happy as I'd pictured it. She slowly shakes her head, her shoulders sagging, making her body look like it's inwardly imploding, and the reality hits me. We're not going back to London.

Cut to black.

"Ooh, power cut," says Uncle Henry excitedly, completely failing to read the mood of the room. "Good job you found those candles, eh, Coco?"

"We're not going back, are we?" I say quietly.

Min shakes her head. "Bob's sold the flat. He just wanted me to go up there to sort out the sale of the furniture and to return a few items."

"And Robin?"

She snorts. "Was never going to give me my job back."

"But the clothes," I say, struggling desperately to understand. "Where did the money…?"

"Gardening leave," she explains. "My contract always had a three-month notice period and Robin was just trying to do me out of it. Scumbag."

"So we're staying here," I say slowly. Fear and dread

153

flooding over me as I watch the dream of going home slip through my fingers.

Min nods.

"But I don't want to," I say, my voice rising with indignation. "I want to go home to my mates. And my school and the flat."

"Coco," murmurs Min, but I don't let her continue.

"I hate living here!" I screech, standing up suddenly, sending my chair clattering noisily to the ground, where it instantly falls to bits. "This house is a dump. It's falling down round our ears."

Uncle Henry clears his throat. "I think that's a little unfair." But, as if to emphasize my point, a scattering of plaster drops from the ceiling into his untouched, and now cold, baked beans.

"And you," I say, hurling my words at Min. The ones I'd promised myself I wouldn't say. "Would you even have told me about my grandma if Uncle Henry hadn't?"

Her silence speaks a thousand words.

Cut to black.

Part 2

THE STRUGGLE PHASE

STRUGGLE *[STRUGH-uhl]*
Verb
To contend with an adversary or opposing force.
Noun
A war, fight, contest of any kind.

PHASE *[feyz]*
Noun
A stage in a process.

The Struggle Phase
Physiology. The inevitable contractions the human body makes in response to water submersion. Commonly known as the Mammalian Diving Reflex (MDR).

Pathetic Fallacy

If my life were a film, it would show a montage of me sitting in numerous pensive shots, staring out at the sea, tears rolling down my cheeks, with seriously mopey music full of piano chords and gentle violins.

The reality, as ever, is so much more boring. The weather's rotten and matches the mood of everyone in the house, which is solemnly quiet save for the crackle of Min's record player and Uncle Henry's erratic typing.

I flick through the photo albums, looking for answers. And while it does fill in the blanks about Min's life, answering all sorts of questions about who she and my uncle used to be, it just throws up more about my dad and his side of the family.

The storm hits that evening. Battering the house with a scary intensity. The horizon is a blurred black line of nothing, just a grey sea merging with the storm-clouded sky: bleak and wild and mesmerizing rolled into one.

By morning, the harbour is a mass of white foam. Boats rocking wildly as they're flung about. White spray shooting into the air with boom after boom as the waves compete to be the highest hitter.

I draw my chair up to the window, pulling the duvet round me like a protective cocoon, to watch the advancing waves build like a cavalry of white horses with flowing manes as they mount their attack. As the wind grows, so too does the sea, gathering into massive swells that are rammed against the coastline in a domino effect, and with it my anger and irritation as the fury suddenly surges out of me like a lungful of pent-up air. Why should I keep my existence secret from my family?

I fling open my bedroom door, having decided to have it out with Min, regardless of how she might react, only to be confronted by the kind of surreal scene that makes you wonder whether you're actually dreaming. The attic stairwell now resembles a trickling stream complete with running-water sound effects.

"Er, Uncle Henry?" I call out nervously. "You'd better come—"

My next words are drowned out by the crash of tumbling glass, followed by a loud creak and a whoosh as the stream turns into a river.

"What the—?" gasps Min, appearing in her bedroom

doorway, her black dressing gown hanging limply over her scrawny figure. "Henry!" she yells. "HENRY! The roof's finally given up!"

Looks to camera – I know the feeling.

"My research," gasps Uncle Henry. "The fish, my laboratory."

"I'll get a mop," I say, jumping into action at the sound of another loud crash.

"Get the dustpan and brush while you're at it," he calls. "And bin bags. We'll need plenty of those."

But I soon realize we're going to need a lot more than that. It's like the house has been hit by a tornado that's ripped a giant hole in the roof, rain hammering in and the storm raging directly above us. In films, this would be called *pathetic fallacy*, where the weather reflects the mood of the main character. Spot on in this case. Dark black rain clouds full to bursting. Sheets of lightning dramatically tearing up the sky and the odd crack of ominous thunder to replicate our misery.

"What about the fish?" I gasp.

"It's rain," snorts Min. "I *think* they'll survive."

"Actually, sudden changes like this can be uncomfortable … if not dangerous," says Uncle Henry anxiously. "It depends on the fish's body type. Scaly fins might—"

"Now is NOT the time to talk about this!" snaps Min. "What can we do? We can't exactly take the fish tank downstairs."

Uncle Henry grabs a couple of giant beakers. "No, but we can carry the fish in these."

"Erm, Uncle Henry?" I say nervously, pointing at a thin stream of smoke coming from beneath a pile of broken glass. "Something appears to be on fire…"

"It's an exothermic reaction," he says, grabbing a beaker of rainwater to douse it, his expression oddly alive, like he's enjoying this spur-of-the-moment experiment.

The storm rages on as we work to clear the fish tank. The wind howling through the roof and rattling at the windows, whipping up the papers into a frenzy, making me feel like we're about to land in Oz. And as I open my mouth to ask, "What next?" my words are suddenly drowned out by an almighty crack when, with a puff of smoke, *I disappear…*

Secret Lives

I hear them shriek a string of expletives, then their terrified faces appear cautiously above me through the newly created hole in the attic floor. Lying on my bed among fragments of plaster and wooden floorboard, I stare up at the ceiling of my bedroom and start to cackle.

"What are you laughing at?" frowns Uncle Henry. "A fall like that could break your back."

"Yeah, but it didn't," I gasp as big, hysterical gulps of laughter burst out of me, which quickly turn to tears as the disappointment of losing my home takes its toll.

Uncle Henry disappears from view, leaving Min to stare down, looking awkward, like she's missed her cue. Then the sky suddenly stops flashing above her and a silence spreads over the house. Uncle Henry appears at my side, pulling me into an awkward hug.

"It's OK," he whispers, just as another part of the ceiling comes crashing down, knocking us flat on our backs, which makes Min splutter with such infectious laughter that we're soon all laughing as if it's the funniest thing that's ever happened.

For the first time in a long while, it feels like one of those moments when the plot changes, jolting everyone out of their misery. A storyline that continues once Steve the builder has been over to cover the roof, with promises to be back to fix it soon. Min sweeps up the remnants of the laboratory, even offering to wash my clothes, while I return the fish to their tank under Uncle Henry's strict supervision.

~~~

"What are you doing?" I ask the next morning when I come downstairs to find Min clomping about in the front room, dragging about and rearranging furniture as if she's found a new purpose.

"Something I should've done yonks ago," she replies. "A little help perhaps?"

Together we shift the table to the window where it looks out over the overgrown garden and sea beyond. Min places an old sewing machine and a large dustbin bag of clothes on it.

"Ma's," she explains. "With any luck, there'll be some proper vintage pieces that I can alter. I used to be pretty nifty with a sewing machine. Made all my clothes back in the day. Would've gone to fashion college if I'd got the A levels."

Looks to camera — yet another thing I didn't know about her...

"What've you got there?" she asks, nodding at the photo album in my hand.

"I'm up to 2003," I say. "Think it's gonna be a corker."

She snorts. "Ma used to spend hours doing those. Pictures laid out all over the floor. Spent more time looking back at the past than living in the moment."

"Sounds like everybody who lives here," I murmur.

Min stares at me, studying my face with narrowed eyes as if she's contemplating her next move. "You're trying to find pictures of them, aren't you?" she says quietly.

I nod. "I don't see how I'm supposed to live here, knowing that they're my family."

"But that's just it, you're not," says Min. "All they will ever see is that I'm your mother. The person who last saw Billy alive. They hate me. They'll hate you too."

"Then tell me what happened," I reply. "Without the Romeo and Juliet bit. Let me make up my own mind."

"We were just kids…" she says as she starts to tell me her version of events. "We used to hang out in the cave beneath this house. Morvoren."

Looks to camera — I knew there was something Uncle Henry wasn't telling me.

"I'd sit around reading while Billy painted me," continues Min. "He even did one on the cave wall. It was beautiful… Anyway, we had a massive row the night I told him I was pregnant. He was worried about what his parents would say. They never liked me…" Her voice cracks. "He wasn't thinking straight. Stomped off out of the cave, knowing that the tide was coming in and that the storm could have altered the currents. But even the strongest of swimmers…"

She pauses to wipe away tears with the back of her hand. "I followed him. Tried to save him, but he was too far away…"

I suddenly understand why she's never told me this before.

"Sarah was on the beach; she saw the whole thing. Called the lifeguard, but it was too late. There was nothing either of us could do…"

"Why didn't you drown?" I ask.

"I didn't fight it," she says simply. "And they'll never forgive me for that, Coco. You don't know them like I do. They'll want you to take their side. This divided town is testament to that. I can't lose you too. Please say you understand."

"OK," I mumble.

Looks to camera – well, what else can I say?

About Time

"How about we eat out tonight?" suggests Min. "Not sure I can face cooking after all the cleaning I've been doing."

I eye Uncle Henry hopefully. "D'you think you could walk that far?"

He shrugs. "Well, if a Stimpson's goby fish can climb a hundred-metre waterfall, using its mouth—"

Looks to camera...

"—it's about time I tried," he laughs.

"Give me two ticks," I call, excitedly dashing up to my bedroom to dig out something that's not covered in plaster, and returning to find Uncle Henry still in his dressing gown. "You're not wearing *that* out, are you?"

He frowns. "Yes. It's comfy."

"But it's full of holes. You can't wear pyjamas!"

"Why not? Fish don't change their outfits to go out.

Why should I? Actually, goldfish do. There's a Pleco fish that will literally suck the slime coat off them…"

"Are you suggesting I'm the Pleco fish in this scenario?" I say.

Uncle Henry nods. "Kind of."

"Ready?" asks Min, appearing at the top of the stairs.

My jaw drops at the spectacle. I needn't have worried about what *I* was wearing. Uncle Henry looks like a hollowed-out scarecrow in his sleepwear and Min, in a floor-length gold kimono, four-inch heels and wrapped in a vintage golden fur, looks like a lion. Now all I need is a tin man and a dog.

Looks to camera – if only!

The reception in the Plaice 2 Be is stunned silence. Locals and tourists alike turn to stare as if we're celebrities, though it's Min they're really looking at.

"Where's Henry?" she asks.

"Collapsed on the supermarket bench," I say. "I told him we'd meet him back there."

Min rolls her eyes, then, seeing someone she knows, she wanders off, leaving me to get the food.

"Hi, Amy," I say, giving her my brightest smile. Guess she's going to be a friend now that I'm living here. "You on school hols yet?" I ask. Silence. "Think the weather's set to improve tomorrow. Good job cos we've got a hole the size of London in our roof!" Not even a twitch. "D'you fancy going to the beach sometime?" I add, somewhat hopefully I must admit, given her continued frostiness.

"Well, aren't you going to answer her?"

I turn to see Wanda, her long grey hair tumbling down in tangles, a towel slung across her shoulders and a wetsuit hanging round her waist. "We must stop meeting like this," she laughs, her face glowing with pleasure.

I laugh with her. The words, "You're my grandma," sounding so loud in my head, I don't know what to say.

"You all right?" she asks.

I nod mutely, the words now flashing in front of my eyes.

"Amazing surf today," she says. "Those waves were all-time perfection. Best it's been in years." She fixes a stern look on Amy. "I hope you're not being rude, Amy Enys."

Amy stares at us both, the red flooding her cheeks, and, with a surly expression, she says, "Salt and vinegar?"

"Yes, please!" I reply, beaming as if she's offered me the Crown Jewels. "If you fancy hanging out, you know where I am. Bye, Wanda!" I quickly gather up the food parcels, eager to escape for fear of blurting out my secret.

We eat the fish and chips perched on the supermarket bench, watching the surfers glide in on the epic waves.

"Did you know a cod becomes sexually active at three

or four years old?" says Uncle Henry, staring pensively at his food. "The female lays up to five million eggs and most of those will be consumed by other fish and sea creatures."

I lower the piece of fish I was about to eat.

"You're putting her off her food, Henry," laughs Min. "Careful, darling, or the seagulls will have it."

"Not hungry anyway," I murmur. Too busy thinking about Wanda.

Uncle Henry snorts. "Remember when that seagull nicked your chips, Min? You cried about it all evening."

"Did not," she protests. "Well, maybe a bit. But Ma wouldn't buy me any more and you wouldn't share."

He frowns. "Yeah, I did."

"Oh." She sighs happily. "That was such a good summer, wasn't it? Before things changed and Pa died. Remember that campfire we had?"

"Which one?"

"The one where Ma had a go at Sarah for skinny-dipping. This would be a perfect evening for a campfire."

They both sigh, staring off at the horizon, lost in a joint memory I can't share.

"Why don't we have one then?" I say, feeling desperate to create some of my own.

But Uncle Henry shakes his head. "Not tonight, Coco. I think I've travelled far enough. We've still got to sort out where you're going to sleep."

"Yeah, you're not sharing with me again," moans Min.

"It was like you were running in your sleep last night."

"Where am I supposed to go then?" I say. "There's only one other spare room with a bed and that's covered in dustbin bags that you won't let me move."

Min rolls her eyes. "That's cos I'm halfway through sorting them out. You can strip your bed, can't you?" She nudges me in the ribs. "I'll even help you if you like."

Jumpcut to me struggling to change the sheets on my own. Clouds of dust dancing in the air as the occasional bit of plasterwork falls on my head.

I'd moan but this place feels different. Uncle Henry and Min reminiscing rather than quarrelling – let's just hope it lasts!

PISCARY BAY TIDE TIMES

Wednesday 17th July

HIGH TIDE:	06:13	HEIGHT:	6.10 m
LOW TIDE:	12:34	HEIGHT:	1.40 m
HIGH TIDE:	18:30	HEIGHT:	6.30 m

Waxing Full Moon

SUNRISE:	05:31	SUNSET:	21:25
MOONRISE:	21:02	MOONSET:	04:49

Babysitting

If Min and Uncle Henry can make friends, so can I. So goes the commentary inside my head the moment I wake. Things are on the up; the plot really has changed for the better. I can feel it in my bones.

Min is sitting with the sunlight washing over her in the newly ordered front room. Her sewing machine set up by the window, blue skies and azure sea as the backdrop and her favourite tunes crackling on the record player accompanied by crooning seagulls and the beat of the waves crashing against the rocks below.

She looks different. And it's got nothing to do with the bright orange, wide-legged, halter-neck trouser suit.

"What?" she asks, wrinkling her nose.

"Have you started using that cleanser I gave you?"

"No," she snorts. "Nothing water and a bar of soap

can't do. You off out?"

"Yeah. Going to make some friends."

"In that?" she says, nodding doubtfully at my hot pants and cropped T-shirt.

"Yeah," I say lightly, refusing to be drawn in.

"Oh," she murmurs. "OK. See you later then."

∼∼∼

"Morning, Jan." I wave as I skip happily past the Burbank.

"Good morning, *kochanie*," he replies, his silver suit reflecting brightly in the morning sunlight. "You out early."

"I'm off to make some friends," I tell him happily.

"Good luck!" he says.

"Thanks," I call, skipping away.

A loud rap on the glass of the *Hej!* window stops me in my tracks as I see Ingrid working on another display, furiously waving at me. Dressed in a beautiful tartan red jacket cinched in at the waist over a white shirt and a pair of skinny jeans, she looks as fierce as ever.

"*Hej*, Ingrid," I say, poking my head round the door to ruffle Ned's head. "You're looking good today."

"*Hej*, Coco!" she cries. "You always say the right thing. Off somewhere nice?"

"Going to make friends with this town," I tell her.

"*Wauw!*" she laughs. "Good luck!"

I soon realize that the problem with my plan is that everyone my age is still in school and, without any money left, I can't even hang out in Screams. I decide to visit Adele instead, hoping that maybe she'll give me some more babysitting.

"Hi, Adele," I say brightly, finding her on her hands and knees, scrubbing mournfully at the doorstep to the annexe.

She glances up, quickly dabbing her eyes with the back of her hand. "Oh, hello," she says in a false, bright tone. "Just cleaning up this mess. You would not believe the way those women left the place. Sick everywhere. I had to take all their deposit."

"Need some help?" I ask, seeing my in.

Adele smiles. "Thank you, darling, but no. Honestly, if I'd known how hard it would be to do this, I might have reconsidered. Actually, could you pick Sprout up from school at three? Take her to the beach perhaps?"

"Course," I say eagerly.

"Just make sure you watch her," Adele adds. "She's the adventurous kind and, if you don't keep an eye on her, she'll be up a tree or stranded on a rock before you know it. Grab her swimming things, would you?" she says, waving me away. "Her room's such a pigsty – your guess is as good as mine. Here, let me give you some cash for an ice cream too. Only one scoop, mind. And don't let her go in the sea without a wetsuit on. Bring her home for six and I'll cook you both fish fingers."

I smile to myself. This must be what it feels like to have a mum who's around more. Although, come to think about it, isn't that what I've got now? Funny, it hasn't changed a thing…

~~~

"What flavour do you want?" I ask Sprout when we finally get to the front of the queue. Screams is crammed with kids crowding round the counter. Bennie and his mum are rushed off their feet as usual.

"What can I get you?" asks Bennie.

I grin. "I'll have some salted car—"

"Oi, oi!" cries Leo, suddenly jostling in front of me.

"Er. D'you mind?" I say, frowning indignantly at his back.

He glances over his shoulder. "Sorry, didn't see you there… Salted caramel, please, mate," he says with a grin and all Bennie can do is shrug apologetically.

It's like the supermarket all over again as they start a lengthy chat about the sea conditions, while I slowly start to wilt. For some reason, this boy really gets my goat.

"Oi," I say, prodding Leo in the shoulder. "Pushing in is one thing, but now you're just delaying on purpose."

He slowly spins round and, with a smirk, leans back on the counter, taking a lick of his ice cream. It infuriates me. Reminds me of the way Uncle Henry winds Min up. "All yours," he says airily.

"D'you fancy him?" whispers Sprout. "Your face went funny."

"No!" I gasp. "He walks around as if he owns the place."

"He's a Fish," she laughs. "Mummy says he thinks he's better than the rest, but that he's not. I actually meant him though." And she nods in a not-so-subtle way at Bennie.

I laugh. "No. I like him though. Seems kind and thoughtful. I'm hoping that if I stick at being friendly, he'll eventually crack and we can be mates. You know, kind of like a remora fish?"

Sprout's expression remains clueless.

"They attach themselves to sharks for protection," I explain, and she nods knowingly as if I'm making complete sense.

"It's not working so far, is it?" she sighs. "Cassie Enys – that's Amy's sister – says that you're never going to be accepted."

"Oh. Well… They don't know how determined I can be," I say. "They haven't got to know me yet, have they?"

"No, but…"

"Trust me," I laugh. "I just need more time."

Sister Act

On the third day in a row of babysitting, I'm attempting to build a giant sandcastle with Sprout on a small patch of the town beach while keeping an eye on the local kids in case they say hello. No luck so far.

"What's going on over there?" I frown, spotting a lifeboat zipping across the water.

"Probably just a mermaid," says Sprout airily. "Mummy's got a whole load of them booked in. They come down for the weekend to become mermaids, then go swimming in their tails, thinking they know it all, and quite often get swept out to sea by the current. The lifeguards are always bringing them back. Mummy says it's the Pengellys' fault."

"The Pengellys?" I say, trying to hide my excitement.

"Yeah, they run *Part of our World* and Mummy says it only encourages them."

"I thought you meant a real mermaid for a second," I laugh.

Sprout giggles. "Course not, silly. I'm nine, not seven! Come on, race you into the water."

"Not without your wetsuit, you won't."

"Oh," she whines. "Why can't I go in without one, like you? Mummy's such a worrywart."

I shrug. "That's what she wants and, besides, you can stay in for longer with a wetsuit."

"How come you don't have one then?"

"Because I really am a mermaid," I smirk, flicking my imaginary flowing locks behind me as if I'm Ariel. And the fact that I can't afford one…

Sprout shrieks with delight. "You're never."

"Am too!"

"Then where's your tail?"

I grin. "Well, duh! It only appears when I'm in the water. Obviously. You should see it – it's beautiful. Shimmering pinks and purples, oranges too. Flecks of copper that catch the sunlight."

Sprout gasps, her eyes wide with wonder, temporarily forgetting that's she's too old to believe. "Can I see it?"

"Course," I laugh. "But wetsuit first…"

~~~

"D'you know everybody?" Sprout asks later when we're walking along the high street. "Because you've said hello to everyone we've passed so far."

I giggle. "Jan's so kind. He always makes me smile."

"They do a yummy afternoon tea at the Burbank," Sprout says with a sigh. "Ingrid's a bit scary. She doesn't like it when I go in there with ice cream, but she daren't say anything. Mummy's one of her biggest customers," she adds proudly.

"I'm sure she is," I laugh. "Ingrid's nice when you get to know her. Just got to say the right thing is all."

Sprout frowns. "So who were the family in the car that you waved to?"

"I don't know!" I laugh. "I was just thanking them for letting us cross."

"Oh. Mummy only ever raises a single finger and Daddy doesn't thank anyone. You're a bit weird, aren't you?"

I snort. "What, because I'm being friendly?"

"It's more than that though," she says. "You're always trying to air-kiss everyone."

"It's what I'm used to."

"Yeah, but you blew that last car a kiss!"

I shrug. "Felt like the right thing to do. They all looked pretty gloomy. Did you see the kids in the back arguing? I just wanted them to know that I was grateful after all the other cars that hadn't bothered to stop. I've always done it. Imagine how it would feel if someone did it to me. You know, waved or blew me a kiss, or hugged me even. It would make me feel good, so I wanted them to feel that way too."

"Definitely weird," says Sprout decisively. "People aren't like that around here. You're going to confuse them."

"Yeah, well, maybe if they started being a bit nicer to each other, stopped fussing over what group they fall into, they might be happier."

Sprout squeezes my hand. "I think you're nice. Even if Leo doesn't. And Bennie's just a silly sea bass if he doesn't become your friend."

I smile down at her, feeling happy.

"What are you smiling at?" she asks.

"Just wondering if this is what it feels like to be a big sister. I always dreamed of being one. Playing together, talking, going on outings, that sort of thing."

Sprout stares at me as if I'm half mad. "That's not what it's like. Shiv hates me. She's always yelling and thumping me. If I go in her room and ask her to play, she screams about not having any privacy. She's boring. Always got her nose in a book or studying. You're *much* nicer. *You* actually play with me."

"Oh, I'm sure that's not true," I laugh, feeling flattered.

Sprout nods firmly. "'Tis. She thinks I'm an annoying brat who gets in the way and makes everywhere messy."

"You?" I cry in mock horror. "Messy? Never!"

PISCARY BAY TIDE TIMES

Saturday 20th July

LOW TIDE:	02:09	HEIGHT:	1.40 m
HIGH TIDE:	08:02	HEIGHT:	6.00 m
LOW TIDE:	14:21	HEIGHT:	1.50 m
HIGH TIDE:	20:19	HEIGHT:	6.20 m

Gibbous Moon

SUNRISE:	05:34	SUNSET:	21:21
MOONRISE:	21:24	MOONSET:	08:58

Sibling Rivalry

I'm back at the Old Barn the next afternoon. Adele is going to collect Shiv from school so I'm babysitting Sprout while her dad, Simon, takes a work call. It's beginning to feel like I live here.

Looks to camera – I wish.

"Are you excited about Shiv coming home?"

Sprout shakes her head. "Nope." Then, slamming down her penultimate card on the kitchen table, she yells, "Uno!" and bursts into laughter.

She frowns suddenly. "Last time I saw her, she hit me."

"That's not very nice," I say. "Why'd she do that?"

Sprout shrugs. "Dunno. Why are you so interested?"

"Oh, I was just thinking, since she's my age…"

"She won't like you," says Sprout quickly. "She's a bit of a snob and you're … different. Sorry."

"Oh," I murmur, feeling like my balloon's been popped. I had thought we could be friends. Now I'm not so sure...

"Don't look sad," says Sprout, rushing over to throw her arms round my neck. "You've still got me. And I'm your first friend, aren't I?"

I smile. "Yes, you are. What's the hug for?"

"You said you liked being hugged," she replies, failing to suppress her giggles. I stare at her with narrowed eyes.

"You wanted to see my hand to make sure you're sure going to win," I gasp. "Hazel Quarter—"

"Sprout, what are you doing?"

A change comes over Sprout as soon as her big sister walks in the door. It's like she reverts to being the baby of the family, throwing her sister a stroppy look and vying for my attention.

"Sprout, get off her," snorts Shiv, attempting to prise her sister's hands from their stranglehold round my neck. "You're being too much. Hi," she says, grinning at me. With shoulder-length brown hair framing a friendly looking face, she's hardly the villainous troll that Sprout described. "I'm Shiv."

"This is Coco," says Sprout, jumping in. "She's new here and she's *my* friend. Did Mummy tell you about her?"

Shiv laughs. "Yes, all the way home."

I step forward as if I've only just remembered it's my cue. "Hi, Shiv," I say, greeting her with my usual air kisses, which she fumbles over and ends up kissing me on my mouth, making her blush bright red to the tips of her ears.

"You're not supposed to kiss her on the lips, Shiv," sniggers Sprout. "Don't you know anything?"

"More than you do," retorts her sister, punching her lightly on the arm.

"Ow!" shrieks Sprout, completely overreacting. "That hurt!"

"No, it didn't."

"Yes, it did," insists Sprout. "Mummy!" she cries, dashing from the room. "Mummy! Shiv hit me!"

"Sorry about her," laughs Shiv. "She's a bit overdramatic."

"Yeah," I say. "I was half expecting you to appear in a cloud of black smoke the way she described you."

She giggles. "Don't tell me. She said that I never allow her in my room and I'm constantly telling her to go away."

"Pretty much."

"Sprout comes into my room every single morning at six a.m. and goes on at me to play," explains Shiv. "Then she touches everything I own. Even my make-up. And she leaves the bathroom in a mess – toothpaste all over the sink, wet towels on the floor. Doesn't even flush the loo after a poo! And she comes in when I'm in the shower. I basically have no privacy."

"Ah," I say, beginning to see the other side of the story.

"Mummy, tell her she can't hit me," demands Sprout, appearing with Adele in tow.

"Delley, there's sick in the courtyard," says Simon,

appearing suddenly. A tall man with wavy brown hair, greying at the sides. He nods hello to me and rushes over to give his eldest daughter a hug, while poor Adele frowns at us all, looking like a rabbit caught in the headlights.

"You need to tell her, Mummy," insists Sprout.

"It was a joke punch," laughs Shiv.

"Tell you what," I say, jumping in. "How about we go for a swim? All three of us. It's a gorgeous day and I haven't been yet."

Shiv wrinkles her nose at her watch. "Town beach'll be heaving by now."

I smile. "That's not where I was thinking of…"

Dreams and Aspirations

I've discovered a short cut down an alleyway of one hundred steps from the Old Barn to the supermarket, meaning we don't have to walk through town. And it gives us the most amazing view of the sea. Shiv stops at the top and sniffs the air, her eyes closed, smile wide with pleasure.

"I've missed that smell," she gushes. "And these hills. These views."

"But not the sea or the beaches?" I say.

She shrugs. "Not as bothered. Probably because the only time I come home is when the Zombies are here. Hard to get excited over a thin strip of sand."

"It's not like that where we're going." I grin.

"How come you haven't taken me to this beach before?" complains Sprout.

"Can't make friends on a deserted beach," I retort.

"With the Fish, you mean?" says Sprout sniffily.

I shrug. "With anyone."

"Is that why Shiv hasn't managed to make any friends then?"

Shiv and I exchange a look before she thumps her sister lightly on the arm. "How's it working out for you?"

I sigh. "Meh. I know most people by their first names at least."

"More than Shiv knows," giggles Sprout.

"All right, Sprout," mutters Shiv irritably. "Mum says that your mum's the original Cuckoo. Apparently, Mum went for a drink with her and Tania and came back with a humungous hangover and all the latest gossip about the celebs your mum's met."

"Like who?" I ask, feeling the familiar irritated sensation of yet another person being impressed by my mother.

But Shiv just shrugs. "Dunno. I'm not bothered by that sort of thing. I'd rather watch a wildlife documentary. With the exception of *Big Mother* of course. I love that show."

"Oh, of course," I laugh, finding her attitude rather refreshing. "Me too. Actually, I want to make documentaries one day."

"Gosh, really?" she gasps. "How wonderful! It sounds like you had a seriously glamorous life in London. Way more exciting than this place. Why did you move here?"

"Didn't have much choice," I say.

"And what about your dad? Where's he? Sorry," she adds, seeing my twisted expression. "I'm being nosy. Just a pleasant change to have someone new to talk to around here. Feel free to tell me to shut up."

I giggle. "No, it's OK. I don't mind. It's kind of nice having a normal conversation." I lower my voice. "No offence to your sister, but she's kind of…"

"Annoying?"

"I was gonna say young." I hesitate, briefly toying with the idea of telling Shiv my secret. A problem shared is a problem halved and all that, but I promised Min. "My dad's a director," I say.

Looks to camera – hmm, not sure starting a friendship with a lie is a good idea.

"Bob Seymour."

Looks to camera – well, he is my sort-of dad…

Shiv frowns. "You didn't take his surname?"

"They never married and Min didn't want me to," I say, stopping at the cliff-path gate and feeling relieved that I can change the subject. "Here we are."

"Oh my gosh, Shiv!" shrieks Sprout excitedly. "I didn't know this place existed, did you? It's like being on a deserted island. Oh, this changes everything. Summer is going to be awesome."

"Careful," calls Shiv, laughing as her sister bounds eagerly down the path. "No wonder Mum wants to get her hands on Cliff House," she tells me. "She'd kill for this kind of USP. Mind you, half the Cuckoos in town want it too. And the Fish, I shouldn't wonder. You wouldn't believe the rumours about what it's like inside."

I laugh. "Like what?"

"Oh, I don't know," sighs Shiv disinterestedly. "I'm not really into interiors like Mum. I'd rather have my nose in a science book. I want to be a hydrologist one day. They solve problems regarding water quality and its availability. Maybe climate science too, gathering data from the sea," she explains and it's my turn to be impressed. She's so clever.

"You'd like my uncle then," I say. "He's into marine life too. Fish specifically. He keeps on telling me these strange facts. Like last night—"

"I thought you said this was a private beach?" interrupts Shiv, pointing down at the beach where a group of kids are sunbathing. Their wetsuits, surfboards and diving paraphernalia strewn across the sand.

I nod.

"Then they're trespassing." She frowns. "Come on."

The Outsiders

I clamber after Shiv as she strides confidently down the footpath, as if confronting a group of trespassers is all part of a normal day. Nothing seems to faze her. It's amazing.

"Excuse me!" she calls. "You can't be here."

Cut to a shot of Leo Tremain looking every bit the beach bum in trunks and rash vest, his messy surfer hair falling into his eyes, skin turning a warm brown, in the way my skin's started to go too.

"Oi, oi," he cries, throwing a scornful look at Shiv. "Should've known you'd act like lady of the manor. 'Cept it's not your land, is it? It's hers," he says, turning his disdain on me. "Funny you never said anything the other day when we saved your life."

I blush. "I was trying to save your life actually. And it's not like that. It's just… Well, we were looking forward to having this place to ourselves…"

"It's a private beach," insists Shiv. "Belongs to Cliff House. She's got every right asking you what you're doing here."

"Well, would you look who's back," says Amy, sitting up and shielding her eyes from the sun. "Home from La-di-dah Land. Mummy bought any more houses lately?"

"It's Hertfordshire actually," snaps Shiv. "It's not my fault what my mother chooses to do. And, for the record, I'd much rather live here all year round."

"Like we care," snorts Leo.

"You're not our people," Amy agrees. "End of."

"What the hell does that mean?" I laugh. "This Fish and Cuckoo thing is a load of rubbish, if you ask me."

"We didn't," snarls Amy.

"Course it's a load of rubbish," pipes up Bennie, side-eyeing Shiv. "It's a silly term that our parents dreamed up."

"So why use it?" I ask.

He shrugs. "Habit, I guess."

Leo shakes his head. "Nah, it's more than that. It's things like your superior attitude. You come sweeping down here as if you own the place."

Looks to camera…

"Her family does," snorts Shiv.

"Look, I know you don't like Min," I say.

"That's an understatement." Leo's scowl deepens, if that were even possible. "We've been using this beach for years."

192

"Yeah, illegally," counters Shiv, standing her ground.

Whoa. She's quite a force to be reckoned with. The thing is, I'm not sure it's helping. And do I really mind if they're here too?

"What's going on?" asks Sprout, glancing around with a puzzled expression. "Can I go over to the rock pools with Cassie?"

Shiv nods. "Don't go in the sea without telling me though. You know what the—"

"Yes," she calls over her shoulder. "Stop being a worrywart. You're being like Mummy."

"You can't swim properly," retorts Shiv, though this is said to Sprout's back as she runs away. "You need to leave," she tells the group. "This is Coco's uncle's land and she'll … report you if you don't."

Looks to camera – will I?

"Ooh, get her," scoffs Amy. "Sorry, but I ain't shifting for no Zombie."

"Please don't call me that," I say. That term gets right under my skin, which I guess is what it's designed to do.

"Yeah, she lives here now," says Shiv.

"Cuckoo then," counters Amy.

"Look," I say, beginning to bristle, "we just came down for a swim."

"We just came down for a swim," mimics Leo in an annoying, whiny tone, which, despite seeing my uncle do it to Min a thousand times, I fall for immediately.

"Don't do that," I say.

"Don't do that."

My face burns with irritation. "I mean it."

"I mean it…"

"Help! HELP!"

I turn to look out to sea. Cassie is frantically waving at the cliff face, where Sprout is clinging on desperately to a rock surrounded by water.

"How did she manage to get all the way out there?" I ask, gasping as an outgoing wave smashes against the rock, nearly toppling her into the sea again.

"Sprout!" shrieks Shiv, her face paling with fear. "Oh my God, you've got to help me. She can't swim. Not in that!"

The Rescue

I sprint down the beach, diving quickly into the sea, my only focus on saving Sprout. The tide may be going out but it's rough today and it isn't easy to swim.

"Coco – wait!" calls Leo, catching up to me in a few strong strokes. "There's a rip out there. If she jumps in the wrong place, she could be swept out to sea again. You both could."

I stare at the calm patch of water with waves crashing either side. It looks like the best place to be and I say as much. But, rather than his usual eye-roll, he shakes his head calmly. "That's exactly how you spot one."

"So, what do we do?" I say, feeling helpless. "We can't exactly leave her there until the tide goes out. If one of those waves knocks her in..."

Leo studies the water, his eyes narrowing as he

concentrates. "We need to make sure we stay the other side of the rock. See that?" he says, pointing at one of the trespasser signs. "That's the entrance to Morvoren Cave. There's a channel that runs between the cave and the rock she's on that causes the rip. There's another one beyond it too, but not as strong. If she jumps in that side, she should be fine. But listen, if either of you do get caught, don't fight it. The rips around here will defeat even the strongest of swimmers. You've just got to go with it. You'll eventually pop out of it and wash back in with the waves. Got that?"

I nod, feeling like I'm in safe hands.

"Help!" screams Sprout, looking terrified. "The wave carried me out here. Help!"

"It's all right," Leo calls gently. "We're here to save you. But listen, you need to do exactly what I tell you, OK?"

"You can trust him," I tell her as Sprout looks at me for reassurance.

"I want you to jump in the water," explains Leo. "It's OK," he adds as she starts to protest. "But I need you to aim out to sea."

Yet more protests. I don't blame her. "Do not jump towards the beach whatever you do. The rip that got you there will take you even further out."

"I can't," says Sprout, panicking.

"You can," says Leo.

"I'll be there to catch you," I tell her. Easier said than done. Because trying to swim closer while the rough waves are crashing down *and* steer clear of the rip is nigh on impossible.

"Let's do this," says Leo decisively. "Come on, Sprout. You can do it! Jump. We'll catch you, I promise."

"Jump, Sprout!" I yell. "Now!"

With a terrified yelp, she jumps into the sea, landing just in front of me where she thrashes her arms around, and I grab at her to bring her to the surface.

What I'm not expecting is how much she feels like a lead weight – a flailing one – and I immediately sink under in my efforts to keep her above the water. I resurface just in time to take a breath and then I'm under again, unable to keep us both afloat. Holding my breath, I swim under the water, my lungs burning with the effort as I kick with all my might against the outgoing tide.

Suddenly I feel a firm hand on my back and I'm pulled upwards and into the arms of Leo where I gasp for breath, holding a tearful Sprout in a firm grip as he propels us in. Soon the three of us are scrambling to the shore where Shiv is jumping up and down frantically. She pulls Sprout out of my arms and into hers as soon as she can.

I lie back in the shallow water, panting for breath. "Thanks," I tell Leo. "You were amazing out there."

He grins. "So were you. Most people would have panicked in that kind of situation."

"Yeah, well, I'm not really the damsel-in-distress kind of character, you know."

He chuckles to himself. "Yeah, I'm beginning to realize that. Next time I'll leave you to drown, shall I?"

I laugh. "Not gonna be a next time. Especially now I've got these!" I point to the flippers I'd treated myself to with the babysitting money from Adele.

"Those?" he scoffs, comparing them to his own, which dwarf mine by some margin. "Think you're gonna need a bigger pair…"

Champions

The atmosphere has changed on the beach. It's no longer us and them as everyone crowds round Sprout, throwing towels over her shoulders and asking if they can get her anything. And, when Leo and I join them, we're both treated to the pats on the backs of champions.

"Oh, Sprout," scolds Shiv, through a fountain of tears. "What on earth were you doing out there?"

Sprout smiles sheepishly. "Cassie bet me that I couldn't reach the cave entrance," she replies, cuddling into her big sister. "I fell over in the shallow water and the next minute I was being dragged out to sea. It was pure luck that I managed to grab hold of that rock. I'm so sorry, Shiv."

"Cassie," hisses Amy. "You know that cave's out of bounds."

Her sister shrugs. "You're always talking about it."

"Am not."

"Leo does," counters Cassie. "He's always on about going in there."

"When?" gasps Amy. "Have you been earwigging at my bedroom door? I've told you not to do that." She storms across the beach, her little sister trotting in her wake, trying to keep up with their argument.

"Good save, James," says Bennie, extending his hand solemnly, which I take to be an olive branch.

"Thanks." I grin. "Oh and use the beach whenever you like. I don't mind. Plenty of room for us all…"

~~~

"What's so special about Morvoren Cave?" I ask Sprout as we climb the cliff path home.

"A mermaid lived there."

"A woman died there, you mean," corrects Shiv.

"And turned into a mermaid," counters Sprout.

"That's just a legend," mutters Shiv. "Mermaids don't exist. You can't have half mammal half fish."

"Then what about the carpet of sparkling mermaid tears?" demands Sprout.

Shiv stares at her, wide-eyed. "Oh, you've seen inside the cave, have you?" She rolls her eyes. "Honestly, Sprout. You scared the life out of me. Promise me you'll never do that again."

Sprout nods earnestly. "You won't tell Mummy, will you?"

"*We-llll…*" Shiv sighs.

"You can't!" gasps Sprout. "Oh, please. She'll never let me out of her sight again."

"OK." Shiv sneaks me a wink. "I suppose I don't need to tell her but … only if you promise not to come in my room before nine a.m. for the rest of the week."

"Eight," says Sprout. "Eight thirty?"

"This isn't a negotiation."

"Fine."

"Bet it lasts all of one day," mutters Shiv, watching her sister prance off happily ahead of us.

"Were you really going to tell Adele about her?" I ask.

Shiv snorts. "Course not but I needed to get something out of it. Mum would just blame me anyway. Why weren't you watching her like a hawk, Siobhan?" she says, mimicking Adele perfectly. "You should've read her mind and known that she was going to fall over in shallow water… Good job you were there," she says, squeezing my hand. "Thanks for saving her."

"It was all Leo," I say. "If he hadn't been there, I'd never have known about that rip." I stop in my tracks, suddenly hit by a major realization. "Did you see the way we worked together? We weren't Fish or Cuckoos or … Zombies. We were just kids looking out for each other."

"And?" Shiv frowns.

"It's obvious!" I cry. Well, it is to me. "This plot needs a rewrite."

"Plot? Rewrite?"

"Yeah," I say, my excitement building. "You know like in films? The narrative's all wrong. It's got bogged down in ancient history and today proves that. We can get along; everyone just needs reminding that we're all the same underneath. And I'm the linchpin. I'm going to give this town the happy-ever-after it deserves…"

WIZIWISDOM

MORVOREN CAVE

Fake news! <small>(edit)</small>

MORVOREN CAVE IS A MYTH. END OF. And here's the proof:

1. The idea that a cave might exist somewhere under the grey cliffs of Piscary Bay, accessed by a series of labyrinthine tunnels that run for miles, is quite frankly ludicrous. Almost as stupid as the rivalry between the self-proclaimed Fish and Cuckoos.

2. Then there's the story of a beautiful young woman getting lost when she followed her dog into the tunnel, finding herself trapped when the tide turned. So far, so good, though I suspect whoever made this up had been watching too much Wizard of Oz… But this fairy tale doesn't have a happy ending. Both the young woman and dog were drowned in the strong rips that can be found in Piscary Bay and − here's where it really is crazy − she turned into a mermaid. Yeah, right! As if a mammal could ever live in cold water for that long.

3. And finally, there's the cave itself, which has been elaborately described, despite NO ONE EVER HAVING SEEN IT. I mean − a staircase made of green stone? Come off it! A carpet of mermaid tears (see my comment above). A self-portrait of a hauntingly beautiful woman staring down from the cave wall, which, so the story goes, is said to shimmer with an eerie green glow from a sea of stars. That's just the effect of the many bioluminescent organisms that can found locally…

26th July 17:08
This page was last edited 15 years ago

Excerpt from the Piscary Post:

TRAGEDY OF MORVOREN CLAIMS ANOTHER LIFE

Morvoren Cave is to be officially cordoned off following the death of an eighteen-year-old man, known as Billy Pengelly. The tragedy happened during Thursday night's storm when Mr Pengelly and seventeen-year-old Minnie James tried to exit the cave and were caught in an unexpected rip thanks to the strong winds causing a higher than predicted tide. Cliff House owner, and mother of the survivor, Mrs Brenda James, wasn't available for comment.

A Line in the Sand

My master plan is beginning to work, and each day we successfully share the beach, albeit either side of a line that Amy's drawn.

"Be careful on those rocks!" yells Shiv, keeping a beady eye on her sister. "She's not listening to me. And she was in my room at six thirty this morning." She sighs. "So, tell me again how you're going to solve a long-standing rivalry? Sharing the beach hasn't exactly changed things."

Baby steps is a perhaps more accurate description for the progress I've made. Because, try as I might to recreate the kind of camaraderie of last week, I can't seem to get it back and the line in the sand might as well be a brick wall for all the conversation we haven't had. Maybe today will be different without Amy here. She's made it very clear that she doesn't like me.

"They should be more grateful," tuts Shiv. "You didn't have to share. I wouldn't have."

"Good job you're not me," I laugh.

"You're very persistent, aren't you?" she says. "I admire that, truly I do, but... You don't know these people. The Fish own this town, or at least act as if they do. Believe me, Sprout's tried with Amy's sister. She's always complaining about how she has to do what Cassie says in order to stay friends. I bet that's why she went near the cave."

"Not because she wanted to see the mermaid tears or the green stone staircase then?"

"Someone's being doing their research," laughs Shiv.

"Just Wiziwisdom." I leave out the fact that I also researched my dad's accident. "D'you think it's true?"

"What, the mermaids?"

"No! The idea that there's a cave full of labyrinthine tunnels that are lit up by glittering organisms. Bio-something."

"Bioluminescence," says Shiv.

"Yeah, that," I say. "Apparently, it's the most common form of communication on the planet."

Shiv frowns. "I thought you hated science."

"I do. Made the mistake of asking Uncle Henry about it last night. He went on about some chemical reaction between Lucifer and oxygen."

"Luciferin," giggles Shiv.

"Oh," I laugh. "I wondered what he meant. Anyway, I'd love to see it. How'd you know all this stuff? You're very clever."

"I read."

"So do I," I retort.

"Books, not Wiziwisdom. You know anyone can update that website, right?"

"Oh," I gasp. "That might explain why my Uncle Henry's page talks about him being born with scales. Someone must be having a laugh… Maybe it's not true about those Neptunian Awards either." I stand up. "I'm going in for a swim. You coming?"

Shiv sits bolt upright, staring incredulously at me. "Wait. Your uncle is *Henry* James? But he was… He is… Oh my God! I can't believe I didn't put two and two together." Her face spreads into a huge beam.

"What?" I say.

"That he lived here," she gushes. "He was really set to be someone once upon a time. Won the Neptunian Award two years in a row and that never happens."

"That's real, is it?" I say.

"It's the most coveted award in the marine-biology world," Bennie pipes up, sitting as close to the line as possible. I think he fancies Shiv. "Goes to scientists who have gone above and beyond with their research," he adds. "We've only explored around five per cent of the world's oceans. Imagine what kind of fish are waiting to be discovered. *That's* the sort of thing winners of the Neptunian Award think about." He laughs. "People around here have no idea what sort of science royalty he is!"

I leave the two of them deep in conversation about evolution, and wade into the water. Within a few short steps, I've dived under, enjoying the prickly feeling of the cold tickling my sun-baked skin and I pull myself along the seabed until I reach Leo who is busy diving among the rock pools.

It's funny how things look different underwater. Seaweed standing tall like skyscrapers while fish dash around like commuters during rush hour. Everything is given an aquamarine tinge that varies as the sun dips in and out behind the clouds, and which makes the pinks and purples of the seaweed pop.

I follow Leo out to sea where we resurface close to the trespasser signs. "So, this is the legendary Morvoren Cave? It doesn't look much. Where's the entrance?"

Leo points down. "It's submerged. You can't get in until low tide. Not easily anyway."

He dives back under and motions for me to follow him until I can make out the black hole of the cave entrance. Then, sticking close to the cliff edge, we dart in and out of the nooks and crannies of the submerged rock pools, now completely transformed by the high tide. Leo points out seaweed-crusted crabs scampering along a wedge of rock splattered with sparkly pink patches. Sound is muffled down here and I feel as if I'm moving in slow motion. Like there's no pressure from the real world. It makes me smile and when I glance over at Leo I can see he feels the same way.

Down here there are no lines in the sand. We're just two people fascinated with the underwater world.

PISCARY BAY TIDE TIMES

Monday 29th July

HIGH TIDE:	03:21	HEIGHT:	5.50 m
LOW TIDE:	09:54	HEIGHT:	1.80 m
HIGH TIDE:	15:49	HEIGHT:	5.70 m
LOW TIDE:	22:24	HEIGHT:	1.70 m

Waning Crescent Moon

SUNRISE:	05:45	SUNSET:	21:10
MOONRISE:	02:42	MOONSET:	19:06

The Entrance

I can't stop thinking about Morvoren Cave. And it's not just the fact that it's tied to my dad either: it's the stories that seem to surround it. I need to see it! And, using the tide-times website, I've realized I can pinpoint exactly when I can get near the entrance.

"Why are we here so early?" yawns Shiv.

"It's nine thirty," I laugh, waving at Leo and Bennie as they stride across the sand, fishing spears and catch in hand.

"What're they going to do with those?" Sprout frowns.

I nod towards a pile of wood. "Cook them, I expect."

Sprout wrinkles her nose. "I like toast for breakfast."

"And I like sleep," mutters Shiv. "What are we doing here?"

"Yeah, the sea's miles out."

"That's the point, Sprout," I retort. "I thought we could

check out the cave entrance."

"We?" says Shiv, fear spreading across her face.

"We won't go in," I say. "At least not today. I just want to have a look. It sounds fascinating."

Sprout's face lights up. "I'll come! I'm dying to see the mermaid."

"There is no mermaid," retorts Shiv. "I'm sick of being your babysitter. Why couldn't Mum arrange a playdate for you?"

"I'm not a baby!" shrieks Sprout. "And, besides, my friends are all on holiday."

"What about Cassie?" I suggest.

"Doesn't like me any more."

"Oh, why not?" I ask.

"Because I'm friends with you," she replies. "*Amy* doesn't like you."

"You don't have to repeat everything you hear, Sprout," hisses Shiv. "It's not *all* true. We're not going and that's that."

Except it isn't and they launch into their usual sibling bickering, which could rival Henry and Min in volume and pettiness.

"You're here early again," says Leo, flinging his mask and flippers on to the sand while Bennie sets about lighting the fire.

"I wanted to explore Morvoren."

"Morvoren?"

I nod. "Yeah, only the entrance. Maybe a bit more. The tide's at its lowest just before ten. Fancy coming?"

"What, with her?"

"No, she's not keen."

Leo glances at Bennie.

"'S'all right," says Bennie, gesturing at the fire. "I've got this. You go."

It's a long walk over the wet sand as we pass rock pools revealed by the outgoing tide. Sticking close to the edge of the cliff, we eventually reach the row of trespasser signs dotted high above us, and where the sea is about to reach its lowest point. The excitement surges through me when I spot the opening in the cliff face.

"Is that it?" I cry, rushing over, feet slapping in the shallow water.

Leo nods, his eyes alight like mine.

The coolness coming from the cave is something else, like it's a natural air-con unit that sends shivers down my spine as I climb through the entrance. A short distance inside, I crouch down to where the hole shrinks to about a metre in diameter, and has barely legible words in large red letters, haphazardly painted round the top.

"*P OUT IN OUT*," I read. "Pout in out? What's that mean? Is this like in *Lord of the Rings* where you have to solve the riddle for the cave to let you in?"

"You've been watching too many films," snorts Leo, running his hands across the rock surface where oranges run into turquoise blues and purples. "I've never been this close. Mum's always been very clear about that."

"Which has just made you want to see it more?"

He laughs. "Yeah. That and her stories of the maze-like tunnels and dark, subterranean corridors. There's supposed to be this awesome natural staircase in there. If you get the right conditions, it glitters like a sea of stars. Something to do with a chemical reaction with oxygen."

"Yeah, biolumin-something," I say. "Light gets emitted when oxygen mixes with… I forget what's it called."

"Bioluminescence," he laughs. "I'd love to do a night dive in it. Happens frequently down here. It's beautiful."

"Wow," I murmur. "I'd love to capture that on camera."

We fall into silence, staring at the black hole and hoping that one of us will be brave enough to venture in, but knowing that we shouldn't. There are enough signs telling us that.

The spell is broken when Leo turns to go back and I can't help but let out a little sigh of disappointment.

"You're different to the other Zombies," he says.

I grimace. "That's an awful term."

"It's meant to be," he laughs. "Cuckoo then."

"That's worse. I didn't steal your home."

"No, but their mum's doing a good job of it," he says, pointing at Shiv and Sprout. "Do they have to be here every day? People are beginning to talk."

I laugh. "You don't have to listen to them, you know. Bennie's not bothered by her."

"He should know better."

"He does," I snort. "He's taken the time to get to know her. Maybe you should try it..."

~~~~

"You were ages out there," moans Sprout when I flop on to the sand, tingling with excitement. The sound of sizzling and the smell of freshly caught mackerel mingle with the waft of burning firewood, filling the air enticingly.

Sprout grabs hold of my arm and pulls me on to our side of the line. "Will you build a sandcastle with me? Shiv's been too busy nattering with that silly sea bass," she mutters, throwing a sidelong glance at Bennie. "I think she's got a crush on him."

"Leave her alone, Sprout," scolds Shiv. Then casting an eye on me she adds, "You took your time. Thought you'd actually gone in for a minute."

I shake my head. "No, not today at least. Leo's keen on it, I think."

Shiv snorts. "Surprised *he* let you hang out with him for that long."

"You could've come with me," I say. "How's Bennie?"

"Shiv's got a crush on him," sings Sprout gleefully.

"Oh my God, shut up!" shrieks Shiv, covering her

burning cheeks. "Bring on Wednesday when she goes to summer camp. I'll be able to have lie-ins again. Watch the movies that I want to watch…"

"How about having a campfire?" I suggest as an idea takes hold. "We could invite everyone. Make it a party. You could talk to Bennie and it might be a good step forward in my master plan."

Looks to camera – and maybe Leo and I can actually go inside Morvoren this time.

PISCARY BAY TIDE TIMES

Wednesday 31st July

HIGH TIDE:	05:06	HEIGHT:	6.20 m
LOW TIDE:	11:34	HEIGHT:	1.10 m
HIGH TIDE:	17:27	HEIGHT:	6.50 m
LOW TIDE:	00:01	HEIGHT:	0.90 m

New Moon

SUNRISE:	05:49	SUNSET:	21:07
MOONRISE:	04:38	MOONSET:	21:00

Hurdles

Convincing everyone to come to the party doesn't turn out to be quite as easy as I imagine, and I have to use all of my negotiating skills to make it happen. Shiv bows out immediately, telling me she's the last person for the task, and I can soon see why she's reluctant. I've had tentative yeses from Bennie and Tania's son Abe, plus two from girls I got chatting to in Screams. Amy won't give me an answer either way and I think Seth only agrees to get me to go away, since he can't leave the kiosk. That just leaves Leo.

"I'm having a campfire," I tell him. "Tomorrow night. Thought it'd be nice for us all to get to know each other."

He frowns. "Why?"

"So there'd be less fighting."

"You're living in cloud cuckoo land," he snorts.

"Maybe," I say lightly. "But I also thought it would be a

good opportunity to explore Morvoren Cave."

"Morvoren. At night? You sure?"

"Why not? It'll make it feel more like an adventure. It'll be dark anyway and there's a low tide around midnight. We don't have to go in far and we might get to see the sea of stars."

He bites his lip, thinking. "All right. You're on…"

Fade up on the scene of my future success. The one where I actually manage to get everyone talking.

The weather's been glorious all day, not a cloud in the sky, leaving it a bit cooler than the last few nights. The perfect opportunity for us to huddle round a campfire. I've even been down to collect driftwood and have left it in a giant pile well away from the water.

Shiv turns up at the house promptly at seven p.m. I am nowhere near ready, thanks in part to an impromptu dip in the water after I'd gathered the firewood. But also because I want to make an entrance. I am my mother's daughter in that regard.

"It's Shiv!" I yell down the stairs. "Can someone let her in? Uncle Henry?"

I hear him grumbling as he huffs and puffs his way to the front door. "Hello," he says. "You must be Shiv. I'm Professor Henry James."

"Hello, sir," comes her formal reply. "It's such an honour

to meet you. I loved your paper on fish who climb. It was ... magnificent." She sounds ridiculously nervous, probably been practising that speech all afternoon.

"Hey," I call, leaning precariously over the bannisters. "I'll be as quick as I can."

"Take your time," she replies.

"You like fish," says Uncle Henry, leading her into the corridor. "What's your favourite?"

"Mandarinfish," I hear Shiv reply. "I know it's poisonous, but it's so beautiful..."

Looks to camera – I think she'll be OK.

I take my time getting ready. This is an important night and, if it's going to go the way I've planned, everything has to be right, including the costume...

~~~

Shiv is deep in conversation with Uncle Henry, something about skin and mucus – I daren't ask!

"All set?" I ask and, by the irritated look on Shiv's face, I'd say not.

"Where are you off to?" asks Uncle Henry.

"We're having a campfire," I tell him.

"Where?"

"Down on Cove Beach."

He looks surprised. "Did you ask my permission?"

Looks to camera – permission?

I laugh nervously. "Er ... no."

"Well, maybe you should have." He frowns. "Have you checked what the tide's doing? How many of you are there? You're not going in the sea, are you? It's dangerous."

I wait patiently with my breath held, letting him get his fears off his chest. Better out than in. Then I reassure him. I've worked hard convincing everyone to come to this party – I'm not about to fail at the last hurdle.

"It's low tide just after midnight," I say. "Ten people max and yes, I know all about the rips. Don't worry, Uncle Henry. I've got this covered."

Sensing his defeat, he slumps back. "Stay out of the water then. And no swimming or alcohol."

"Yes, Uncle Henry," I sing, then poke my head round the door of the front room where Min is engrossed in her sewing, fabric spilling over her legs like a waterfall. "I'm off now. Do I look all right?" I ask, giving her a twirl in my carefully selected outfit – plaid shirt, denim shorts and hoodie. It's what everyone's wearing around here.

She glances up, concentration still etched between her eyes.

"It's … different," she mutters miserably.

Looks to camera – says the grown woman wearing a velour catsuit.

I breathe in and hold it there, the familiar feeling of tension welling up in my chest. I'm not going to ask her what's wrong. Shiv's waiting for me. Although from the sounds of it she's started another conversation with

221

Uncle Henry. But no, I'm not going to be drawn into this now. I'm just not. I can't—

"What's wrong?" I ask.

She shrugs. "Dunno… Just been feeling down today. Dwelling on what we had in London. I miss it…"

She could have done with realizing this two weeks ago, but OK.

"Can't really talk about this now," I say. "Shiv's waiting…"

"Where are you going?" she asks.

"Having a campfire down on Cove Beach. You gave me the idea actually," I say, thinking that I'll flatter her out of her mood. Big mistake.

"That's a great idea," she gasps. "Here." She produces a lipstick from her pocket. "Can't have you going out without a bit of lippie, can we?" Then she whispers, "Did you want me to nip out and get you a bottle of something? I don't mind."

I shake my head quickly. Can't think of anything worse. But she's not listening.

"I could bring it to the beach, if you like," she says. "A party's just what I need. This frock can wait…"

Looks to camera – no, no, no, no, NO!

"Erm," I gasp, struggling to find the right words. "Maybe another time? Finish your dress. Bye then." I hastily make my exit, dashing back into the kitchen and forcefully yanking Shiv by the arm as I go.

Friends

I wipe my mouth with the back of my hand the moment we're out of the door. I don't need my mother's lipstick. It's the wrong colour for one thing. And thank goodness I talked her out of coming with us. Rule number one of any decent adventure movie is to get rid of the parents.

Shiv and I walk in companionable silence down to the beach, our arms laden with crisps and fizzy drinks. I've known her for less than two weeks, but it feels like we're becoming firm friends. She's just so clever, like every word that comes out of her mouth is thought through and intelligent. Christ knows why she's hanging out with *me*.

"Wow," sighs Shiv, looking star-struck. "I just had a conversation with *the* Henry James. Two if you count them separately. I mean … just … wow."

Well, it makes a change from the usual impressed noises

my friends in London used to coo about Min.

"Are we talking about the same Henry James?" I laugh. "The dressing gown, the wild hair…"

Shiv shrugs. "Just signs of a brilliant mind," she says. "He's got better things to think about than what he should be wearing. What's he working on at the moment?"

"No idea. To be honest, it's all I can do to keep him off the subject of fish. It's like it's the only conversation he's comfortable with."

Shiv sighs. "I know the feeling."

"But you're so … together! I bet you have tons of friends at school."

"You'd be backing the wrong seahorse if you did that," she laughs. "I'm not like the other girls at school. They're more into what they look like and social media. It's so boring."

Awkward glance to camera…

"Honestly, I'd rather study than post on Instagram. So, what about you? What did you like doing in London?"

I giggle. "Posting short films on Instagram and vintage-clothes shopping?"

Shiv howls with laughter as her face turns a deep shade of crimson. "Oh, I'm so sorry," she gushes. "I didn't mean it like that. You're not like any of the girls in school – you talk to me for a start."

"Why wouldn't I?" I laugh. "You're so interesting… Oh my God, they actually came!" I halt at the top of the cliff path from where I can see a small cluster of people standing round the now lit campfire.

"D'you know all of them?" gasps Shiv, stumbling on the narrow path down.

"Yes," I frown. "You must know Esther and Freya."

She shakes her head.

"What about Anna? Her sister's in Sprout's class."

"How do *you* know them?"

"I talk to people," I say. "Why, don't you?"

"Not if I can help it."

"Why not?"

"Because I don't know what to say," she admits.

"Talk about what interests you then," I suggest.

"Science and maths, you mean?"

Looks to camera – well, it's a start.

"Talk to Bennie then," I say. "The two of you were getting on well the other day."

"But he's a Fish…"

"And?"

"What if he won't speak to me?"

"He will. Come on. I'll introduce you to the others…"

Cinderella

I leave Shiv standing awkwardly beside Esther and Freya, looking like she'd rather be anywhere else. Their attempts at conversation are met with barely audible mumbles. Funny, I never noticed how shy she was before.

"Bennie! Amy!" I cry. Overexcitedly, I'll admit, but they're the first of the … well, the others to arrive. "Glad you could make it."

"What are you doing?" Amy shoves my air kisses away. "You're so la-di-dah it's painful."

I frown. "It's the way I say hello to all my friends."

"I'm not your friend. I'm only here because Bennie persuaded me."

"Don't hold back, will you?" Bennie grimaces nervously.

"Look, I don't think we've got off to the best start," I say, giving her my twinkliest smile. "But if you'd just give me a chance and get to know me... That's what this campfire is—" Amy splutters into her hand. "It is possible to get on with people from a different background, you know."

"Not here it isn't," she sneers. "Honestly, you and your superior London attitude. Swooping in, thinking you can change things as if you're something special. Life's easy when you get to look down on everyone else from your ivory tower, isn't it?"

"If you mean Cliff House, it's falling down round our ears," I retort. "And I don't think that."

Amy snorts. "Yeah, right. The air-kissing, the constant talk about the TV industry and all your fancy clothes."

Looks to camera – they're from a charity shop.

I give her my brightest smile, thinking that will help. It doesn't. "I just want us all to be friends."

"Yeah, well, it's not working, is it?" she says, pointing to one side of the fire. "That lot's the Fish and that there's the Cuckoos. It's hardly like they're mingling, is it?"

"But it doesn't have to be like that," I insist somewhat feebly, given it's said to the back of her head. "Why doesn't she like me?" I ask Bennie.

He sighs. "Just history repeating itself. Leo and Amy were an item before you came along. Just like Min took Billy away from Amy's mum."

"I'm not after Leo." I frown. "Just trying to be friendly. Where is he anyway?" I ask, glancing at my watch. Still three hours until midnight.

227

Bennie shrugs. "It's his gran's birthday. Said he'll be along later. Maybe…"

I try not to watch the clock. Try not to look out for Leo's arrival. Try to focus on having a good time. But it's no use and I end up feeling like Cinderella waiting for the stroke of midnight. Because that's when the adventure begins. That's when I get my first look inside Morvoren Cave and I can't wait.

"I'm going home," says Shiv.

I frown. "But it's only eleven."

"And Mum will be wondering where I am."

"But you haven't talked to Bennie yet."

Shiv shakes her head. "I'm not like you. I don't get on with— Who's that?" she gasps, and I turn to see my worst nightmare.

Min – dressed in a huge flouncy ball gown, complete with towering heels, picking her way across the sand – looks exactly like my fairy godmother. Except in this case it's embarrassment she's conjuring up rather than help.

"That's Min," I sigh. "Look, go, before she sees you," I say, hastily pushing Shiv towards the cliff path. "You don't need trouble from both our mothers…"

If attention is what Min wanted when choosing that outfit, she's certainly succeeded. As well as mortifying me.

"I bought you that bottle just in case you changed your

mind," she says, her eyes darting round the party, checking everyone out.

"I don't drink," I growl. "And I don't want you here. You're my mother. And what do you look like?"

"Now who's being the mother?"

"Heels on a beach," I hiss. "Who does that? It's embarrassing."

Min stares at me. "I do. And I'll wear what I like, thanks. If you're embarrassed, then that's *your* problem. At least I don't look like … a lumberjack," she says, waving her hand disdainfully at my outfit. "Not many people here. I thought you said this was a party. Oh, hi!" And she picks on the nearest person – Freya – greeting her with the kind of effortless air kisses that I never quite manage. "I'm Min and you are?"

Looks to camera – urgh.

She's always been like this with my mates. Overly familiar. Thinking they're interested in what she's got to say. Thing is, they usually are…

By eleven thirty, my mood has hit rock bottom. Min is in full party mode, regaling the few who remain with stories about the celebrities she's met, telling them things that I'm pretty sure she signed a non-disclosure agreement about. Leo still hasn't turned up either. I was rather relying on his local knowledge to get us in and out of Morvoren Cave safely.

"…and then she went to the loo," Min is saying, "completely forgetting that she was still wearing a—"

229

She stops suddenly, her face paling as if she's seen a ghost.

"Leo," I gasp, jumping up. "You made it."

"Who's the fairy godmother?" he mutters, extracting himself awkwardly from my hug.

Min pushes past me to greet him. "I'm Min," she gushes. "Leo, isn't it? Let me get a good look at you." And she studies him at arm's length, by which time he's looking seriously uncomfortable. "It's uncanny," she murmurs.

Looks to camera – what is?

"I held you when you were days old," she laughs. "That makes me sound ancient."

"That's cos you are," I growl, pulling Leo away from her, eager to get her out of the spotlight. "Did you bring the head torches?" I ask. "There's no moon and it's a bit too dark without them. I thought we could—"

He shakes his head, staring levelly at Min, his jaw working ten to the dozen. "I can't be here. Not with her."

"I know she's annoying," I say, "but she's harmless."

"Tell that to my uncle," he says solemnly.

"Your uncle?"

"Yes. He drowned here because of her."

Looks to camera – wait, what?

"But you're not a Pengelly."

"No, but my mum is," he growls.

And I watch him go, my mouth stuck in a frozen O, because, if Billy was his uncle, then Leo is my cousin.

Us and Them

"What happened after I left the other night?" asks Shiv when we meet on the beach a few days later.

"Disaster," I say. "Min predictably made an absolute spectacle of herself, which made everyone leave early, and then she upset Leo as soon as he turned up." *Oh, and he's my cousin!* "He stormed off in a huff and Amy took the opportunity to rub it in my face."

"That's typical of her," says Shiv. "I thought you were getting somewhere. I was even going to congratulate you on your success. I mean, not many Fish turned up, but getting Bennie and Amy there was something. And Leo. Especially him. What did Min do?"

"What she normally does," I mutter, feeling like if I say any more I'll blurt out something I'm not supposed to.

"Maybe it's a good thing. We get the beach to ourselves

at least. And there's no Sprout. That means we can do whatever we want."

"Let's go for a swim then," I suggest. "Tide's on its way out again."

But Shiv wrinkles her nose. "Maybe later."

Looks to camera – she never comes in the water.

"We could try exploring Morvoren Cave," I say. "Leo and I were going to do it the other night before Min spoiled everything."

Shiv gasps. "So that's how you convinced him! But it's dangerous, Coco. Someone died there years ago." She goes on to tell me everything I already know about my dad's death, and the intense desire to tell her my secret flares up again.

"Yeah, I know all that," I say. "But…" The words stick in my throat. I can't say anything, I promised Min, and no matter how angry I am with her at the moment—

"They're back," says Shiv.

I turn to see Leo, Bennie and Amy, along with a group of other kids who I don't recognize, striding confidently down the cliff path.

"Do you want them here?" she asks. "You're within your rights to tell them to leave, you know." And she stands up to confront the newcomers…

~~~

The campfire from the party, now reduced to a pile of ash, sits forlornly between our two groups. I sit, staring at it, absent-mindedly poking my toe in the charcoal that's like tea leaves, as if they might give me the answers I need.

"We're not shifting," says Amy. "If anyone should leave, it's you."

So goes the conversation of the last half an hour.

"All I'm saying is if you want to share this beach, you're going to have to be a lot nicer to Coco," says Shiv, standing her ground. She's trying to stick up for me, only I don't think it's helping.

"You're just like your mother," sneers Amy.

Shiv shrugs. "What, a successful and determined woman? I'll take that as a compliment, thanks." Bennie chuckles and Amy throws him a furious glare.

I sneak a glance at Leo's annoyed face. Is that what my dad would have looked like? I want to yell, "You're my cousin!" but don't. Would he act differently if he knew?

"Well?" says Shiv, using an authoritative tone of voice that makes me cringe and immediately riles the others. Predictably, they all start bristling and muttering how they're not moving. Hard to see a way out of this. It's worse than when Uncle Henry and Min have one of their rows.

"Look," I say, "we're not going to get anywhere like this. I meant what I said the other day, about sharing the beach. Only Shiv's got a point. It's too small for us to keep on arguing like this."

"You know, I've been using this beach my whole life," says Leo. "And we've never needed permission. Never had to kiss up to anyone to use it either. Until you came along."

"I know how to settle this," says Amy suddenly, nodding at the water with a nasty glint in her eye. "Last Fish Floating. You can play against a proper contender this time. How about it, Leo? Winner gets the beach for the day."

"That's ridiculous," murmurs Shiv. "You can't. They're … Fish. It's a set-up."

But I shrug her off, spurred on by the challenge. And I've been practising every day. Swimming along the seabed. I'm pretty sure I'm getting good. Good enough that I reckon I'm in with a chance anyway.

"All right," I say. "You're on."

Mission: Impossible

Two strides in, I run my hands through the water, allowing the trickling effect of sand and sea through my fingers to calm me down. I focus on the crashing waves round my thighs, trying to ignore Leo's smirk, like he knows he's going to demolish me. Is this a mission impossible?

Three, four, five strides more and I look back to the shore. Shiv and the others standing apart like strangers. Am I walking into a trap?

I dive under the next incoming wave, enjoying the cold nipping at my shoulders. I've got this. I've been swimming in these waters for over a month. My breath holding has never been so good.

"Fish at the ready," calls Amy, holding up her hand.

Leo nods and gulps in a massive breath of air.

"Cuckoo?"

I reluctantly nod, flinching at the label. Then Amy slams her hand down and yells, "Go!"

I push forward, face down in the water, arms floating in front of me, slowly counting out the Mississippis the way I do in the bath. The first minute goes by fine, though I'm putting all my effort into not being distracted by *his* presence. Hard with the waves rocking me nearer. Oh, and the thought that he's my cousin!

Mississippi sixty-three. Mississippi sixty-four.

I spot him staring directly at me. Trying to psych me out no doubt. Well, it won't work...

Mississippi eighty-one. Mississippi eighty-two.

He's still watching me. I try sneering, but I'm not sure it comes across that way. I probably look more like Brian in this big diving mask. A thought that makes me splutter, sending a smattering of bubbles shooting to the surface.

Two minutes...

I shake my head from side to side, willing myself to relax, then make the mistake of looking up into his eyes made cartoon-wide by *his* diving mask, which makes me want to laugh again and another stream of bubbles trickles out. He motions for me to go up, but I'm really not falling for that.

Two and a half minutes... I really want to breathe!

Three... I'm closing in on a PB. I can do this!

By three and a half, I feel like I'm going to explode. How long *can* he hold his breath for? My diaphragm is spasming like mad and the blood's pounding in my ears; all I can think about is taking a refreshing gulp of sea air.

Mississippi... I can't remember where I've got to. I'm not thinking straight. I need to breathe. Give me air. Give me...

Cut to a shot of me bursting to the surface, breathing in *the* most delicious gulp of air. Never has it tasted so sweet. Until I realize I've lost. Leo is still floating there comfortably as if *not* breathing is the most natural thing in the world.

"All right, you don't have to show off," I snap, prodding him on the shoulder.

He stands up suddenly, breathing sharply in and out, in quick succession. I brace myself for the smug, self-satisfied smile and gloating, but instead he frowns at me with a wonky look of confusion.

"Loser!" chants Amy, pressing her L-shaped finger and thumb in my face as I wade out of the sea. "The beach is ours now."

"Yeah, for today," mutters Shiv, throwing a towel round my shoulder and a dirty look at Leo as we traipse miserably back up the cliffside. "I'm sorry, Coco. That was all my fault. I just didn't like the way they were treating you."

"I know," I say. "I went along with it. I thought I could beat him."

"How? His dad was the best freediver in town until he ran off with a Zombie. That's what Mum said. Who do they think they are? It's your beach!"

"It's OK." I shrug. "I don't mind." And I don't. Because – thanks to Leo's puzzled expression – I know what I've got to do.

"How can you not mind?" demands Shiv.

"Because I know how to fix things," I laugh. "And Leo's the key to all this."

"Leo!" she scoffs. "If he's the focus of your project, you've got your work cut out."

"You didn't see the way he looked at me," I say. "He was definitely impressed by how long I could hold my breath for, and I've just got this feeling that it means something. I can do this, Shiv. I'm a people person. I'll impress them with my sparkling personality."

"And which one is that again?" she laughs.

"The one that doesn't end up thumping you," I snort. "Come on. Race you back to Cliff House…"

Ghosts

It's taken nearly three weeks for the builders to start work on the roof, during which time I've been sleeping beneath an enormous hole in the ceiling. Whenever Uncle Henry goes up to the attic in the middle of the night to pace around, I get woken up either by the sound of him muttering or the feeling of plasterboard pattering on my face.

Now covered in scaffolding and with scores of builders swarming about, Shiv and I turn up at the house to find Min standing outside the front door with a tray of teacups in her hands, overdressed as usual in a beautiful turquoise gown that's so long it's trailing in the rubble.

I take a deep breath; we haven't spoken since the party.

"Guests, darling," she drawls. "Really?"

"This is my friend, Shiv," I tell her. "Adele's daughter."

"Hi, Miss James," says Shiv, offering her a formal

handshake, which immediately hits the wrong note. Min hates being lumped in with the adults.

"SHUT UP!"

The yelling comes from inside the house, making us all jump.

"His Lordship's had a relapse," explains Min. "Miserable sod. Not coping very well with all this." She wrinkles her nose. "Where exactly do you expect to hang out? Your room looks like a building site."

"SHUT UP!" comes the yell again.

"What's he doing here?" Min frowns, and I spin round to see Leo running his hands nervously through his hair as he traipses up the garden path. "You've got a nerve coming here," she says. "You ruined my daughter's party!"

Wry look to camera…

"I ought to have you arrested for trespassing," she hisses.

Now she sounds like Shiv. This isn't the way to solve things. There's a reason Leo's here and I think it's a good one.

"There's no need for that," I rush to say, giving her a pointed stare to go away, which she ignores completely. "Min," I snap. "D'you think you could give us some space?"

"It's my house," she mutters sulkily and it's only thanks to another bout of yelling from inside that she actually budges.

"Take a seat," I tell Leo, gesturing towards the sofa swing, which he declines. "Suit yourself," I say lightly, pulling Shiv

240

on to the seat with me, where we trail our feet back and forth amid the dirt and dust. "Did you want something?" I ask, giving him my sweetest smile. I need to play this right. "Cove Beach not enough for you, you came for the house?"

A smile at last!

"You weren't kidding when you said it was a wreck," he snorts and perches on an upturned bucket lying among the debris and scaffolding poles. "Look, I'm sorry about earlier. It wasn't a fair game."

Subtle smile to camera.

"Is that so?" I murmur, outwardly keeping my cool while my head is exploding with triumphant fireworks.

"I'M GOING OUT. THIS—" Uncle Henry storms past, albeit at a snail's pace, the air filled with colourful expletives as he yells about the noise and mess, tossing a miserable look in our direction.

"Professor Henry James," sighs Shiv, going goggle-eyed as if she's seen a celebrity, while Leo mutters, 'Wow,' under his breath. What is it about my family that makes them so fascinating to everyone else? I mean, Shiv's met Uncle Henry already.

"So, how long can you hold your breath for?" I ask Leo.

"Nearly five minutes?" He pauses. "Didn't expect your uncle to look quite so—"

"Decrepit?" I say. "Yeah, he's been ill for the last decade. Not that anyone in this town has bothered to notice…"

241

I can't help myself. "So, how d'you go about building up your breath hold?"

Leo shrugs. "Practice? There's a whole load of apnoea exercises you can do. Anything anaerobic basically." He frowns. "Where did you learn to hold *your* breath like that?"

"In the bath," I say, which makes him snort.

"Seriously?"

I nod.

"Wow! And you've never learned to freedive?"

"No."

He hesitates, biting his lip while he thinks. I do exactly the same thing.

"Meet me on Cove Beach tomorrow morning at eight. If you like, I'll show you the ropes… There's a mermaid trip going out on the boat next weekend. You could come as my guest?" And he flashes his twinkly smile – the people-pleasing kind that I use when I want something – which means that I've won.

"OK," I say, glancing at Shiv. "But only if she can come too."

Looks to camera – well, this is the perfect opportunity for me to put my action plan in motion, isn't it?

Mothers

Turns out Min was right about my bedroom being a building site. Quite why she didn't think to ask the builders to cover my things with a plastic sheet, I don't know. So we're back at Shiv's house, lounging on her bed, watching YouTube videos of professional mermaids in an attempt to convince Shiv that she should come on the trip.

"I don't know," she says, wringing her hands anxiously.

"You don't have to dress up as a mermaid, if you don't want to," I tell her.

"Wait, you can dress up as one?"

"Yeah. I saw a box of tails when I was on that other boat trip. They were quite beautiful actually, if you're into that sort of thing."

She nods thoughtfully. "Sprout would be dead jealous, but... I don't know," she sighs. "Don't get me wrong, I can see how it fits into your master plan, but … Leo's a Fish, Coco. They hate *all* outsiders. Fact."

I roll on my back, feeling a flush of disappointment. "So no then."

"I didn't say that. Just worried about Mum finding out. She's a worrywart. Didn't let me cross the road on my own until I was twelve and that was only because I downright refused to hold her hand. There's no way she's saying yes to me going freediving, let alone being a mermaid."

"Don't tell her then," I suggest. "I don't tell Min anything."

Shiv rolls on to her back to join me. "What's with her ball-gown obsession? I've never seen anyone dressed like that on the beach or the middle of a building site, come to think of it. She's very glamorous. Her skin's flawless."

"I know," I snort. "Only uses soap and water as well."

"She doesn't have a skincare routine? How is that even possible with that much make-up?"

"Yeah, she's always been a bit different," I sigh, rather wishing she wasn't. Kind of sick of everyone being so impress—

"Seemed a bit ridiculous to me," says Shiv.

Looks to camera – no one has ever reacted to Min like that. Not even Bob.

"She's quite moody, isn't she?" Shiv continues. "You were different around her. Like you were treading on eggshells… D'you wish she wasn't so different?" she asks, narrowing her eyes at me as if she's mind-reading.

"That she was the kind of mum who baked cupcakes and read you bedtime stories when you were little?" She snorts. "Having a mother who models herself on the winners of *Big Mother* isn't all that, you know."

"But Adele's a lovely mum," I say.

"Helicopter mum, more like. I can't do anything without her sticking her nose in. It's exhausting. I just wish she'd let me grow up."

"Min's never been like that," I sigh, feeling like I've missed out. "I've always been able to do what I want. Like I could, say, sleep over here and not tell her. She wouldn't even notice."

"Mothers. Who'd have them?"

"Yeah, there's a reason why they're written out of film plots first," I mutter. "If my life was a film…"

"You need a break," says Shiv firmly. "How about we have that sleepover that she's not going to notice you having? Your house is a right mess. I should've thought of it sooner. You've been walking around with plaster dust in your hair for weeks."

Looks to camera – have I?

"Oh, please say yes," she begs.

"OK," I laugh, thrilled that I get to have a proper shower and sleep in a nice bed.

"Excellent!" she shrieks. "Now, let's watch another of those mermaid videos. We need to practise looking serene… I'm being a worrywart, like Mum," she explains.

"And I definitely don't want to be. Besides, I wouldn't miss getting one up on Sprout, even if I can't actually tell her. She'd blab to Mum in a shot. But it's on one condition. Two, actually."

"What?"

"No filming me while I'm asleep," she says. "And we read up about freediving. I hate going in unprepared and, where there's a risk, I want to know what the science is behind it."

I giggle. "You're so like my uncle…"

Becoming Ariel

Being a girl who loves swimming and all things glittery, when I was offered the opportunity to join the Mermaid Academy, I naturally jumped at the chance. So imagine my surprise when I found myself not in the water, but a classroom. Welp!

Turns out that becoming a mermaid isn't as easy as donning a fishtail or finding the right waterproof mascara. Oh no! Posing gracefully while holding your breath, not looking cross-eyed and staying under the water takes real skill. And one that I definitely didn't have. I soon realized I would have to master the science of freediving if I was ever going to make my lifelong dream of becoming Ariel a reality…

Excerpt from Aquatic Life *magazine:*

…these Sea Nomads are as at home under the water as fish, having lived in and around the south-east Asian waters of the Philippines, Indonesia and Malaysia for centuries. Diving, fishing and often spending up to five hours in the water per day, they are able to manage huge breath holds of up to thirteen minutes, amid growing evidence that Darwin's theory of evolution has been at work…

Excerpt from The Big Blue Blog:

Every Full Breath You Take

To a scientist, there is a fascinated horror at the idea that someone might voluntarily starve their body of oxygen in their hunt for the euphoria of a dive. Placing themselves quite unnecessarily in the grey area between life and death. And yet to divers it's all part of the experience. There are those too who might argue that freediving is a holistic experience of being at one with the water that has nothing to do with science. But I beg to differ.

In this article, we will cover:

- APNOEA – How to hold our breath beyond our usual comfort level.
- EQUALIZATION – What we have to do to adjust our bodies as the atmospheric pressure changes.
- MDR – The signs to look out for during the struggle phase.
- EUPHORIA vs HYPOXIA – Knowing when it's time to head back.
- SAFETY – How we should never freedive alone.

The Ropes

In true unpredictable English-summer style, the weather is horrendous the next morning. Grey sky, grey seas and the air as cold as autumn. It's all I can do to convince Shiv to get out of bed to come with me.

"Come on," I say, trying to coax her with a plate of toast.

"But it's cold," she moans.

"So, wear your dryrobe."

"And it's raining!"

"Dryrobe," I insist. "Look, this is the beginning of something big. And, if we're going to learn how to be mermaids, we have to start with the basics. That means static ap-something."

"Static apnoea," laughs Shiv. "God, you really don't retain anything, do you? OK, fine. I'm coming. But only because you need me…"

Fade up on a training montage. Me – sprinting along the beach while Leo shouts in my face. Me – cracking up laughing when he falls over in the sea from jogging backwards. Him – looking amazed at how good I am at this. Him – throwing his arms round me and telling me how pleased he is that we're cousins...

Maybe not that last one.

The reality is much more boring of course and consists mainly of me sprinting down the beach, then holding my breath as I walk back slowly the other way.

"When are we getting in the water?" I moan after several mornings of this routine, and by which time Shiv has thrown in the towel and taken to sitting huddled in her dryrobe.

"I don't need to be taught how to run," I say. "I did that in London. I want to be able to freedive like you. You're the best, aren't you?" Imitation is the best form of flattery after all.

"Fine," he laughs. "Tomorrow morning nine a.m. Tide will be coming in nicely and the forecast looks calm. Don't be late..."

"This is the relaxation phase."

Cut to a shot of Shiv and I lying on our backs in the middle of the sea, hands clutching a line as we stare up at the cloudy sky.

"When you're ready, you'll take it in turns for your one

full breath and then roll on to your front. I'll gently tap parts of your body if I see them tense up and you will – hopefully – give the OK signal. When you feel like you want to come up for air, slowly stand up and complete the surface-breathing process that I taught you yesterday. The key thing is to remain as relaxed as possible."

"Right," says Shiv seriously. "And this is called static apnoea, right? How long will we be face down in the water for?"

Leo assesses her with a frown, barely bothering to conceal his contempt. The idea that he'd love her once he got to know her having gone out the window the moment she turned up in her dryrobe and flash wetsuit. *All the gear, no idea* springing to mind.

"You'll probably last thirty seconds tops."

But, if she's bothered by his narky attitude, she doesn't let on. "That long!" she gasps. "Gosh. I'm not sure I can do this."

"Don't then," he says bluntly.

"So I'll go first, shall I?" she says, unperturbed.

I watch from behind my fingers as she makes her first attempt at floating on her front. It's as though her whole body is made of wood. Shoulders up round her ears, tensed as if she's waiting for the worst to happen. I barely get to ten Mississippis.

"How'd I do?" she asks hopefully.

"Let's just try again," I suggest. "But this time relax."

Twelve Mississippi. Thirteen Mississippi. Fourteen Mississippi.

Shiv rolls on to her back, gasping for air, eyes wild as if she's hating every minute.

"Ten seconds," says Leo.

"Fourteen," I frown.

He shrugs. "Not much either way."

Shiv's face crumples with annoyance. "Well, there's no need to rub it in. I'm not a natural freediver, big deal—"

"Why don't I have a try?" I say.

But their bickering goes on and on, and I'm almost grateful to roll on to my front, except I can still hear them at it, albeit muffled. I feel my body tightening up and the intensity of my diaphragm spasming is too much to bear.

"…who d'you think you are?" Shiv is saying when I come up for air.

Leo frowns at me. "Two minutes. What happened?"

"You," I snap. "How am I supposed to relax with an argument going on overhead?"

"Nothing to do with me," he mutters.

"Nor me," bristles Shiv. Then, taking a breath, she holds her hands up. "OK, fine. I'll go."

"It's about time," snorts Leo, but this is said to Shiv's back as she wades out of the sea.

"You need to try to drown everything out," he tells me. "Let your mind *and* body go, yeah? Think of it as entering a different world where you're leaving all your troubles behind."

I make it to nearly four minutes this time. Thanks in part to reciting the lyrics from 'Bohemian Rhapsody' – a distraction technique I read about online – but I also got what Leo meant about leaving the outside world behind. I felt so much more relaxed.

"Not bad." He grins. "You're a natural. It must be in your DNA."

Looks to camera…

"Wanna try again?" he asks. "But this time try taking a bigger breath before you turn over. See, that's Shiv's problem. She's like everyone else. Only uses about a third of her lung capacity. If you fill up to your diaphragm, that's two-thirds, and then, when you're comfortably full, your chest will rise naturally, filling the rest."

This time I make it to four and a half. I can't believe it! It feels so crazy to be able to hold my breath for that long, while at the same time feeling so natural. Of course, there's the added bonus that I'm not stressed. How could I be? I'm learning to freedive with a cousin I never knew I had! Someone I actually really like. It's as if we've got this inbuilt bond.

"How long have you been freediving?" I ask him.

"My whole life," he says. "Dad showed me what to do as soon as I'd learned to swim. It's where I feel most at home in the water, you know?"

Looks to camera – do I ever!

The temptation to blurt out my secret plays loudly in my head as if the voice-over artist is ignoring the director. And, no matter what I do, I can't get them to shut up. Surely things would be simpler if I could just tell everyone the truth…

~~~

"Bye, Leo. See you tomorrow!" I call.

"What's tomorrow?" sighs Shiv miserably from her spot on the rock, huddled in her dryrobe, wetsuit lying abandoned in the sand.

"Duck-diving."

"Urgh," she grunts. "Count me out. How long did you manage?"

"Four and a half minutes," I reply. "Leo's a great teacher."

Shiv snorts. "For you maybe. How come he's so friendly with you? What've you got that I don't?"

Looks to camera – shared DNA?

"The ability to hold my breath for the duration of 'Bohemian Rhapsody'?" I giggle, but she doesn't smile back. "I'm working on him."

"Are you? I preferred it when it was just the two of us."

"Come on, Shiv," I say. "I'm going to make this work. I promise. There must be a chink in his shiny fish scales somewhere. Look, why don't I come back to yours again?" I suggest, glancing up at Cliff House looking sad and forlorn against the grey skies. The roof is now covered

254

in hideous bright blue plastic, making it stand out like a sore thumb. The thought of sleeping there again isn't a particularly compelling one.

"I've got plenty more good film ideas that we can watch, and it'll be just the two of us…"

PISCARY BAY TIDE TIMES

Saturday 10th August

HIGH TIDE:	01:32	HEIGHT:	5.20 m
LOW TIDE:	08:14	HEIGHT:	2.20 m
HIGH TIDE:	14:11	HEIGHT:	5.10 m
LOW TIDE:	20:49	HEIGHT:	2.20 m

Gibbous Moon

SUNRISE:	06:04	SUNSET:	20:50
MOONRISE:	17:31	MOONSET:	01:22

Dead Nervous

The day of the mermaid trip arrives with perfect filming conditions: a blue, cloudless sky, gentle breeze and calm sea. I'm fully prepared for a day on the boat, Shiv having found an old raincoat of Adele's and a thick woolly jumper that's still got the tags on. Neither are very me, but I think it looks all right paired with my jeans and Converse.

"Good morning, girls," calls Jan cheerily as we walk past the Burbank on our way to the harbour. "Where you going?"

"To be mermaids!" I cry excitedly.

"Rather you than me," he laughs.

"Don't," whispers Shiv. I think she's nervous.

"*Hej*, Ingrid!" I call, spotting her opening up the shop, Ned sitting patiently at her feet, though he springs up when he sees me. "Hello, Ned," I gush. "When am I going to get to take you for a walk?"

"Whenever you like," laughs Ingrid.

"You're on," I say happily. "Just not today. We're off on the mermaid boat trip."

"Perfect day for it," replies Ingrid.

"Don't," hisses Shiv, bustling me along. Yep, really nervous.

"Oh, hi, Bennie! Hi, Mrs Khatri!" I call out. "We're going on the mermaid trip with Leo today." But I don't get to hear their reply, if there is one, as Shiv steers me forcefully away by my elbow.

"Do you have to tell everyone our business?" she mutters.

Looks to camera – seriously?

"You don't know what it's like living in a small town," she says. "Everyone knows everyone, and they talk."

"Yeah, that's what I like about this place. I could go days in London without seeing someone I knew. Stop worrying."

Jumpcut to a long pan of the harbour where the first tourists of the day are queuing up to clamber on to the boats.

Excited look to camera.

"You're not going to film me, are you?" says Shiv anxiously.

"Not if you don't want me to," I say, watching as a *Part of our World* minibus draws up on the concrete ramp and a stocky bloke with the trademark Pengelly floppy blond hair, blond stubble and wraparound sunglasses climbs out, closely followed by Leo.

Looks to camera – is that my uncle?

"Coco," whispers Shiv, tugging on my sleeve. "I'm a bit nervous. I—"

"Don't worry," I mutter, feeling distracted by my newfound family. "It's gonna be fun... Hi, Leo," I call, jumping forward. "Is that your uncle? Is he happy for us to come along?"

Leo nods. "Yeah, but we need to get you the right wetsuit. No way you'll last out there otherwise. You know what happened last time..."

～～～

Fully kitted out in a two-part wetsuit consisting of thick leggings and a hooded jacket that poppers up like a leotard, boots, gloves, mask and of course enormous clown flippers, I needn't have worried what I looked like in Shiv's hand-me-downs. This is next-level ridiculous!

"Uh-oh, here comes trouble," laughs the skipper of the boat.

"Oh, hi, Dave," I coo, running over to give him a hug, since I figure that's better than the air kisses.

"See you've learned your lesson about wearing a wetsuit then," he grunts, backing hastily away from me.

I grin. "Absolutely! This is my friend Shiv Quartermain by the way."

"Aye," he replies, eyeing her warily. "I know who she is."

"We're here as Leo's guests," I tell him proudly.

"Are you now?" comes the confused reply as he motions

for us to climb onboard where we take a seat at the bow of the boat so that I can film a good angle of us leaving harbour.

And action!

Open on a wide shot as the boat slowly meanders out of the harbour, gently rocking up and down, sending a light splatter of sea spray over everyone that produces a chorus of squeals. Cut to a shot of the sparkling blue sea frothing as the boat picks up speed towards its destination, the wind now whipping my hair about, sun toasting my face.

"This is wonderful, isn't it?" I murmur.

Cut to a shot of Shiv's green face. She pushes my phone away, muttering, "Don't," under her breath.

"You all right?" I ask. "Are you seasick? We've only just left harbour."

She shakes her head. "'S'not that," she whispers. "It's the water."

Looks to camera...

"What?"

"I learned to swim in a pool," she explains. "Not the sea."

"What difference does that make?"

"The sea is deeper. It's the thought of all that water beneath me. I don't like it." Shiv pauses to exhale slowly. "I've been trying to tell you. I'm dead nervous. The theory's fine – it's the thought of actually putting it into practice..." She shudders. "I had a terrible nightmare last night. Dreamed that I was stuck underwater. It won't really be like that, will it?"

"Course not," I say. "But why did you agree to all this?"

She grimaces. "Wanted to hang out with you. When I said I don't have many friends down here, I meant … *any*."

"Oh, Shiv," I gasp. "You don't have to get in the water to please me, you know. Just see how you feel when we get there."

Shiv grins. "Mum was right about you. I knew you'd understand." She exhales slowly again, training her eyes on the sea. "OK … I can do this. I can do this. I can't do this! What if I get stuck underwater?"

"You won't," I laugh. "Just remember the breathing process that we practised yesterday. There's really no pressure."

"Apart from the atmospheric one," she retorts. "You will remember to equalize your ears, won't you?"

"I know what I'm doing, Shiv," I laugh.

"Good," she sighs. "I'm glad one of us does…"

Pure Escapism

Fade up on a calm azure sea, my head full of the gentle piano music that I'll add as the soundtrack later on; the actual sound being marred by the very real and dramatic sound effects of Shiv throwing up over the side of the boat. Poor thing.

"Here, take one of these," says Leo's uncle, Noah, handing her a blister pack of anti-seasickness pills. "There're always a few people who can't find their sea legs." He pauses. "Aren't you Adele Quartermain's daughter?"

She nods, gulping down the proffered pill with a swig of water.

"And I'm Coco," I say.

He nods curtly at me. "Yeah, I know who you are. They're here with you?" He asks Leo with a confused frown. "Right, I'm just gonna run through all the theory for these mermaids."

"Listen to what he says," whispers Leo. "You'll need it when we're out there," he says, nodding at the sea, making Shiv pale further.

"I know you're all excited about becoming mermaids," says Noah over the top of the noisy chatter. "But I want to review the theory while Skipper gets us to our first location… Yes, yes," he chuckles, as groans ripple out among the course participants. "But we want you to be *safe*. Now, who can remember what happens when we breathe?"

Cut to a shot of my bored face.

"Your lungs absorb the oxygen from the air and get rid of the carbon dioxide," whispers Shiv, managing to answer between gagging.

"And what happens when we hold our breath?" continues Noah, oblivious to the star pupil in his midst.

"The carbon dioxide builds up in our bodies, eventually triggering an impulse from our brain telling us to breathe," she mutters.

"How d'you remember all this?" I whisper.

She frowns. "It's basic biology. You'd remember it too, if you gave science a chance."

Jumping into the water in a thick neoprene wetsuit is a completely different experience to when I swam with the seals. I feel like I really could stay here forever, despite what Uncle Henry said about mermaids freezing to death.

"You coming?" I call to Shiv. "It's gorgeous in the water. You might feel better once you're in."

And, after much stressing and faffing about, she finally jumps in with a loud, messy splash, bursting to the surface, fear lighting up her eyes, and thrashing her arms about as if she's drowning. I'm by her side in a few short flutter kicks.

"It's OK," I say. "You're fine."

"I'm not fine," she splutters. "I'm terrified. Why did I do this? I'm going to drown!"

"You're not going to drown," I say calmly. "For a start, your wetsuit is like a flotation device. Lie on your back and look up at the sky. Here, I'll do it with you." And together we roll on to our backs, Shiv clinging to my wrist for dear life. Yeah, this really isn't gonna work...

"Come on," says Leo, joining us in the water. "I'll set a line up over there. We can practise our duck-dives and equalizing."

"What – in the middle of the sea?" gasps Shiv, looking horrified. "Can I just...? Let me..."

"You don't have to do this," I say.

"You can always stay in the boat," suggests Leo.

Shiv's mouth sets in a determined line and she begins kicking out to sea, her flippers making a hell of a splash in my face. "I just need to run through the theory of duck-diving first," she says.

Leo frowns. "But it's easy."

"For you maybe," she retorts.

"Let her do it, would you?" I say, giving her an approving nod and Leo a grin.

Shiv's breaths are about as calm as if she were about to jump off the side of a building. "So…" she says. "With the forward momentum of a single flutter kick, I point my arms and body down like I'm making a right angle with my hips, then I point my legs vertically and the downward force will help push me underwater."

Leo nods and then suddenly disappears, his legs sticking out of the water as if he's aiming for a handstand on the seabed. He resurfaces seconds later with a grin.

"Kick, right angle, downward force," mutters Shiv. "Got it." But, no matter how hard she tries to imitate him, her fins don't leave the water and she turns to me, her face full of panic, hating every second of this.

"Look, go back to the boat," I whisper, glancing nervously at Leo.

"He doesn't want me around, does he?" she sighs. "Been dropping enough hints. Fine then. Just … take care, all right?"

~~~

Slowly but surely, I ease my way down the line, squeezing my nose together with one hand to equalize my ears, singing to myself, feeling relaxed and comfortable with my breath hold, despite the rather odd sensation of being completely upside down in the water. Leo, out of the

265

corner of my eye, watches my every move.

I continue on, looking around me, taking everything in. The fish scurrying past, the way the sun hits the blue-green water, diffracting into separate rays, how it gets colder the further down I go, then wondering if there might be any seals down here. And still I press on…

I start thinking about how good I am at this. Wouldn't it be something if I made it as far as the weight on the end of the line? I wonder if anyone else this new to it has done that before? I bet Leo would be impressed. How long did Noah say it was? Twenty-five metres?

Freeze-frame! Twenty-five metres? That's nearly the length of the Oasis outdoor pool!

I make the mistake of tilting my head to look down into the dark depths of the water where I can see the suspended weight close by. It's the wrong thing to do because it hurts my ears, and all I can think about is how far I've come and that I've got to travel the same distance back. *All without breathing.*

Looks to camera – I'm twenty-five metres down! Twenty-five metres! Jumpcut to a shot of me frantically turning myself the right way up, eyes wide with fear.

Then I catch sight of Leo beaming at me. Gesturing with his hands for me to calm down and relax, and suddenly I stop panicking and begin to feel what he's feeling. How being down here under the water is pure escapism. I don't feel human.

Looks to camera – OH MY GOD! THIS IS AMAZING!

At around twenty metres, the pressure of all the water above us takes effect and my body suddenly feels like a stone as I start to sink. Then I stop moving completely and it's like I'm free-falling. It's a beautiful feeling, like being suspended in mid-air. My body is weightless. I feel free. I could get used to this.

The Little Mermaid

Lunch is eaten on a small deserted beach where the shallow water is warm and clear and a perfect place for the mermaids to find their tails.

"Are you going to try one on?" I ask Shiv, as we watch the course participants waddle around in their mermaid outfits – weird long tails made from swimming-costume fabric that cling unflatteringly to their legs like tights, with matching bikini tops. I expect they'll look more the part when they've attached the foam monofins in the water. Or at least I hope so.

Shiv shrugs.

"You all right?" I ask. Again with the dismissive gestures. I don't know what I've done wrong. "That copper one would look good on you," I say. "I could ask Leo…"

"You haven't spoken a word to me since you got out

of the water," she says suddenly. "Leo this and Leo that. What am I even doing here? If you just wanted a camerawoman, you should have at least asked."

I wince. She's got a point – although her camerawork is pretty shoddy from what I've seen… "I'm sorry," I say. "I thought we were going to have a good time, but you don't like—"

"Swimming," she sighs. "I know. I should've told you sooner. I was just … worried you wouldn't like me any more."

"That's crazy," I laugh. "I love spending time with you. You're strong-minded, funny, clever and you know so many things. You remind me of my uncle."

Shiv's face lights up. "So it doesn't matter that I don't like swimming?"

"Of course not. Look, I'm sorry," I say. "I didn't mean to leave you out. I'm just so excited about freediving. I've never experienced anything like it. It feels like I was born to do it. Let's hang out here and watch the photoshoot instead. I can come another day."

"No," says Shiv decisively. "We came out here to be mermaids and that's what we're going to be. I can do this. Mind over matter."

"Oh, thank goodness," I laugh. "Because there's a cave Leo wants to show me. You have to dive down and swim along a tunnel to get there."

Shiv shudders. "A tunnel? You're insane! Maybe I'll just be your lookout. I'm sure I can do that much."

~~~

Fade up on the lush green coastline where the waves lap quietly against the granite-grey rocks. The sun casting its rays for a dramatic scene, turning the water aquamarine blue and as clear as a tropical ocean.

Cut to shot of me loving it.

There's no rope to hold on to this time – we're doing a free immersion – but I've been given strict instructions by Shiv to stay close to Leo. Together we head into the submerged tunnel. It's like exploring another world and again I feel like I've escaped from all my worries. It's so peaceful down here. I've always got music on, or I'm talking ten to the dozen, or there's an inner monologue playing. Who'd have thought silence could be this relaxing? I feel so happy and light-headed. It's bizarre.

The tunnel grows dark and, just as I'm beginning to get a bit scared, there's light ahead and we resurface into a small cave spotlit by a shaft of light coming from a hole high up in the rocks, making the water shimmer all around.

"Wow," I gasp. "This is amazing."

Leo grins. "I told you, right? There are tons of these caves along this coastline."

"Like Morvoren?"

He nods. "I'd love to find out if the legend is true," he says, his eyes sparkling. "There's apparently some portrait in there. Some people say it's a cave painting from thousands of years ago."

Looks to camera...

"I've never met an outsider being that good at freediving so easily," he continues. "You're amazing."

I grin. "Thanks. So are you! I can see why you're always doing it. It's addictive, isn't it?"

He nods. "Want to keep going?"

"Maybe a little bit longer," I say, feeling the opposing pulls of continuing this adventure versus worrying about leaving Shiv for too long.

"Why did you bring Shiv?" asks Leo.

"She's my friend," I say. "And I want the two of you to get along. She's so clever. Knows everything about freediving. Well, the science anyway. Just a shame—"

"She hates the sea?" he laughs. "Well, she's missing out. There's another pool further along. Should take about three minutes to get there. If you think this one's amazing, wait till you see that!"

Meet the Parents

Feeling high on the adrenaline of adventure, Leo and I grudgingly make our way back out to sea. I'm not sure how long we've been gone, but I'm pretty sure Shiv is going to be annoyed. As I get closer to the surface, I spot her flailing around in her mermaid tail upside down, one hand trying to grasp at the rocks, the other clasped to her ear. And, in direct contrast to my expression of euphoria, hers is one of pain and distress.

"Ow, ow, ow!" cries Shiv, now collapsed on the floor of the boat, with a towel thrown round her shoulders, her mermaid tail ripped to shreds in her haste to get onboard. "It hurts! Someone make it stop."

"It's all right," I murmur, clambering quickly out of the water to be by her side. "It's going to be OK."

"No, it isn't," she sobs. "It's throbbing. I can't keep upright.

The pain. The noise!"

"You've perforated your eardrum," says Noah. "It's what happens if you don't equalize the pressure in your ears. What were you doing freediving on your own? It's dangerous."

"I was going to look for them," Shiv replies. "They were gone too long."

Leo and I exchange guilty glances.

"What were you thinking, leaving her on her own?" demands Noah. "She's scared of the water."

"We left her sitting on a rock," says Leo.

Noah snorts. "Try explaining that to your mum. Adele Quartermain's been on the phone apparently. She's fuming. We're to head to the harbour immediately…"

~~~

The boat ride back is without the magic of earlier. Shiv whimpering in my arms, partly from the pain, mainly with the fear of facing her mother. And, when we pull into the harbour, I see three figures standing on the jetty. Adele, with her hands on her hips, looking like an angry bull. Sarah, standing back slightly, her hair in a long blond fishtail plait that reminds me of Elsa and shooting an icy glare to match. And finally Min, a good head shorter, wearing an oversized dress and a man's overcoat, looking like… Well, a child in dress-up actually.

"Siobhan Evelyn Quartermain! What *did* you do?"

shrieks Adele. If there weren't a gulf of water between her and the boat, I'm pretty sure she'd have pounced by now.

"Mum, I can explain," says Shiv loudly, then promptly bursts into tears.

"What's wrong?" frowns Adele. "Why's she shouting?"

"She perforated her eardrum," I explain.

"See, this is exactly what I mean," hisses Adele, turning to Sarah. "Is it normal practice to let children go out on boat trips alone?"

"They're. Not. Children," replies Sarah. She's clearly said this already. "It's in the terms and conditions, if you'd bothered to read them. Anyway, they were guests of my son apparently." And she gives Leo a look to say that they'd be having words later too.

Min is the only one who hasn't spoken and, if anything, looks as if she's not sure why she's here, as if she's been given the wrong casting call.

"Well?" says Adele, giving her a withering look that makes her jump forward to deliver her lines.

"Did you have a nice time?" asks Min. "Picked a good day for it at least."

"A good day for it!" shrieks Adele.

"It's only a boat trip. Coco's already been on the seal one. I used to take them all the time."

"That's hardly the point," replies Adele, blinking hard. "They could have drowned."

Min snorts. "Yeah, right. This one's like a fish. Can't keep her out of the water."

"My daughter nearly drowned," growls Adele, going quite pink in the face.

"No, she didn't," frowns Sarah. "Noah, tell her what happened." But his explanation is not what Adele wants to hear.

"Your son left my daughter on her own in the middle of the sea?" she says angrily, her eyes flashing with fury.

"On a rock," says Leo.

"Yes, well, he shouldn't have done that," replies Sarah grimly.

"And where were you?" demands Adele, turning on me. "I thought you were her friend."

"I am."

"Well, if that's how you treat your friends, I'd hate to be one of your enemies. Friends look out for each other. This was your idea, wasn't it? Shiv has never done an adventurous thing in her life. She's not like Sprout – thank goodness." Adele rounds on Min. "Someone like you may allow your daughter to go gallivanting off as she pleases…"

"What's that supposed to mean?" demands Min.

Sarah rolls her eyes. "That you're a menace to society?"

"Look," sighs Min, "if you lot want to tell yourself that I'm the villain of this piece, that's fine by me. But I'm done trying to please you. Come on, Coco. We're leaving."

Bristling

Min doesn't speak a word to me on the way home, though to be honest I'm not inclined to speak to her either. I still haven't forgiven her for spoiling my party and she's certainly not making settling in here very easy. As soon as we get home, she slams the door behind us, sending a shower of plaster down from the ceiling, and I know I'm in for another temper tantrum.

"Well, that was embarrassing," she splutters. "Sarah I can understand, but the way that woman looked at me. Miss High and Mighty. It's not my fault Shiv doesn't tell her anything or that I've got a headstrong daughter. I haven't seen you for days! It was all I could do to stop my brother from calling the police."

"Coco," says Uncle Henry, shuffling into the corridor. "Are you OK?"

Min rolls her eyes. "See?"

"I'm fine," I say, frowning. Why's everybody worried about me?

"Where've you been these last few days?" he demands.

"Shiv's. We had a sleepover."

"For four days?" he splutters.

Sidelong glance to camera…

"And you didn't think to tell us?" he demands.

I frown. "Why would I? I've never told Min before."

Uncle Henry looks astounded. "Well, you need to start now, young lady." Young lady! "I was awake half the night worrying about you."

"I'm sorry," I say, bristling at the unfamiliar dressing-down. "Didn't think you'd notice. It's what I've always done… Look, why don't I cook us some tea? I bet you haven't eaten properly without me around and you look like you need cheering up. Adele gave me a cooking lesson."

"Why?" mutters Min. "You already can."

"Yeah, but better things than beans on toast." I grin. "Adele knows everything. Makes the most amazing cupcakes *and* her own popcorn with individual toppings. Bet you she could win *Big Mother* hands down."

"Bully for her," growls Min, watching me like a hawk studying its prey while I bustle round the kitchen. "What are you so happy about?"

"I can be happy, can't I?" I remark. Her miserable face

is the antithesis of mine. But I don't want her to ruin this feeling. I feel like I've been floating on cloud nine all afternoon. "How about we do favourite thing?"

She shrugs. "Got nothing to be happy about."

"Well, I loved freediving," I say, blithely ignoring her. "It was amazing. I felt so happy."

"The effects of oxygen starvation more like," snorts Uncle Henry.

"But I held my breath for nearly five minutes," I tell him. "That's a personal best."

"Five?" he says, his expression changing. "But that's … what the Fish can do. You've never done it before."

"I know. I'm a natural at this! You'd have loved it. It was teeming with fish," I say. "There's a deserted beach."

"Hobson's Point," says Uncle Henry.

"You can get to this set of caves along a narrow corridor of rock and seaweed."

"A gully," he adds. "Sounds like Pendorn Caverns."

"That's them!" I cry. "They were amazing. Never seen seaweed like it. Purples, greens and reds swaying in the water, shoals of silver fish darting around. I'd give anything to be able to film it. It was like swimming in a giant aquarium."

Uncle Henry laughs. "How d'you think I got into studying marine life? There's a lot to be said for seeing things first-hand, and the coastline around here is full of such caves and gullies."

"Like Morvoren?" I ask.

Uncle Henry shifts uncomfortably in his seat and shoots Min an impenetrable look, which she returns with a narky one. The one that tells me she's spoiling for a fight.

"You're not to go there," he says. "It's too dangerous. Min," he hisses. "You're her mother. Do something."

Looks to camera…

Min slams her hand on the table as if this is the final straw. "And what would you know about parenting, eh, Henry?" Yep, she's definitely spoiling for a fight. Thing is, so am I…

"Oh my God, would you two just stop?" I shriek as they launch into their usual diatribes. "You're supposed to be adults," I say. "It's pathetic."

"You're pathetic," retorts Min. But for once she doesn't rant about how terrible a daughter I am. She flounces off from the argument into the front room where she puts on the record player at high volume.

I'd laugh if it weren't so depressing. Who's supposed to be the teenager here?

"What are we going to do about her, Uncle Henry?"

He sighs. "Well, even the Fiffer Faffer fish has to grow up eventually."

"Except we're not fish."

"More's the pity," he snorts and shuffles out of the room.

Clip Show

My life suddenly takes on the feel of a clip-show episode – old footage being woven into current scenes to show the way a plot line has developed – as I review footage and begin the lengthy process of editing my film together.

Simultaneously, I try to elicit responses from Shiv and Leo. I might not be in trouble – Min is actively ignoring me, and Uncle Henry is being his usual hermit-like self – but I'm worried that my friends are. Neither Sarah nor Adele seem like women who would put up with much nonsense.

11 Aug

ME 15:30
Hey! U ok?

SHIV 15:31
Meh

ME 15:32
She's rlly mad then?

SHIV 15:32
...

Fade up on my first ever glimpse of the sunset over Piscary Bay, the pinks and oranges making it look like a watercolour as the title appears – 'Coming up for Air' by Coco James.

Zoom in on a lone dog walker who I now realize is Ingrid. Cut to a shot of Cliff House looking like a formidable silhouette against the dusk backdrop, followed by a dimly lit close-up of Uncle Henry peering at me through the letter box while Min barks at him to let us in. Cut to black.

12 Aug

ME 18:21
Freediving was srsly amazing ... u ok?

LEO 18:26
...

Fade up on an exterior of Cliff House sitting pretty in the morning light, followed by a long hand-held shot of my hand

281

reaching to open doors, with the odd look to camera, as I explore the house. Long dissolve into a wide shot of the aquarium. Focus pull on a tight shot of Brian's goggle-eyed expression. Cut to a shot of Uncle Henry, his face growing animated as he tells me one of his fish facts.

Some things – unlike life – end up on the cutting-room floor. Things like Leo brushing past me at the supermarket or shooting daggers at Shiv on the beach. I want to paint him in a good light after all. Min doesn't get such easy treatment. There wouldn't be any footage left if I cut out all the times she's been a nightmare.

ME 20:00
Wld it help if I came & apologized?

SHIV 20:01
No

Cut to a shot of the storm raging outside my bedroom window. It looks amazing, though the sound is a bit muffled. Then comes some footage that Shiv shot of me and Leo in the water. We look so similar it's eerie! I'm surprised no one's noticed.

Cut to a shot of the mermaid trip. Me looking positively euphoric in all my pieces to camera, Shiv green and miserable. Shiv standing to one side, staring miserably at Leo, while I laugh and joke with him from behind the camera...

Why didn't I notice? Why did I insist on her coming?

All those times she wouldn't get in the sea with me, beyond paddling, are now plain to see from the footage I have of her.

But it's Shiv's unwitting voice-over that really floors me. "What am I doing here?" she mutters. "It's Leo she's after. Why would she be interested in someone like me...?"

13 Aug

ME 07:30
R U mad at me?

SHIV 7:30
...

Cut to a shot of the three mothers standing solemnly on the jetty as the boat moves in slow motion towards our unknown fate. Cut to black. End credits.

ME 23:30
I'm sorry...

I watch the film back with a mixture of emotions. Worry because I've clearly not been the friend to Shiv that I thought I was being. Excitement because I think the film's actually rather good. It could do with some shots in the sea, and it definitely needs a better soundtrack, but all in all it's not bad for my first short film. What I need is a professional opinion and I know just the person to send it to...

Troublemaker

In just a few days, the news of our escapade has spread like wildfire through town. Jan wants to know how deep I got, while Ingrid apologizes for telling Adele, with the explanation that she'd come into the shop to pick up Sprout's birthday present. Mrs Khatri gives me such a disapproving look that I daren't even venture into Screams.

"Her bark's worse than her bite," laughs Wanda, pausing for a breather outside the Plaice 2 Be, her shopping spilling on to the pavement.

"Here, let me help you," I say, gathering up the bags.

"Oh, thanks, lovey," she says. "I'm surprised to see you around town. I hear Adele Quartermain is still on the warpath. You're a bad influence on Shiv apparently. And for that matter my grandson got an earful from his mother about you too. Funny, you don't strike me as being like Min at all. You certainly don't look like her."

"Yeah, I look like my dad," I reply in a strangled voice, the temptation to say something rearing its ugly head again. "Would it help if I apologized to Sarah?"

Wanda's face spreads into a beaming smile. "I like a girl who faces her problems head-on. Takes courage being an outsider around here, you know…"

~~~

The Pengellys' end-of-terrace cottage sits high up on the opposite side of the bay, among a higgledy-piggledy mass of buildings overlooking the harbour; with a bay window stuck on the front, it's got a perfect view of everything, including Cliff House and the sprawling vista of the Old Barn, which looks more like a house in the Hollywood Hills.

"Come on in then," says Wanda. "I'll put the kettle on." And she disappears into the kitchen, leaving me to make myself at home.

The front room is small and very lived in. Mismatched furniture wedged in everywhere. Walls lined with portraits and seascapes. The mantelpiece littered with photos, which I'm instantly intrigued by, given that they're of my family. Noah and Sarah from young to middle age in just a few snaps. Awful school pictures of Leo, which makes me splutter out loud, then loads of Billy, including the ones I'd seen in my grandmother's album, only with Min cut out.

"He was a looker, wasn't he?" says Wanda, thrusting a steaming cup of hot tea at me. "That was my Billy," she adds, nodding sadly at the photo.

"Yeah, we've got the same one in in an album at home. He looks the spitting image of Leo," I say, running my fingers along the mantelpiece. "I love old photos. Not sure we'll feel quite the same in the future when we look back on our perfect selfies."

Wanda snorts. "You'll all think you were mad! Believe me. You get to my age and start seeing everything in a different light. How's Henry?" she asks, beckoning for me to take a seat.

"Getting there," I say. "He's taking it step by step."

"He took my advice then," she muses. "I should go and see him. That's very remiss of me. It's been far too long. Poor thing. The way this community hasn't stood by him. Making up all these ridiculous stories. You'd think they had nothing better to do. Pass me that photo album, would you?" she says, pointing at the coffee table. And together we flip through the album pages, which are nothing like the ones at Cliff House. No order or timeline, just a mishmash of photos glued in haphazardly.

"They were a pair," cackles Wanda, pointing to two boys standing proudly side by side, arms round their surfboards.

"Is that Uncle Henry?" I gasp.

Wanda nods. "They were magnificent surfers in their day. I should know – I taught them. And your mum. Up and out every morning they were. Either swimming, surfing or diving. They loved the water. I couldn't get them out of it. Even in the winter."

"Bet Min didn't," I mutter ungraciously, thinking of her poor circulation.

Wanda snorts. "Oh, she was the worst! Used to bunk off school to be with Billy. Her pa was not a happy man the day she missed her A-level exam, I can tell you."

"What was she like?" I ask.

"She was a troublemaker, is what," snaps Sarah, shutting the front door with a click. "What are you doing here?"

I grin nervously, wondering how best to play this. Repentant with a touch of sparkle, or completely remorseful?

"Came to say sorry," I murmur, choosing the latter. She doesn't look like she'd be fooled by my dazzling smile. Better keep my air kisses to myself too…

"What for?"

I stop. For Min? For existing? For trying to be friends with my cousin? All of the above?

"For cutting short the mermaid trip," I eventually decide on.

"Yes, there is that," mutters Sarah. "But it was that Quartermain girl's erratic behaviour that ruined the day for everyone else. Not you."

"Oh, thank you for being so understanding." I smile, giving it my twinkliest all, hoping that I can win her over, as a sudden and immense desire to fall into her arms and let the words come tumbling out washes over me. "You're my aunt, Sarah," I'd say. "I'm your long-lost niece." And we'd hug it out.

"You're just like *her*…" mutters Sarah scornfully.

Nervous look to camera.

"I know Min's not the easiest person," I murmur, "but if you could just see it from her point of—"

"I bet she didn't tell you that she's the one who made him go in the cave," says Sarah, fixing her cool blue eyes on me. "In the middle of a storm. Who does that? Billy knew better, but he was like a lovesick puppy trailing round after its owner. She was a troublemaker with all her thirst for adventure and scant regard for authority. And it got my brother killed. So no," she adds, "I don't need to hear her side of the story. You can't ever excuse her behaviour…"

As I trudge back down the hill, Piscary Bay stretches before me in all its technicolour glory, except I'm so livid I barely notice it. The two stories are so similar, only Min seems to have edited out some of the key scenes. And we all know that she's been doing *that* my whole life. Who's to say she's not doing it now? How can I trust a word she says? And how can we go on living like this? Her – eternally branded a troublemaker – and me, tarred with the same brush. No, it's over. This whole thing. I'm done.

Cut to black.

Part 3

EUPHORIA

EUPHORIA *[yoo-FAWR-ee-uh]*

Noun
A state of intense happiness and
self-confidence.

Psychology
A feeling of happiness, confidence or
well-being.

Ray Of Hope

I don't realize I'm doing it until I get as far as the Burbank Hotel. I'm holding my breath. The grittiness grating in my lungs reminding me of the anger pulsating through my veins.

"*Kochanie*," calls Jan. "You all right? Someone looking for you."

I sigh. Another person who wants to have a go at me no doubt.

"Why the sad face?" he asks. "He's a very handsome man. Looks like someone famous."

Bob. It must be! He's the only person I know who looks as much like a movie star as Min.

"He asked whether I know Coco James," says Jan, "and I replied, everybody know Coco James." He grins. "He went that way."

If my life were a film, this would be the moment it starts raining as I dash down the road, the music launching into an upbeat pop number. Then I'd arrive, drenched to the skin, and fly into Bob's arms, a close-up on my ecstatic face as he spins me around, thrilled to see me again. Unsurprisingly, in real life, the sun burns bright and I'm huffing and puffing, sweat running down my bright red face in rivulets by the time I catch up to him. No actor worth their salt would allow a close-up looking like this.

"Bob!" I yell, spotting him standing barefoot in the sand, looking as mesmerized by the water as I am, his gleaming white trainers hanging limply in his hand. A welcome mirage wearing a blue velvet blazer that matches the colour of the sea, his warm brown skin glowing in the sunshine. "BOB!" And I launch myself into his arms, promptly bursting into tears.

"I can't get over you being here," I say, clutching his arm, wanting never to let go, while we watch the surfers and bodyboarders come shooting in on the waves.

"I had a week spare," says Bob. "But it's your film that made my mind up. Didn't exactly paint Min in the best light. What's going on?"

I tell him everything. The secrets, Min's teenage tantrums, the judgemental community. "It's just not working," I say. "I can't do it any more. Min is a total nightmare. I want to come and live with you."

Bob puffs out his cheeks, frowning at the sea. "This isn't like you," he murmurs. "You're always so upbeat and positive."

"Yeah, well, things have changed," I mutter. "I've changed."

"*Hej!*" cries Ingrid, striding out of the sea with her surfboard. Quite how she manages to keep her red lipstick so perfect, I don't know. She's like Min in that regard. Maybe it's something that comes with age...

"*Hej*, Ingrid," I reply. "She's one of the nice ones," I tell Bob. "She owns *Hej!* You'll love it... How's the surf today?" I ask.

Ingrid grimaces. "Crowded with bodies. It's like the apocalypse out there. Who's this young man?"

I laugh. "This is Bob."

"Ah, the sort-of dad you were telling me about!"

"Hello," says Bob, shaking her hand.

"*Hej*," she replies, surveying him with an approving look. "The Zombies are getting better-looking, eh?"

I giggle. "Yeah, but don't tell him that..."

"She was terrifying," whispers Bob when she's gone.

"Ingrid?" I laugh. "Oh, she's a pussy cat."

"Lion more like," he mutters.

"Wait until you meet Uncle Henry then. What with him looking like a scarecrow and Jan looking like the tin man, I feel like I've landed in Oz."

Bob chuckles. "Still thinking your life's a film then?"

"Course," I laugh. "It's the only thing that keeps me going, knowing that the plot can still change."

He frowns. "And you want that to happen now?"

"It needs to," I sigh. "Speaking of which… What did you actually think of my film?"

"It was … good," he says after a lengthy pause, during which I have shrivelled up with terrified anticipation. "I liked the sweeping panoramic shots and the way you've gone in super close on your subjects. It certainly looks good and the soundtrack you've used works well, but…"

I inhale sharply. Nothing good comes after a 'but'.

"It's missing something," he says eventually.

Looks to camera – and there it is.

Perhaps I'm not in the best frame of mind for this after all.

"It's rubbish, isn't it?" I say and as Bob flings an arm round me, squeezing me tight with the kind of hug that I wish Min would give me sometimes, my shoulders sag and the tears flow.

"Don't cry," says Bob. "You didn't let me finish. What I was going to say was… Here, open this." He produces a neatly wrapped, boxed-shape present. "I think it might help with your film."

I rip it open, the anticipation being too much because I think I know what it might be.

It is! "An underwater camera?" I gasp. "Oh, Bob.

Thank you so much. It's just what I need."

He grins. "Call it an early Christmas present. Besides, I can't wait to see what you produce. Your film's got potential, Sunshine. But you're going to have to learn to take criticism on the chin. Doesn't get easier, I promise you that. Now, are you going to lead the way to this Cliff House of yours? I'm intrigued. Your film made it look appalling. Like some kind of set from a horror movie – *The Haunted House of Scary Bay*," he adds, swiping his hand across the sky as if it's already a headline title.

"And that was me editing it in its best light," I giggle. "Can I show you around first? There's so much to see. Where I swim every day, the ice-cream parlour, the gift shop, the harbour, this legendary cave…"

Bob frowns. "For someone who's just said they want to come back to London with me, that's a long list of things you like about this place. Tell you what, I'm starving, and I hear they do a mean afternoon tea at the Burbank Hotel. How about you go and get that awful mother of yours and bring your uncle too? We'll make a celebration of it…"

Think Pink

The interior of the Burbank Hotel is something else. The decor is so dark in contrast to its bright exterior that it takes a while for my eyes to adjust to the sudden dimness. Everything is black. Walls, furniture, chairs, floor. The reception desk is made from a long piece of shiny black marble on which sits a giant black vase full of flowers. Vibrant colours of orange, yellow and deep maroon interspersed with flourishes of green, which, set against the black backdrop, looks like a Dutch master's painting.

"Coo! This has changed a bit," murmurs Min. "We used to call it the Ocean Dive on account of its spit and sawdust clientele. Bet they're proper miffed about this upgrade. Still it's a nice improvement, isn't it, Henry?"

"I made it," he gasps, collapsing on to a sofa and looking around him in awe as if seeing the world for the first time.

Through a wide arch, my eye catches on the grandest stairwell I think I've ever seen. In direct contrast to the black lobby, the double staircase is stark white. White marble steps, with a white balustrade and white walls complete with white artwork, all lit by a giant white glass chandelier. It looks like the stairway to heaven!

"Can I help you?" A young man suddenly appears in front of us, looking like a silhouette in his black uniform.

"We're here for afternoon tea with Bob Seymour," announces Min loudly, which draws several looks in our direction. Probably because she's still wearing her sunnies and they make her look like a movie star. Her whole get-up does.

Afternoon tea is served in a bright pink dining room. Candy-coloured walls, floor-to-ceiling glass windows swathed in deep pink velvet, looking out on a courtyard garden full of pink flower beds. In the corners of the room are giant pink planters out of which grow enormous palm trees – not pink, thankfully – then table upon table laid with fuchsia-pink tablecloths and glass vases with pink daisy-like flowers garnishing them.

Min wanders in, gasping her approval, and causing more heads to turn. Her coral summer dress with matching hair wrap and contrasting patterned silk kimono of course fitting in perfectly with the candy decor, as if she'd planned it.

And, lounging comfortably against the pink velvet banquette in his latest-of-everything-wear, Bob looks like he belongs here too, bringing my hastily pulled-on outfit choice and Uncle Henry's scarecrow attire into uncomfortable focus.

"Bob Seymour!" shrieks Min at the top of her lungs – yet more looks – and she rushes into his arms, giggling like a schoolgirl.

"Would you look at you," he laughs, holding her at arm's length. "You're looking … well."

"You sound surprised," she replies. "What's she been telling you?"

"Nothing," he says breezily. "I already ordered for us," he adds, gesturing to the table laden with a delicate pink china tea set and large three-tiered silver platter brimming with sandwiches and cakes. "I hope you're hungry…"

~~~

"So, have you missed us?" asks Min, nibbling on the corner of a gluten free egg sandwich, while I devour mine in two hungry bites. "Are you here to beg us to come back?"

Looks to camera – do I actually want that?

Bob snorts. "I came because your daughter sent me her film. That house of yours looks amazing. Tons of potential."

"Potential to bankrupt us," mutters Uncle Henry.

"Wanna buy it?" asks Min hopefully. "I'm not kidding."

"You can't sell Cliff House," I whisper. "It's our home."

"It's falling down," says Min, taking a gulp of tea. "Costing us a fortune to repair. Be easier to pull it down and start again. We could probably build ten high-end apartments."

"No," I gasp, recoiling at the thought and feeling angry that she'd even suggest it. "It would spoil the bay. Bob! Don't let her talk you into this." I turn to Uncle Henry. "You don't agree with her, do you?"

He shrugs.

"But I thought you were dead against it. You already told Adele where to go."

"Oh, she's been sniffing around, has she?" scoffs Min. "Her friend's mother," she explains to Bob. "A regular *Big Mother* wannabe, if ever there was one."

"Stop being so mean," I say. "Adele's lovely."

"You would say that," laughs Min.

"What, because she's kind to me? Asks me how my day's going? Makes me hot chocolate with marshmallows and even hugs me? That's what a mother's supposed to do."

"Oh wow," says Min dryly. "If I'd known it was *that* easy..."

"Oh, shut up," I snap, feeling the resurgence of my anger from the conversation with Sarah. Something I haven't yet talked to Min about.

"Coco," warns Bob, glancing around. "We're in a restaurant."

I try biting my lip and swallowing down the words that

301

I usually manage not to say. But today I'm mad that she's been lying to me all this time and I'm sick of tiptoeing round her.

"Look at the state of you," I say, ignoring Bob. "You're a liar and a—"

"Don't talk to her like that," warns Uncle Henry.

Looks to camera – he's defending her?

"She's doing the best she can," he adds.

"She needs to grow up," I burst out, feeling like I've been holding my breath for months, the euphoria of coming up for air fuelling my anger like oxygen to a fire. "Acting as if she's a teen—"

My diatribe is interrupted by a young man standing nervously at Bob's side, staring at him with such incredulity it's as if he can't believe he's really there. "Excuse me," he says. "Are you … someone? You look like a film star."

Bob grins. "Just a TV director."

"Oh. Can I have your autograph then?"

"Sure."

"Is she famous?" asks the autograph hunter, nodding hopefully in Min's direction.

Looks to camera – oh, for heaven's sake!

"No, she isn't," I growl. "Go away."

"Coco." Bob frowns. "What's got into you?"

"You haven't been here," I say lamely. "You haven't seen what she's become. She lied to me about my dad."

"No, I never," shrieks Min.

Eye-rolls to camera.

"Liar," I hiss.

"Am not—"

"Can we calm down, please?" says Bob solemnly. "I'm here to help. Now kindly watch your tone. Both of you."

Making Amends

Standing in the middle of the room, my attention is firmly fixed on my phone screen, where the three torturous dots have been pulsating for the past hour, as if Shiv is writing a thesis of a response, telling me how bad a friend I am. I realize this now. Having watched my film over and over, it's the only conclusion possible.

23 Aug

SHIV 17:35

...

"Ow," I hiss, as I'm pricked for the millionth time. "You're hurting me."

"Stand still then," mutters Min, pins sticking out of her tightly pressed lips as she alters her old school blazer.

Bob's gone, having exerted his calming influence and got us all talking, not shouting, again. And, for once, it actually feels like it might last. Something's changed in Min. She's started being useful and got me enrolled in the local comp. I start in a few weeks. I'm dreading it.

"What are you sighing about?" asks Min as my phone pings with a message from a London friend.

"Shiv's ignoring me," I say. "Hasn't returned my messages in weeks. I don't think she likes me any more."

"Of course she likes you! She burst an eardrum doing something she absolutely loathes, all so that she could spend time with you. Maybe if you put down the camera once in a while, you'd actually see what people are feeling." She pauses to arch a perfectly shaped eyebrow at me.

Looks to camera – she really means her of course. She hasn't changed that *much.*

"You've been so focused on fixing a community that doesn't even want fixing," she says, "trying to make friends with the enemy, that you haven't noticed what's under your nose. Namely, Shiv."

I frown. "I thought you didn't like her."

"It's her mother I can't stand. There," she says, sitting back to survey her handiwork. "I think you're done."

"This is hideous," I sigh. "Never had to wear a blazer and tie in London. Why do I have to start now? There's only a year left of GCSEs."

Min snorts. "It's not that bad."

"Easy for you to say," I frown. "I'm not like you. You're—"

"Just trying to help, darling," she says. "I know you like to pitch me as the villain in your life – and I don't mind, they do have the best backstories after all – but give me a break. I'm trying my best."

"I was going to say effortlessly cool actually."

She laughs. "Well, thank you. I only appear cool because I don't care what people think, you know."

"Except for Wanda and Sarah," I argue. "Why didn't you tell me that it was your idea to go in the cave?"

"Because I feel guilty. Every day." Her voice cracks. "Don't you think I regret making that decision? That I'd change it if I could? Life's not a film, Coco. You can't reshoot the scenes that you don't like. It's taken fifteen years and coming back here for me to realize that. We were just kids."

Looks to camera – I think Min may have grown up more than I've given her credit for.

"It was the place we escaped to," she explains. "Where no one else would follow for fear of getting lost in the tunnels. It was our place."

"So how did you find your way out?" I ask.

She smiles sadly. "I marked the route with nail varnish… Look, I should've told you, I'm sorry. But I knew they'd turn you against me."

"They haven't," I say.

"Good," she sighs. "Because nothing's going to change

306

their opinion of me. Not even you. They want to make up the narrative that fits *their* story, not mine… I've made my peace with that. But…" She stops, biting nervously on the corner of her lips. "If you want to try being a part of their family, I won't stop you."

"Really?" I say, feeling so shocked it's as if my eyes are standing on stalks.

She nods. "Yes, really."

My phone pings with another message. Still not Shiv.

"Look, do what you do best with Shiv, eh?" says Min. "She'll come around. They always do. You're a social butterfly. Just like your dad. Oh, and take your Uncle Henry for a walk, would you? He's been pestering me all afternoon. Think of it as having a dog," she adds, sensing my reluctance.

"Does that mean we can get one?" I retort, which doesn't even get an answer as Min goes back to staring out at the sea. And, for the first time since we've been here, I notice just how relaxed she looks. Colour in her cheeks, tiredness washed away. Maybe she is happier here. Can I really tell the Pengellys who I am without ruining that?

Sea of Stars

Since making it as far as the Burbank, and with help from Bob, Uncle Henry has started taking evening walks.

"Min said that I can tell people about my dad if I want to," I say to him. "Except I don't know if I should."

"Have you worked out the pros and cons?" he asks.

"Not yet." I take a deep breath for courage, feeling worried that I won't like the outcome. "It might make it easier fitting in, I suppose. And I'd have a whole other family to get to know."

"Min and I not enough for you?" Uncle Henry laughs.

I giggle. "Too much… But what if Wanda and Sarah don't accept me? What if I make things worse for Min? She seems and looks so much happier down here. What if they turn against her all over again?"

Uncle Henry inhales slowly. "You know, in Japan, they

eat pufferfish. It's called—" He clicks his fingers. "Fugu! A delicious but deadly delicacy. People literally risk their lives to eat it."

I frown. "People would eat Brian if they had the chance?"

"Well, yes, but that's not my point," he mutters. "I meant that you're brave to be trying to fix things around here. Still going at it in the face of such toxicity."

Looks to camera – oh.

"But maybe," he says, "it's time to stop trying so hard. All the nerve in the world won't make people change. Not if they don't want to. Min's testament to that. She's only changing because she wants to, not because of you. If you feel like you want a relationship with Wanda and her clan, that's up to you."

"That's what Bob said," I say. "I suspect he had a word with Min about it too."

Uncle Henry smiles. "He's a wise man, that Bob. Amazing handle on Minnie. I've never seen her be so open with anyone. You're different around him too. More … relaxed."

I giggle. "Relaxed?"

"Yes. You told him where you were going and what you were doing. You talked to him."

"And I don't with you?" I say, feeling bad. "Mind this narrow bit, Uncle Henry," I add, grabbing hold of his hand.

We walk on in silence, each of us concentrating on the path ahead until we've reached the bottom. Uncle Henry glances back up the hill, his eyes wide with disbelief.

"You made it," I laugh. "Next step the sea."

He chuckles. "One day maybe."

The skies are clear tonight, lit up with an awesome display of stars like a vast galaxy of fairy lights. The kind of night sky that in a film would have several shooting stars appear at key moments. Uncle Henry and I sit, watching the tide roll in, mulling over what we can and can't change about our lives.

One of the signs above Morvoren has come loose, flapping gently in the breeze as if to say, *Don't forget about me!*

"What's Morvoren like, Uncle Henry?"

He sighs. "Never seen it."

"What? But didn't you write that Wiziwisdom article?"

"Yes, to put people off," he says. "I based it on what Min told me. No idea if any of it's real."

"So there isn't a green marble staircase that glows under the right conditions," I say, feeling disappointed. "No mermaid tears, no sea of stars?"

Uncle Henry shrugs. "It's always sounded a bit too much like the *Wizard of Oz* to me. Min was obsessed with that film. Your guess is as good as mine."

All of a sudden, I know I want to go there. See for myself the place where Min and my dad used to hang out. Find out whether the legend is true. I could film it for everyone to see. Show them the tunnels. It might help…

Then, as the sun finally disappears, the most extraordinary thing happens. The waves lapping against the shore explode suddenly with tiny blue neon dots as they hit the sand. An actual sea of stars. It exists!

"Bioluminescence," I murmur. "It's a sign…"

PISCARY BAY TIDE TIMES

Saturday 24th August

LOW TIDE:	05:33	HEIGHT:	2.30 m
HIGH TIDE:	11:33	HEIGHT:	5.00 m
LOW TIDE:	18:05	HEIGHT:	2.40 m
HIGH TIDE:	00:16	HEIGHT:	5.00 m

Waning Quarter Moon

SUNRISE:	06:25	SUNSET:	20:23
MOONRISE:	00:33	MOONSET:	15:39

WIKIWISDOM

Slack water

Slack water is a period of time at the end of each rising and falling tide, when there is little or no movement of water in or out. Depending on location, it usually last between 2.75 and 3 hours.

The Early Bird

I'm up and out early the next day, the sun well into its morning routine, slowly casting a warm yellow light across the sea, marking the start of a new day. An exciting day. One in which I plan to get my friend back onside and with an adventure in mind too. In fact, I'm so excited to tell Shiv about the sea of stars that I'm outside her house before I stop to think she might not answer the door to me. Fortunately, it's Sprout who does.

"Coco!" she squeals, wrapping her arms round me. "What are you doing here?"

"Hello to you too, munchkin," I laugh. "How was camp? You glad to be back?"

She wrinkles her nose. "Not really. Mummy and Shiv haven't stopped fighting about you."

"Sprout, who's at the door?" demands Adele, appearing

in her dressing gown. "Oh… It's a bit early, don't you think?"

"Sorry," I say. "I just wanted to speak to Shiv."

"Well, she won't want to talk to you," she retorts and launches into a lecture about how much she trusted me and how I'd led Shiv astray.

"Mummy," hisses Sprout, tugging on her sleeve. "Stop it. You're being embarrassing." But, since Adele is clearly on a roll, Sprout disappears into the house and I'm thankful when Shiv soon appears in her place.

"Sprout needs you," she sighs. "She's climbed up on the kitchen counter, trying to get at the marshmallows."

"For breakfast! Why didn't you stop her?" gasps Adele, dashing towards the kitchen, where I hear her shriek at Sprout about the dangers of climbing and eating too many sweets.

"Hey," I say with a nervous grin. "Thanks for that."

Shiv frowns. "That wasn't for you. Just don't need my mother fighting my battles for me. What d'you want?"

"I came to say sorry," I say. "I haven't been much of a friend, have I? Only realized that when I looked back at the footage. You forgot that the camera was on. I heard what you said."

"Oh, I'm sorry, did my performance spoil your little film?" she sneers. "You were just using me. Admit it."

"That's not true."

"Oh no? For someone who said they wanted to fix things

around here, you've spent an awful lot of time sucking up to that Leo Tremain." She frowns. "You left me alone on a rock in the middle of the sea for an hour."

I grimace. "I'm sorry. I got carried away with the freediving. I just wasn't expecting to love it as much as I did. And I'm good at it. That's not a feeling I'm used to."

Shiv rolls her eyes dismissively. The kind of thing someone who's never struggled does and it riles me.

"You didn't tell me that you didn't like swimming in deep water until we were in it," I snap. "What was I supposed to do?"

It's Shiv's turn to grimace, but then she changes tack suddenly, narrowing her eyes – there's obviously something else bugging her. "I know about your dad by the way."

Looks to camera – what?

"Mum said she saw you in town with him."

Looks to camera – what?

"Bob Seymour," she says. "People talk in this town – I know he's not your dad. I can't believe you lied. What else have you been keeping from me?"

"Nothing."

"Then why did you lie?"

"Because…" I say, searching around for a reason and coming face to face with the only one. "Because it was easier to tell you that than the truth. And, well, the fact is … Leo's my cousin!"

And the secret is finally out.

After some serious grovelling to Adele, and thanks to Shiv's backing, we curl up in her lounge, with things feeling like they're finally back on track.

"Let me get this straight," says Shiv incredulously. "Billy Pengelly was your dad, which makes you Leo Tremain's cousin *and* a Fish, a Cuckoo and a Zombie."

I nod.

"And Min has been insisting that you keep it a secret from everyone all this time?"

I nod again.

"Here we go, darlings," trills Adele, arriving with a tray laden with food. Steaming mugs of coffee, fresh fruit, a plate piled high with croissants and another with hot, buttery, home-made fruit toast. "Wasn't sure what you'd like," she says. "But do say. I can always make something else."

"Oh, thanks," I say. "This is too much as it is."

"Not at all," she laughs, sitting down in a nearby armchair. "So, tell me, what's that gorgeous man you were with like?"

"Mum!" hisses Shiv, giving her a pointed look. "Go away."

Adele looks momentarily startled then, flushing, she says, "Oh… Yes… Sorry. Is that Sprout calling for me? I'll, er … leave you two to it."

"Thanks, Adele!" I call.

"You know, you don't have to be so grateful," mutters Shiv.

"But I am."

"Well, stop it. You're making me look bad. Now start from the beginning again and give me all the gory details…"

Déjà Vu

It's like old times as we plod down the usual route from the Old Barn to Cove Beach, Sprout bounding on ahead like a puppy on her first walk.

"Come on, slowcoaches!" she calls. "I want to swim!"

"I wish I was as enthusiastic about swimming as her," sighs Shiv. "I can't believe I ever wanted to try being a mermaid. I've had awful nightmares ever since that trip. Keep waking up, thinking I'm surrounded by water and I can't get out."

I grimace. "Sorry. How's your eardrum?"

"Better," says Shiv. "It was my fault. I should've stayed put. But you were gone too long and I was worried. Plus, I saw a seal swimming and I wanted to get a closer look."

"You know Uncle Henry used to go freediving before his illness," I tell her. "He said that the first-hand experience

319

was invaluable to his research."

"Really?"

"Yeah, he made it down to the beach for the first time in a decade last night. We watched the waves explode with blue fireworks. It really did look like a sea of stars. It was wonderful. I wish you'd been there."

Shiv nods thoughtfully. "Perhaps I should take a leaf out of his book then. I've never thought of myself as the adventurous kind, but maybe I should prove Mum wrong…"

"What's Mummy wrong about this time?" laughs Sprout, running back to join us. "Is it because she said that Coco's a bad influence and that she's just like her mum? A Minnie-me?" She frowns. "But I don't see what's wrong with that. Min looks like a movie star…"

"You don't have to repeat everything you hear," mutters Shiv.

"It's all right," I laugh, then Sprout starts pulling at my arm, urging me to move faster. "There's plenty of time for a swim," I tell her. "Low tide's at six tonight."

"Spoken like a true local," snorts Shiv.

I giggle. "It's hard not to notice when I look out at the sea every day. It's one of the things I love about living here."

"Love?" laughs Shiv. "You've changed the script."

"Had to," I say, the wind whipping my hair into a frenzy and making me shiver. "Can't believe the summer's nearly over and we've wasted two weeks not speaking."

"Let's make up for it now then," says Shiv.

We turn down the cliff path, the sea stretching out enticingly in front of us. I can't wait to get in.

"So, what are you going to do about the … you know … big secret?" she whispers.

"What secret?" asks Sprout.

"Nothing," we reply in unison.

Sprout's brow crumples into a scowl. "No one tells me anything," she grumbles. "I'm good at keeping secrets."

"Are not," laughs Shiv.

"Are too."

"Erm, what are they doing here?" Shiv stops in her tracks and frowns. "Is this some stupid last-ditch attempt of yours for a happy-ever-after?"

"No," I say, edging past her and setting off briskly down the cliff path, leaping the last bit on to the warm sand.

Cut to a shot of Leo. I haven't seen him since the mermaid trip either.

"Hi, Leo," I call.

"Oi, oi!"

"You didn't reply to my texts. Did you get into lots of trouble with your mum?"

"Yeah, but she'll get over it," he laughs. "Once Adele Quartermain does."

"She's forgiven me," I say. "I'm sure you'll be next."

He snorts. "Something else will come along. It usually does."

"You know freediving with you was the most amazing

321

thing I've ever experienced," I tell him. "I love being in the sea. Don't know how I ever survived when I was in London. Feels like I've been freediving for years."

Leo glances around him nervously. "Yeah, you're a natural... Look, no offence, but I can't be seen hanging out with you. Especially not Miss La-di-dah over there. The Fish and the Cuckoos go back a long way."

"But they're just labels," I say, laughing out my frustration. "I can't choose between you and Shiv. I don't want to."

He shrugs. "To be honest, Mum's not keen on me being associated with a James anyway. She's made *that* very clear."

Looks to camera – if only he knew how loud the words 'YOU'RE MY COUSIN' are broadcasting inside my head right now.

"It's not you," he adds, drawing a line in the sand. "It's your mum."

Shiv dutifully takes a seat further down the beach, spreading a blanket out, Bennie looking yearningly over at her. Leo lies down with his T-shirt covering his face, and I'm left standing there with a foot in both camps, feeling like I've got to pick a side. Again. But I don't want to!

"I was going to invite you to explore Morvoren Cave," I say airily to the wind. Leo sits bolt upright. I just needed the right hook after all. "I've got a new waterproof camera. I'm going to film it. Thought you might want to come along, but if you can't bear to be in my company…"

"Morvoren Cave," gasps Shiv. "But isn't that dangerous?"

"What's dangerous?" says Sprout.

"Nothing," mutters Shiv irritably. "She wasn't talking to you. Go and play over there," she hisses. "What are you talking about, Coco? We can't go in Morvoren Cave. You remember those boys in Thailand. They were trapped underground for days. Someone died trying to save them."

"This won't be like that."

"How d'you know?"

"Because Min's been in there," I say, glancing nervously at Leo. "And she's marked the route in. Low tide's at nine thirty on Tuesday morning. I've done my research. The slack tide should give us three hours to explore."

"At the most." Leo frowns. "We don't want to get caught in the tunnels when they're filling up."

"So you're coming?" I grin.

He shrugs but the glint in his eye tells me he is. It's the same one I get when I'm determined about something too.

"Then I'm coming as well," says Shiv suddenly.

"What?"

"Imagine what sea creatures might live in there," she tells me. "I might discover something new. You could take photos with your camera and I could show them to your uncle. And, besides, I said I wanted to be more adventurous…"

PISCARY BAY TIDE TIMES

Tuesday 27th August

HIGH TIDE:	02:59	HEIGHT:	5.30 m
LOW TIDE:	09:34	HEIGHT:	2.00 m
HIGH TIDE:	15:29	HEIGHT:	5.60 m
LOW TIDE:	22:08	HEIGHT:	1.70 m

Crescent Moon

SUNRISE:	06:29	SUNSET:	20:17
MOONRISE:	02:15	MOONSET:	18:47

Writing on the Wall

There's a chill autumn-in-the-air wind whipping in my face today, the salt biting at my nostrils, and the sun just breaking through the clouds: the perfect day for an adventure. Something for which Shiv has come seriously prepared. Wrapped in her dryrobe, and straining under a large rucksack, she looks like she's going on a week-long expedition.

"What've you got in there?" I laugh, helping her to lift it off her back on to the sand.

"Food, blankets, first-aid kit," she says. "I had to leave it by the gate last night so that Mum wouldn't see. And then she suddenly told me I was going to have to look after Sprout."

"How'd you get out of that?" I ask.

Shiv grins, her eyes lighting up with glee. "I told her

I couldn't. Things have changed between us – thanks in part to you."

"Me?"

"Yeah. I really admire the way you face problems head-on. Say sorry when it's due and make people feel special. I want to be more like that. Anyway, we had a massive heart-to-heart last night. It really cleared the air. She promised to stop being such a helicopter mum and I promised to stop being such an ungrateful brat."

"Wow." I'm touched. No one's ever told me they admire me.

"What did you bring?" asks Shiv.

"Camera, torch and goggles," I say.

"Is that all?"

"We're only going to be inside the cave for a couple of hours," I laugh. And I'm not even sure the tunnels will be wide enough for her rucksack, but I keep that to myself.

"Oh, is that the camera Bob bought you?" Shiv says. "Let's have a look. Wow."

"I'll show you how to use it," I say. "For all the fish you're going to find… There's Leo. Remember to be nice."

"Aren't I always?" she giggles. "Don't answer that."

"Oi, oi," grunts Leo, glancing at us both, his face wrinkling at the sight of Shiv's rucksack. "How d'you expect to keep that lot dry? There might be a completely submerged tunnel that we have to swim through."

Shiv frowns. "You mean I'd have to go under? Coco,"

she says, beginning to panic. "You never said anything about that."

"Min's not mentioned it," I say. "But maybe leave the rucksack. I'm sure we won't need it."

"OK, fine. But I'm bringing my dryrobe and this."

And, much to my surprise, she pulls out a smaller bag from within her rucksack. What does she think we're going to be doing in there?

And action!

I run on ahead, my feet slapping the wet sand, so that I can get a shot of Leo and Shiv as we walk towards the cave.

Piece to camera: "I'm so excited. After weeks of research, we're actually going inside Morvoren Cave!"

Cut to a shot of a No Trespassers *sign.*

"*Danger, keep out,*" Shiv reads aloud. "*Trespassers will be prosecuted… Maybe we should go back.*"

"What film have you ever seen where the main characters actually take any notice of a sign?" I laugh. "Besides, Min used to come here all the time."

"And look how that turned out," mutters Shiv, giving Leo a surreptitious glance. "*P OUT IN OUT,*" she reads when we arrive at the entrance. "What's that supposed to mean?"

"Keep out, Min's about," I say. "She's got the same sign on her bedroom door, just some of the letters have rubbed off. Did you bring the trail ribbon?" I ask Leo.

"Trail ribbon?" repeats Shiv suspiciously. "What's that?"

"Just a precaution," I say. "It was Leo's idea along with the underwater head torches. We don't want to get lost."

"But I thought you said Min had marked the way... I don't know about this, Coco," says Shiv. "It doesn't feel safe."

"This is just our safety net," I say calmly. "But you don't have to come."

"No, I want to." She takes a deep breath. "I can be brave and adventurous..."

Cut to a shot of me following Leo through the cave entrance, Shiv gripping hold of my hand like she'll never let go, as we feel our way through the corridor, climbing upwards into the unknown.

Cut to black.

The Maze

Piece to camera: "Well, we're inside the cave at last," I say, *running my hands over the smooth yellow rock that I'm sitting on. "It was a steep climb up here and it looks like the tunnel stretches on for miles…"*

Jumpcut to a shot of Leo's back.

As we leave daylight behind, it's soon pitch-black and I'm grateful for the head torches lighting our way forward, leaving the path behind dropping into darkness.

"Over here!" calls Leo, his voice sounding strangely echoey up ahead. "There's a fork in the tunnel."

"Which way do we go?" whispers Shiv.

Cut to a shot of a red letter M painted on the rock.

"That way," I laugh, pointing to it. "I told you. Min did mark the way."

On we creep, Leo unwinding the bright orange trail

ribbon, our feet slapping in the freezing-cold standing water. I shiver involuntarily, blinking hard and trying to keep my camera steady as the tunnel grows uncomfortably narrow and Shiv's clutch tighter. I don't blame her. We've passed so many tunnels, going up and down and around and around, I've lost all sense of direction and it feels like we're in the middle a of a complex maze.

Leo stops in his tracks suddenly and turns to me, looking worried. "That's the end of the ribbon," he says, tying it tightly to a jutting-out rock above us.

Shiv inhales sharply, pouncing immediately on his words as if she's been waiting for the right excuse. "We should go back then."

Cut to a shot of my disappointed face.

"We've got plenty of time," I say, glancing at my watch. "Couldn't we just keep following Min's markings?" I push past Leo. "Let's just walk as far as the end of this tunnel. If there's another fork, we'll turn back. Deal?"

I lead the way this time. My breath firmly held as I take each step, hoping that we'll reach the main chamber soon. The path suddenly drops, halving in height so that it feels like we're crawling through the bowels of this place. My heart is pounding with anticipation … or fear… Both? The thought that Min made this journey *without* the markers…

I push on, this time uphill, the tunnel growing narrower, and, just as I'm beginning to feel claustrophobic and achy from my hunched stance, all of a sudden, we're there.

"Whoa," we say in unison, our voices echoing as we beam gleefully at one another like excited children who've found their presents on Christmas morning.

Cut to a wide shot of an immense cave, lit only by our three wavering beams of torchlight.

Green, orange and purple striations of seaweed cover every surface like wallpaper. Boulders piled on top of each other, small rock pools at their feet full of sea creatures and shells. And, in the middle of all this, lie light green stones smoothed into steps to form a grand staircase. But what really takes my breath away are the piles of sparkling green gems at the foot of it.

"Mermaid tears," I gasp, feeling like I've found Ariel's treasure trove, though on closer examination they're really just pieces of glass smoothed by the tumbling sea.

The soundtrack is suddenly full of *oohs* and *ahs* as more of the cave is revealed. Shiv shrieking about the sea creatures in the rock pools – sadly not glowing – and Leo gasping at the rows of green bottles and candle stumps lined up along a natural ridge high off the ground, all of which are covered in slimy seaweed and salt.

Long, wide pan of the cave as I creep slowly up the stone staircase, trying to record everything, even in the darkest depths.

Then something catches my eye and I lower the camera to get a better look, my eyes trying to adapt to the darkness. I dash forward, beside myself with excitement. At the top of the staircase is a smooth grey wall upon which is carved a portrait of a mermaid with long wavy hair, looking eerily like Min, right down to the stick-thin figure and giant beehive hairdo.

"Leo, Shiv," I gasp. "Look!"

The three of us stand in a row, silently contemplating the giant picture. Me marvelling at how good my dad had been at drawing.

"I swear I've seen that picture before," murmurs Leo. "Or one like it."

Looks to camera…

Shiv tilts her head as she studies it. "Yeah. She looks familiar somehow. She looks a bit like … you."

In unison, they turn to stare at me, their torchlight beams instantly blinding me, making me gasp and stumble backwards. Caught off-guard, I throw my hands up to shield my eyes and my beloved camera flies out of my hand, clattering noisily down the steps into the dark depths of the cave floor. I clamber down to retrieve it, yelping in frustration and skidding on the last two steps where I trip over my feet, landing painfully on my side.

"Coco, are you all right?" yells Leo, jumping down to help me. But he skids on the same steps and the forward momentum sends him flying head first into the pool of mermaid tears.

An eerie silence settles over us for three seconds – I count the Mississippis – as we wait for him to get up and brush himself off. But he doesn't. He lies there, twitching.

"Leo!" yells Shiv, picking her way carefully down the steps. The echoes of her sobbing merge with the ricochets of Leo's cries of pain as I lie there, still winded and gasping for breath.

It seems our adventure film has become a disaster movie.

Too Late

Lying propped against Shiv's shoulder, feet dangling in the pool of mermaid tears, Leo gazes around him, looking dazed and confused as if wondering how on earth he came to be at the bottom of a green marble staircase.

"Ow," he mutters, reaching up to touch the side of his head, then staring, puzzled, at his hands that are now covered in blood.

"Oh my God!" I screech as I catch sight of the wound – a dark black gash on the side of his head. His blond hair is matted and has turned a bright shade of crimson red. "What are we going to do?"

"We need to get him out of here," replies Shiv. "He might have concussion. How many fingers am I holding up?" she asks Leo.

He stares at her. "Three."

"Good," she replies. "Any nausea?"

"Only the sight of you," he snorts.

She pulls a face. "Still got a sense of humour then. That's a good sign."

Leo smiles back weakly.

"Can you stand?" she asks.

He nods but, when he tries to get up, it's on wobbly limbs and he lurches forward on to me. He tries again, but it's like his sense of balance has completely gone as he sprawls against Shiv, groaning with frustration.

Shiv takes a deep breath, her face full of fear, eyes searching around us while she considers what to do. "We'll have to try to lead him out," she says. "D'you think we've got enough time before the tide comes in?"

I stare at my watch. It's gone eleven. "We should have," I say. "But we need to go now."

"What about your camera?" she asks, nodding towards the rocks where it disappeared.

"Leave it," I say. "Probably broken anyway."

With an arm round each of our shoulders, it's slow going. Leo is much taller and heavier than me. A problem made even worse by how much his head's flopping about, like a hand puppet without the guiding fingers. Shiv ends up taking most of his weight, while I feel our way along the tunnel, our feet slapping in shallow puddles where previously there was none.

As I turn the corner, my feet sinking into ice-cold, ankle-deep water, we come to the top of the narrowest and lowest part of the tunnel and my breath freezes suddenly in my throat. It's flooded and, with every new step I take, I know that we can't go any further. The descent is too steep. This must be one of the submerged tunnels that Leo mentioned.

"Coco," says Shiv anxiously. "How much further before it gets wider? I can't carry him like this."

I lick my lips nervously, gulping non-existent saliva down my dry throat. "Er… Stay there a mo," I say, trying to keep my voice light. "I'm just going to check ahead." And, with a little wave, I disappear into the darkness of the tunnel.

Within a few strides, the water is up to my chin, making my neck arch painfully upwards, then, as I take another step down, my feet don't even touch the ground and I'm treading water. The tunnel is completely submerged.

Shiv's face falls the moment she notices my drenched clothes.

"We've got to keep going," murmurs Leo groggily. "Tide's coming in." Seated on the floor of the tunnel, his arms and head flopping forward, he looks exhausted.

"How d'you expect to swim in that state?" snaps Shiv, sounding scarily like Adele. "Not with an open head wound… I can't swim underwater in that dark tunnel," she whispers to me. "That's like making my nightmare a reality."

"But what about Leo?" I hiss.

"He can't stand up straight," she replies in a hoarse whisper. "We'll have to go back to the cave and let him rest. How long until there's another low tide?"

I'm shocked to discover that it's gone midday; it's taken us nearly an hour to get this far. I gulp. "Not for another ten hours."

Shiv's eyes nearly pop out of her head. "We can't stay here that long!" She jerks her head towards Leo. "He's got concussion. He should see a doctor."

"We won't make it in time," I say. "Not with him like that. It's too late. We're trapped by the tide…"

The Darkest Hour

"How long's it going to be now?" whimpers Shiv as we huddle together, Leo's head resting on her lap, the two of them wrapped in her dryrobe. We're sitting in darkness to conserve the torch batteries. We're down to two, since Leo smashed his torch when he fell.

"Five minutes since you last asked," I mutter miserably. "I'm so sorry, Shiv. I should never have suggested this."

"I wanted to come," she replies. "You weren't to know this would happen and I was kind of enjoying it. Right up until, well… You two fell down the hill like Jack and Jill." Our echoing giggles sound hollow. Like we shouldn't be laughing given the situation we're in.

"I'm pretty sure I saw a lobster in that rock pool," sighs Shiv. "Wish I'd got a photograph now. Your uncle was right. Seeing things up close is useful. Can we turn the torches on again? I don't like the dark."

"How are you feeling, Leo?" I ask.

"Thirsty," he mumbles. "I've got a splitting headache too." He frowns up at the portrait. "That picture looks like Min. My uncle must have painted it." His voice is all croaky and faint. Makes me feel scared. What if he...? No, I can't think that way.

"Here, take these painkillers," says Shiv, fumbling in her bag and giving me a wide-eyed look. "Lucky I ignored you and brought this, isn't it?" Leo smiles weakly and, going to close his eyes, he thanks her. "Don't go to sleep," she orders.

"But I'm tired," he moans.

"You can't," she says firmly. "You have to stay awake. What are we going to do? What if...?"

"I'll go for help," I say, jumping to my feet with the decision made.

"But the tunnel's submerged," gasps Shiv, clutching at my wrist. "What if you get lost?"

"I can hold my breath," I say. "And I've got my goggles. I'll follow the trail ribbon out."

"And the rips?" she asks.

"Might not be there," I say, "and, if they are, I know what to do. Leo taught me that."

"But what if this is history repeating itself?" she whispers urgently.

"I've got to try," I say. "Even if you do end up staying here until low tide, there's no way we'll be able to carry Leo out. We need help. I'll be back as soon as I can. Look after him."

After a teary farewell, I walk quickly back along the tunnel until I'm waist-deep in the water. I pause to run through the relaxation phase in my head, an almost pointless task given how tense and scared I'm feeling. Then, with one full breath, I duck under the water and into the submerged tunnel. It's freezing and absolutely nothing like freediving with Leo. I feel terrified. I shouldn't be doing this alone – the first and most important rule of freediving – but what choice do I have? If Leo's concussion gets worse, well…

I come up for air a few minutes later and am relieved to find myself back standing in waist-high water, the trail ribbon above me, secured to the roof of the cave. I take a few steps forward then, all of a sudden, my head torch flickers and the scene is plunged into darkness.

Cut to black.

I turn this way and that, feeling terrified, desperately trying to get my eyes to adjust to the dark. My hands shoot up to the ceiling where I feel around for the ribbon again. It's there. Thank God. If I can just keep my hand on that, I'll be fine.

Cue the soundtrack.

An eerie silence punctuated by the sound of me whimpering. Me talking out loud: "It's going to be fine,

Coco. You can do this." Me counting out the Mississippis, trying to guess where the end of the tunnel is. Me trying to sing with a wavering voice as the fear keeps threatening to overwhelm me.

I come to another submerged corridor and know I've got to swim through it, despite feeling terrified. It's only a short one. I remember it because it's where I stumbled on the steps down and almost dropped my camera. Taking a deep breath, I duck under the water, sticking one arm out ahead of me, the other tracing the trail ribbon along the tunnel ceiling. Slowly, I inch along, kicking with all my might. Hoping that I've got enough breath to get me to the end.

Fade up the menacing violin music, as the scene remains steadfastly black.

My mind is whirring with thoughts of what I'd say to Min if I had one more chance to see her.

Cut to a shot of me coming up for air. Or rather the sound of it – it's still pitch-black.

The tunnel goes up and down, the water ranging from knee-deep to neck-high, and I'm terrified of descending into the next fully submerged tunnel. I know it's coming because it's the long one down to the entrance that's always submerged at high tide. The only way out is by swimming and that could be straight into a rip current that might shoot me far out to sea. Have I even got the strength to swim back to shore?

Just as I'm tempted to turn back, my fear getting the

better of me, my next step is illuminated as if I'm made of electricity and I gasp, running my hand through the water, tiny blue dots of plankton trailing behind them. The sea of stars. It's another sign!

Jumpcut to me wading confidently onwards, keeping a firm grip on the ribbon until I can see daylight and I've at last reached the smooth yellow rock that I'd recorded a piece to camera on earlier.

I'm at the top of the final descent. I just need to keep my head and, if the rips are present, not fight them.

I duck-dive into the water, pulling myself down towards the entrance, and, within a minute, I'm spat out and back to the surface, where the bright light blinds me.

Fade up on a long and empty shot of the incoming waves crashing to the sound of seagulls. A wobbly voice – mine – whispering, "You're going to be OK."

Cut to a frantic set of shots as I look wildly about me, fully expecting the current to pull me out to sea.

But there's no discoloured darker water. No chop. Waves breaking like normal. I cry out with relief. I'm safe.

Cut to a shot of my relieved face.

Fade up on blurry shots of the sea alternating with the grey sky as I swim front crawl with all my might back to the shore.

Cut to a shot of me dragging myself on to the sand, relieved to find Amy and Bennie sunbathing there.

"Help," I croak, my throat sore from the saltwater I've unwittingly swallowed.

Cut to a tight shot of Amy's sneering face.

"What's wrong with you?"

Focus pull on to Bennie frowning.

"You all right, James? I thought you were with Leo."

"I am. I was," I gasp. "He's ... in there. With Shiv. He's injured. Need to get help." And I burst into tears.

Lost and Found

There has been a complete set change since I got back to shore, making it feel even more like a disaster movie. Gone is the bright sunshine, replaced by thick black thunderclouds. White horses rearing up and tumbling down, crashing against the rocks in their haste to retreat out to sea. A lifeboat sits close by, assessing the situation. Now all the shot needs is a helicopter hovering in the sky, being rocked about in the high wind as it searches the water with a spotlight.

The beach is crowded with people. Adele pacing up and down, wringing her hands, talking animatedly on the phone. Bennie's mum offering round cups of tea and coffee. A doctor on standby, talking with Ingrid who has arrived with much-needed blankets. Sarah and Noah doing their last-minute checks of breathing equipment. Bennie studiously tending the campfire, while Amy looks after me.

"Don't worry," she whispers, squeezing her arm tight round my shoulders as I dissolve into a fresh round of tears.

"But it's been hours since I left them," I sob.

"Can't go back in until the tide's well on its way out," she murmurs. "They're in safe hands. You can't do better than Sarah and Noah… They'll have Leo out in no time…" She pauses. "Back to school soon," she says, tactically trying to change the subject. "Typical, isn't it? Right when the Zombies leave, we get to sit in a classroom all day."

"D'you have to sit on different sides to the Cuckoos there too?" I mutter gloomily.

She laughs. "Nah, the teachers are pretty good at keeping things cordial. Guess they've had years of practice… I know it's ridiculous. But it's just something left over from our parents' generation. If anything, it's got worse. Homelessness is pretty bad around here, thanks to all the second-homers."

"But my grandparents bought Cliff House years ago," I say.

Amy shrugs. "What can I say? The Fish are a proud bunch. Especially the Pengellys."

"What's going on?" calls Wanda, striding on to the beach as if to prove Amy's point. "Where's my grandson?" And, as her daughter nods towards Morvoren, she breaks down in Sarah's arms, sobbing, "Not again!"

"They're safe," I say, clambering to my feet, desperate

to put her mind at rest. "Shiv's looking after him. She's got a first-aid kit in there, painkillers, water, snack bars. She knows what to do."

"And whose idea exactly was it to go in there?" demands Wanda, her eyes flashing angrily, giving me a glimpse of the person Min once had to face all those years ago.

"Mum," murmurs Sarah. "You're not helping. Now, tell me again which route you took, Coco."

I frown. "But I'm coming with you. I can show you the way."

"Absolutely not," splutters Sarah.

"It's too dangerous," agrees Noah.

"But I'm the only one here who's been inside," I sob. "Please, I have to. It was my idea. This is all my fault…"

~~~

We don't get in the water until the tide is well on the way out and the lifeguard has agreed it's safe. By seven p.m., the storm has passed, and the sun's rays are beginning to break through the thick grey cloud, creating pools of sparkling silver water on the horizon. But it's getting colder and I'm grateful for the wetsuit and diving mask.

I wade through the waves alongside Sarah and Noah. My aunt and uncle, except they don't know it. Perhaps they never will. I'm pretty certain they won't want to know me if – once – Leo is safe and well. Adele too, I expect. My hunger for a film script has ruined everything.

"Ready?" says Sarah and together we swim towards the cave, where the entrance is still submerged.

I check my head torch for the hundredth time and, with a deep breath, I dive under the water and head back in.

～～～

I hear them before I see them. Laughing and chatting like old friends. And, when I finally get to stand up in the enormous cavern again, I see them at the top of the staircase, still huddled in Shiv's dryrobe, their heads craned upwards, gawping and pointing at the enormous portrait as if they're in an art gallery.

"Shiv, Leo," I call out. "I'm back."

Their startled looks are quickly replaced with happiness, Shiv's squeals echoing loudly round us as she picks her way down the staircase, flinging herself into my arms. "Oh my gosh, you're alive. I was so worried."

"I made it," I cry with tears to match. "And I brought help."

Sarah and Noah suddenly appear in the cave, their eyes wide and expressions of wonder no doubt matching ours as they clamber up the steps to Leo, who is staring at me intently.

"Is he all right?" I ask Shiv.

She grimaces. "I told him. Sorry," she says as I stifle a gasp. "I had to. He kept closing his eyes and then we got into an argument because he wasn't interested in what I was

347

talking about. He's like you – he hates science."

"I don't hate science," I protest. "Not any more."

"Well, he does. Anyway, I ran out of things to say and then he was staring at that mermaid picture and talking about his uncle and how he died and … I blurted it out. I'm sorry. But I did get this," she says, handing me my camera. "It's not broken. You've got some great footage on there."

I smile at her. "To hell with the film. I'm just glad you're safe. The tide's going out and none of the tunnels are submerged. You won't have to do any swimming. Not until we're out anyway. Come on," I say. "Your mum's waiting on the beach."

"Is she angry?" asks Shiv anxiously.

"With me, yes," I laugh. "But she's more worried about you…"

Just Kids

The skies are ablaze in reds and pinks when we make our exit. With Leo propped between Sarah and Noah, Shiv and I walk behind them hand in hand towards the beach where there's a crowd waiting for us round a roaring campfire. Fish and Cuckoos have come together in a crisis. Maybe there's hope for them yet.

In the film version of my life, it would be me being heralded the hero. But my life isn't a film, is it? The reality is that the crowd swarms round Leo and Shiv, pulling them into loving arms. Welcoming Sarah and Noah back amid coos of how brave they are.

"I don't know how to thank you," gushes Adele tearfully.

"I couldn't let the cave take another life," replies Sarah.

And then they're hustled towards the fire where a doctor assesses Leo's condition, and Shiv is engulfed in kisses and hugs from her mum. Leaving me all a—

"Coco!"

I turn to see Uncle Henry stumbling towards me, his walking stick held aloft as he tries to get my attention. "Coco!" he cries. And I run into his arms. "I thought it was history repeating itself," he says, his voice cracking.

"I'm OK, Uncle Henry," I sob. "I'm OK. Where's Min?" I ask as a sudden desire to be with my mum hits me, followed swiftly by my heart sinking. She probably isn't even here. Then, all of a sudden, I see her standing shivering by the fire, dressed for the Oscars in a long black evening gown.

"Coco," she gasps, rushing forward, late for her cue as always. "Darling, you're safe!"

"Where've you been?" I croak.

"Job interview. You're not hurt, are you?" she asks. "What happened?"

"She happened," says Sarah. "Obsessed with exploring that damn cave. Just like her mother."

Min winces, her mouth twitching with the words she wants to say.

"How many lives do you Jameses have to take before you stop?" hisses Sarah.

"I think about him every day, you know," says Min suddenly, looking so hurt I want to jump in and protect her. "Replay that scene over and over, wishing I could make it turn out differently."

"At least you're still alive to do that," spits Sarah.

"Sarah," pleads Uncle Henry, stepping into focus. "This has all been said before."

It's like there's a spotlight on the three of them as the rest of us become a background blur, with a silence so intense it's as if the sound engineer has forgotten to lay the soundtrack.

Then boom! *The clapperboard slams and the director yells, "Action."*

"Oh, poor Min," says Sarah in a mocking tone. "Is this about how we didn't accept you?"

Min frowns. "No. You've allowed time to change your memory, Sarah. All this Fish and Cuckoo nonsense started as a joke. Billy came up with it."

The look on Min's and Henry's faces – everyone's really – is so miserable. Like they're reliving it all. And suddenly I see my family for who they are. Henry, the responsible young man, and Min, the troubled teenager – both still paying the price. And me – the reminder of who they've lost. All those times I've caught them staring when I've given my twinkliest *Pengelly* grin…

"I loved him, Sarah," says Min, her voice cracking.

Sarah snorts. "Loved him? You led him to his death and then you ran off and got pregnant with someone else."

"That's not true," murmurs Uncle Henry. "Billy knew what he was doing. He'd been in that cave loads of times before. We were just kids, Sarah. Barely older than Leo and Coco. Are you telling me that you didn't make any misguided adolescent mistakes?" And he gives her such a loaded look that her cheeks colour.

"So, we're just expected to welcome her back," she splutters. "Her and her daughter who…" She pauses, the emotion getting the better of her. "My son could've died in there."

"I chose to go in there," says Leo, coming to stand beside me, forcing the spotlight on to us. "Coco saved my life."

"And mine," agrees Shiv, squeezing my hand.

"She walked through that cave alone and in the dark," adds Bennie.

"And then she went back in there," finishes Amy.

Sarah blinks as she watches my friends form a semicircle round me and suddenly I feel like things aren't quite so bad after all.

"Aren't you going to tell her?" asks Leo.

"Tell me what?" frowns Sarah.

I shrug. "Would it make a difference? Should it?"

"Yes," he says.

I snort. "So, having been made to feel like an unwanted outsider, you're suddenly going to welcome me with open arms?" I say. "These labels you've been hiding behind are making you miserable. The sad fact is that a tragic death has poisoned you against each other. But that won't bring him back."

I smile sadly at Sarah, joining hands with Shiv and Leo.

"You – we – saved their lives today," I say. "And you didn't think twice about who they were."

Sarah frowns. "I don't understand. What aren't you telling me?"

"I'm your niece!"

I look around me, searching for the source of the voice-over, until I realize the words came out of me, then Wanda steps forward, her face looking like a cloud has been lifted. As if she can see things properly for the first time in years.

"You're Billy's daughter?" She beams at me, eyes starry with tears, her face full of such tenderness. "Well, if that isn't the best news I've had in a long time." And, just like the film version of my life, she pulls me into a hug, cooing with happiness.

"She's right too, you know," she says, turning to the crowd. "All these rivalries that are getting us nowhere – I'm sick of it. I'll hear no more of this Fish and Cuckoo talk. Understand?"

And it's like everyone answers in unison under her reproving gaze. "Yes, Mrs Pengelly."

"Good," she says, looking pleased with the response. "Because I, for one, am over the moon to welcome my granddaughter into this community."

Sighs to camera – the open arms I've been longing for all this time!

Making Memories

Hours later, the sun has long set and even the moon has disappeared, leaving a clear night sky dotted with a thousand jewels, sporadically illuminated by flying embers from the campfire. I sit, staring listlessly at the sea, thinking how happy I feel, euphoric even, at how the plot of my life has changed so radically.

It turns out I have a grandma, an aunt, two uncles and four cousins, plus numerous other relatives once or twice removed – a concept I can't quite fathom. And while I can't say that the community has completely been healed – Min and Sarah just about managed a handshake – there's enough new friendships growing that it can't be too far off. Wanda and Ingrid have agreed to go surfing together for a change. Sarah and Uncle Henry have been talking for so long, I'm beginning to think there's a history to that relationship that I haven't uncovered (yet), and of course there's me and Shiv…

"Guess what?" she whispers excitedly. "I'm doing my A levels here next year."

"How did you manage that?"

She shrugs. "Mum agreed. If I want to study marine biology, it ought to be by the sea. And, of course, there's your uncle. I'd be insane not to tap into that fountain of knowledge. Bennie's going to teach me to swim in the open water too," she says, blushing. "You were right about him. About a lot of things actually."

She nods towards Leo, who, apart from his head now being bandaged, looks back to his old social self, if a little tired. "I never thought you'd really be able to fix this community, you know."

"For a moment, I didn't think I would," I laugh. "Who knew all it would take would be for the two of you to get trapped together in a cave for seven hours?"

Shiv groans. "Don't remind me. I'm going to have nightmares about that tonight."

"You can always come and sleep in my bed," says Adele, coming over to help Shiv to her feet. "That's if you need to. Probably don't, now that you're all grown up. We need to say goodbye, darling – Sprout won't go to sleep until she's seen you apparently."

"Oh, poor Sprout," I coo.

"Poor Sprout?" snorts Shiv. "Are you sure it's not Coco

she wants to see?"

Adele nods. "Definitely you. Though she does adore Coco."

"Yeah, a bit too much," says Shiv, with narrowed eyes. "You need to have the odd argument, tell her she's an annoying brat from time to time…"

"I think you may have just found the reason why the two of you don't get along," I laugh.

Adele gives me a tight squeeze. "Thank you, Coco. For everything. Sweet dreams…"

~~~

"Cousins, eh?" says Leo as I join him and Amy by the campfire. "I told you freediving was in your DNA."

"Yeah, remind me never to play Last Fish Floating with you," laughs Amy. She grins sheepishly. "So you were never really after Leo, were you?"

I laugh. "Not my type. Never was."

"What's wrong with me?" he snorts indignantly.

"D'you really want to go there?" I giggle.

"I've been such a jealous idiot," says Amy. "I thought you were going to take him away from me. Do you think we can be … friends?"

"Are you kidding?" I shriek. "Of course we can… But … what about Shiv?"

Amy laughs. "Yes, even her. Wanda was very clear on that and, besides, something tells me that Bennie won't have a word said against her. The two of them didn't stop talking," she says. "In hushed tones too, like they were sharing a secret."

"I'm glad they finally got together," I say. "They make a cute couple."

"No hard feelings then?" says Amy.

"None. Hug it out?" I suggest. "It's what we'd do in Soho."

"Yeah, well, this isn't Soho," retorts Leo.

"No, it most definitely isn't." I smile.

Looks to camera – and d'you know what? I'm actually all right with that.

The Final Scene

"Weren't you scared when you first went in that cave?" I ask Min later, once the party has faded to a natural end, and all we're left with is our own company and the glowing remnants of the fire.

"I was terrified," she laughs. "Your dad was the brave one. Although it turns out all the tunnels lead into the cave, only some are longer than others. I just marked the shortest route."

Looks to camera – oh.

"But it was so dark in there." I shudder. "My eyes were useless."

Uncle Henry pokes a stick in the fire. "Do you know, there's a Mexican cavefish that has evolved without them? Want to know why?"

"Not really," I giggle. "But I expect you're going to tell me."

"Don't you want to guess?" he asks hopefully.

"They use less energy without their eyes?" I suggest.

"Yes!" he cries excitedly. "That's exactly it. We'll make a scientist out of you yet."

"You know, for someone who walks around looking like a scarecrow, you really are rather wise," I tell him.

Uncle Henry chuckles. "They don't give you two Neptunian Awards in a row for nothing. Not that they're much use when it comes to paying for a new roof, except perhaps to prop it up."

"You're not going to sell the house, are you?"

Min gives me that gappy grin of hers and shakes her head. "Wasn't really considering it. But we're going to have to make some changes. Even me."

"What, you're going to start using make-up remover?" I ask, half joking.

"Don't be ridiculous!" she squawks. "There's nothing that soap and water can't remove."

Looks to camera – except her waterproof mascara…

"No, I meant on the career front," she says.

"We're meeting Adele tomorrow," explains Uncle Henry. "She's offered to help us fix up Cliff House. Min's going to run it as an Airbnb. God help us!"

"Adele's teaching me to cook," says Min, digging him in the ribs playfully. "That You-are-what-you-eat article you left lying around about anti-something foods."

"Anti-inflammatory," I say.

Looks to camera – I actually remembered something!

"Yeah, that. It got me thinking about everything and I've been following it. I feel great. Loads more energy and I'm sleeping better… Adele's worked with the builders down here before, so we'll at least have some chance of getting it done by next year. In the meantime, I'm looking into upcycling clothes. Ingrid reckons there's a demand for it. It's something I've always dreamed of doing. Just took coming home for me to realize. Until then, I've got to get a job. One of us has to pay the bills around here."

"Cheek of it," snorts Uncle Henry. "I've been paying them for years. But I do need to start on a new thesis." He pauses. "I've been researching these Sea Nomads actually. I think there might be a direct correlation between—"

"You do realize we've stopped listening, right?" laughs Min.

Uncle Henry rolls his eyes. "Which is why I'm going back to teaching ignoramuses like you… Tutoring at home in maths and science."

"Yep, still nothing," says Min.

I join in with their laughter, enjoying the fact that their jibes are good-natured for a change. Things feel different, like they're beginning to be more at ease with each other again.

Looks to camera – I wonder if…

"Can we get a dog?" I ask.

Min cackles. "Seriously? Who's going to look after it? Take it for walks? Feed it? Pick up after it?"

"I will," I say. "Isn't that exactly what I've been doing for you two these past few months?"

Uncle Henry bursts out laughing. "Oh, Minnie! You asked for that."

"So did you." She wrinkles her nose. "Tell you what, if you can feed his fish for a month *and* clean out the tank, I'll definitely think about it."

"Hang on." He frowns. "Don't I get a say in this? You have to handle Brian carefully. Took me a long time to learn how to keep a tropical-fish tank. I wasn't born with all this fish knowledge, you know."

Min giggles. "Just the fish scales."

"I knew it was you editing that page about me!" he shrieks. "Stop it or I'll make one up about y—"

"It's the sea of stars again," I gasp as the line of advancing waves is suddenly illuminated.

"The scientific term is bioluminescence," says Uncle Henry.

"Yeah, but I like sea of stars more," I say. "Look!" I squeal. "And there's some dolphins."

Uncle Henry squints out to sea. "Where?"

"Over there! Where the sea's glowing. Can't you see?"

"Not without my glasses, no."

"You're getting old, Henry," laughs Min.

"So are you," he retorts.

"We all are," I giggle, linking arms with them both and hugging them tight.

They might not be the conventional parents I always dreamed of. They might even be the strangest pair in all of Piscary Bay, but they're my family.

Fade to black. Cue the music. Roll the credits...

About the Author

Lou Abercrombie grew up in Essex, studied at Durham University, where she gained a first class Maths degree, and then moved to London, where she worked in television. Lou now lives in Bath with her husband, fantasy novelist Joe Abercrombie, and their three children. As a portrait photographer, alongside projects such as Shooting the Undead (a series that required Lou to learn how to do zombie make-up) and Age Becomes Her (a series celebrating the older woman), Lou's camera has been deftly focused on a large number of children's, fantasy and crime authors.

Lou has always been a keen swimmer, but a chance reading of an article a few years ago, about Lord Byron, inspired her to follow in his footsteps and swim the

Hellespont, a 5km stretch of water between Europe and Asia. Since then she has swum a 10km marathon swim down the River Dart, learned to freedive like a mermaid, swum round Burgh Island and Brownsea Island, competed in the annual Copenhagen TrygFonden swim and completed a night swim with glow sticks. She is always on the lookout for the next exciting swim.

@LadyGrimdark
louabercrombie.com

Acknowledgements

A book about an aspiring film maker would be incomplete without a list of credits. A crew of fabulous people within publishing and beyond who played a vital role in helping produce *Coming up for Air*.

CREW

Agent	Gill Mclay
Editorial Director (at time of commission)	Ruth Bennett
Senior Editor	Mattie Whitehead
Copyeditor	Jane Tait
Illustrator	Anna Kuptsova
Designer	Sophie Bransby
Proofreader	Melissa Hyder

UK Sales Manager	George Hanratty
Digital Marketing Manager	Dannie Price
Campaigns Assistant	Summer Lanchester
Production Controller	Demet Hoffmeyer
Senior Rights Executive	Nicola O'Connell
Sea Advisors	Rachel Ellis
	Julia Knight
	Nick Tettersell
	Ian Donald, Freedive UK
ME Consultant	Bren Abercrombie
Danish Consultant	Barbara Borup
TV Jargon Advisor	Joe Abercrombie
Opinion Offerers	Grace Abercrombie
	Evie Abercrombie
	Ted Abercrombie
Writing Support	Anna Wilson
	Joanna Nadin

Special mention goes to the incredibly supportive
children's book writing community on Twitter who lifted
me up throughout the dark days of lockdown.

Looks to camera: thank you so much! X

Also by Lou Abercrombie

This girl is making waves

FIG SWIMS THE WORLD

Lou Abercrombie